Pride Publishing books by Jason Wrench

Single Books
Twelve Days of Murder
Till Death Do Us Wed

Up on the Farm
Finding a Farmer
Bewitched by the Barista
Sanctuary for a Surgeon

Collections
A Wolf in Billionaire's Clothing: Wolf Island

Up on the Farm

SANCTUARY FOR THE SURGEON

JASON WRENCH

Sanctuary for the Surgeon
ISBN # 978-1-80250-510-8
©Copyright Jason Wrench 2023
Cover Art by Kelly Martin ©Copyright January 2023
Interior text design by Claire Siemaszkiewicz
Pride Publishing

SANCTUARY FOR THE SURGEON

Dedication

This book is dedicated to my mentors in school and life, Dr. James C. McCroskey and Dr. Virginia Peck Richmond. Their encouragement has given me the tools to professionally spread my wings and fly in so many directions.

Acknowledgements

First, I again thank all the amazing people at my Pride
Publishing family for everything they do:
Claire Siemaszkiewicz, Rebecca Scott and Jamie Rose.
As the saying goes, "It takes a village."
I'm glad to be part of the Pride Publishing village.

Second, I also want to thank my fellow Ninja Writers
for keeping me motivated and writing. Last, I want to
thank all my colleagues, family and friends who
inspire me every day.

Prologue

I've seen a lot of things in my Emergency Department before, but staring down at my latest patient had me stumped. I was waiting for the computerized tomography or CT scan to sent to my laptop before transferring my patient to the plastic surgeon on call. I hadn't told my patient yet, but the surgical team was already prepping the operating room. She was still in good humor, so I opted not to stress her out. Some people hear the word 'surgery' and immediately freak.

"Good afternoon, Dr. Betancourt," my boss and best friend Dr. Bryce Camden-Thompson said, coming into the patient bay. "For those of you who are new to this rotation, Dr. Betancourt is one of our trauma surgeons on staff." He then turned to me and asked, "Doctor, what do we have this afternoon?"

I looked up to see why he was being so formal and noticed the string of medical students he had in tow. "Well, Dr. Camden-Thompson, there's a metal rod through the patient's left orbit media inferior quadrant."

"Dr. Chauncy," Bryce said, turning to one of his residents, "do you agree with Dr. Betancourt's diagnosis?"

The resident's eyes grew as he tried to refocus on his attending physician. I stifled a snicker. I could tell the resident had been staring at the patient and not listening to what I was saying. Let's face it... It's not every day you see a stiletto heel sticking out of someone's eye socket.

"Yes, uh, of course, Dr. Camden-Thompson. Dr. Betancourt's diagnosis is accurate."

I tuned them out as I looked down at my patient. "How are you holding up, Ms. Albariño?"

"I just want this thing out of my eye," the six-foot-three-inch individual said.

"You okay with the medical students and residents being here?"

"I already told you, Doctor. Let the children see me in all my glory and idiocy."

The Lady Albariño was a bit of a frequent flyer in the emergency room. The legendary queen had been around the West Village for decades, performing and hosting. Her current attire was a sparkly dress that looked inspired by *Priscilla, Queen of the Desert.*

"Ms....?" Bryce asked the patient.

"I'm The Lady Albariño," she replied. "I would shake your hand, but I'm just as likely to shake your" — glancing down at Bryce's crotch — "since my vision isn't great...for some reason."

There were a few nervous chuckles from the medical students. Still, the residents were doing their best to appear completely affectless. One thing we explain to new students, interns and residents is that you can never look shocked when dealing with a patient. No matter how mangled or gory a patient looks, they're looking to you to be competent and in charge — even if you want to freak out.

"Yes, Ms. Albariño," Bryce continued. "Will you please explain how you ended up with the object in your eye?"

I patted Albariño's shoulder as she began her story for probably the thousandth time since entering the ED. "I was at a gig getting ready when another queen accused me of having an affair with her man — which I most assuredly would *not* be having sex with that beast. That hairy monstrosity would give a Wookie a run for their money. Well, there was a little altercation, and I ended up with Bellatrix Bordello's heel sticking out of my eye."

"Thankfully," I interjected, "the patient can still see out of her left eye, and it responds to light."

Bryce conferred with his group. My cell phone vibrated in my pocket as the ping of an email wanted my attention. I pulled out my phone, looked down and saw it was from radiology. The radiologist summarized, "*We have a left infraorbital canal-orbital floor and posterior wall of the left maxillary sinus fracture with a left maxillary hemosinus. CT scan showed no injury to the optic nerve, superior or medial rectus.*"

"Well, Ms. Albariño," I interrupted Bryce's mini-lecture, "I got the CT scan back, and we will get you up to surgery now. The good news is that your eye is in good condition, so you shouldn't lose any visual function. There is a fracture in your eye socket that will need to be repaired surgically."

"Is that your way of saying you'll have to drug me, Doctor?" The Lady Albariño said seductively. "You could have simply invited me over to your place for cocktails."

"As much fun as I'm sure that would be, I'm afraid my husband would have a problem with it."

The Lady Albariño sighed and threw her hand over her heart like a leading lady from the old silent films. "All the good men are either married or straight."

I smiled and patted her on the shoulder. "Before you go on any dates, we need to have a plastic surgeon get that blasted heel out of your eye. It's not your best accessory."

I left the patient bay and watched as Bryce took the students over to a computer terminal where he could go over The Lady Albariño's CT scan with them in more detail. I got surgery on the line and let them know that The Lady Albariño was being transferred into their capable hands. A minute later, she was wheeled out of the ED.

I went back to the physician's desk area and started my dictation of the case for the hospital chart. I was so lost in my work that I didn't even see Bryce sit down as he slid a cup of fresh coffee over for me.

"Well, that was a first," Bryce said. "I mean...I've read about a heel in an eye socket before in medical journals but never expected to see a drag queen with a scarlet stiletto embedded in her."

"Do you know The Lady Albariño?" I asked.

"Not personally. Richard and I have seen her show a few times over the years."

Richard was Bryce's husband and the other half of Camden-Thompson. I've always known them as the Camden-Thompsons, so I don't really know who was

Camden and who was Thompson before they were married.

My husband, Chance Mercer, is an infectious disease physician at New York University. Even though we both worked for NYU, it had taken a disaster in Mexico City to bring us together. I had been finishing my Surgical Critical Care Fellowship when there had been a giant earthquake right outside Mexico City. I agreed to fly down with a team from NYU to help Doctors Without Borders in the aftermath. Even though Chance was almost thirty years my senior, we had fallen in love. One and a half years later, we were married, when I had been in my early thirties.

"What's Chance up to today?" Bryce asked. "Attending the vigil this evening?" What Bryce had asked about was the annual NYC AIDS vigil that took place every September twenty-seventh for National Gay Men's HIV/AIDS Awareness Day.

"He's attending but not presenting this year. I may walk over to the NYC AIDS Memorial Park at St. Vincent's Triangle on break if things are quiet around here."

The Greenwich Village Emergency Department entrance was less than a block from the park, so this was entirely doable. In fact, I could worm my way through the bowels of the facility and take a side exit that opened right across the street from the park.

"Doctors!" a voice cut through the ED. I looked up to see one of the ED nurses taking a call. "A car drove into a crowd of pedestrians at St. Vincent's Triangle. There was a gathering. Multiple injuries are heading our way. We're the closest ED, so this is an all-hands-on-deck emergency."

Without thinking, I stopped my dictation, downed the cup of coffee and went to the supply closet to put on emergency personal protective equipment. I took a deep, centering breath as I prepared myself for what was about to enter the ED. Out of the corner of my eye, I saw Bryce organizing his medical students, interns and residents into triage teams. The ED was a flurry of activity around me. When the sliding doors opened and the first victim was rolled in, I approached.

"We have a twelve-year-old male who was hit by a motor vehicle. The victim is unconscious..." The EMT read off the vital statistics of the patient.

Without waiting for more information, I said to the closest nurse, "I want a full work-up, including a whole-body CT."

"Yes, Doctor," the nurse said and took over.

The next patient had a bone sticking out of her leg. I told the next nurse to get orthopedics on the phone because we had an emergency surgery. That was what my life was like for the next hour. I quickly evaluated patients, then turfed them to their next destination. Because of our proximity to the accident, we had around twenty victims come through our ED.

After helping Bryce organize surgical teams, I scrubbed in for a two-and-a-half-hour surgery. My patient had internal bleeding from blunt force trauma. Thankfully, I was able to open him up and get the bleeding stopped. The patient would have to undergo a couple of more surgeries before he was on the road to recovery, but we had him stable, and that was all that mattered.

By the time I pulled off my last set of bloodied PPE, I was exhausted. As a trauma surgeon, you learn to turn off your emotions during a crisis. If I let all the carnage get to me, I would be paralyzed in a situation like this. Instead, I took each case as it came. I had to always think three or four steps ahead in my treatment plan to keep on top of my patients. I headed back down to the ED to see if there was anything else I could do to help. I should have been tired, but I always had this buzz of energy after I finished surgery. *Probably adrenaline.*

I looked across the ED and everyone looked haggard. Thankfully, emergency medical services had diverted any noncritical cases away from our facility.

"How are you holding up?" Bryce asked as he came to stand next to me.

"I'm good. You?"

"Same."

"What about your posse?" I joked.

"They performed well. The students and interns did as they were told, and the residents stepped up. I had to order one medical student to leave the ED because he froze. I think this may have only been his first or second rotation."

"Talk about being thrown into the deep end."

"Have you talked to Chance yet?"

"No," I said, the sudden realization hitting me. "I haven't thought about him and not even checked my phone." I reached into my scrubs and pulled out my cell. I was surprised that I didn't have any messages, but sometimes, in the basement of the ED and the operating room, cell reception could be spotty. I hit Chance's number and waited for the call to connect.

He didn't pick up.

I dialed again.

I heard Raul Esparza's rendition of *Being Alive* from the musical *Company* playing lightly. It took my brain a second to register the song…*our* song, the one Chance used for my ringtone on his phone. My heart plummeted as I hit redial and searched for the source. I found a colleague in a back patient bay pulling the sheet over the top of one of the victims. Absently, I hit redial again. When Raul's voice broke through the silence, I took three steps forward and lifted the sheet.

"What are you—?"

I ignored the physician.

Chance's blank eyes stared up at me. I don't know what happened next. The guttural sound that escaped my throat was primal.

Chapter One

The last six-and-a-half months had been a living nightmare. There had been funeral arrangements and memorial services to organize and attend. Then there had been the months of pitying stares. I had become a recluse. I hadn't wanted to deal with friends and coworkers. I had gone to work then gone home. When I ran out of excuses to avoid their offers, I had occasional meals with them. My life had shattered. Richard had recommended therapy on more than one occasion because I was clearly depressed. Of course I was depressed. The man I loved had died.

Chance had been one of three people who had been directly in the vehicle's path when it had run through the crowd. After the NYPD investigation, it was ruled an accident. The car's tire had blown after hitting a metal object in the street, which had caused the driver to lose control of the vehicle. She had tried to regain it but couldn't. I heard through the grapevine that she was now being treated at an inpatient psychiatric facility upstate after she had attempted suicide. The woman hadn't been ready for the media scrutiny and the accident's fallout in her life. Part of me was glad she'd had a mental breakdown, but that was the evil, vindictive side. Another part was sorry for her. As horrible as it was, accidents happened. I saw accidents every day. Some were preventable. Some were not.

I had agreed to another Sunday brunch with Bryce and Richard. I hadn't wanted to go, but I found myself at their door with a bottle of wine. I plastered on my best fake smile and knocked.

"Just a second," Richard's voice rang from the other side. A few seconds later, the door opened. "Darrin, we're so glad you could make it. Brunch is almost ready." He ushered me inside the townhouse as he kept talking. "We're having a quiche I whipped up from scratch. It has a smattering of vegetables with sausage and bacon. I also threw together a mixed green salad and a raspberry tart for dessert." I handed him the bottle of wine. Richard inspected it and nodded before saying, "Good choice."

Bryce came from the backroom. "How are you doing?" he asked me.

"I'm doing…" I left the phrase hanging in the air.

"Well," Bryce said without acknowledging the ambiguity of my statement, "at least you're up and moving around."

I forced a smile and followed Bryce and Richard into the small dining room. The table was set for three. As usual, Richard had set an immaculate table that would make Emily Post jealous. Bryce motioned to a chair, and I took a seat as Richard left.

"So, how are things in your world?" I asked, breaking the silence.

"Richard and I are doing well. We've been looking into surrogacy again. I think Richard's biological clock is ticking. He wants a baby."

"I heard that," Richard's voice echoed from the kitchen next to the dining room. Richard walked in with the salad and placed it in the middle of the table. "And don't let this one fool you," he said, sticking his thumb in Bryce's direction. "He wants to be a doting father as much as I do. We have a lot of love to give a little one."

"Why not adopt?" I asked.

"We talked about that," Bryce acknowledged, "but ultimately we want to have a little baby. We have thought about having one through surrogacy, then adopting her or him a little brother or sister."

"Two kids?" I asked.

"Don't be so shocked," Richard said, returning to the dining room with the quiche. "I'm doing more and more of my work from home. After the pandemic, the firm has embraced remote work, so the timing couldn't be more perfect."

Richard set about serving up the quiche. We spent the next hour talking about a range of topics deemed 'safe' by the group.

After an appropriate amount of time once we'd all eaten, I looked at Bryce and Richard and said, "Well, I need to get to the gym before taking a nap. I'm working the ten-to-ten shift tonight."

"Let me put together a to-go box for you," Richard said. "I worry that you're not getting enough home-cooked food."

Sadly, he was right. Most nights I grabbed takeout or heated something from a box in the microwave.

"Thanks," I said. "It would be much appreciated. You can only eat takeout Chinese so many days in a row."

When Richard left the dining room, Bryce turned and stared at me. For the first time that day, he put on his serious face.

"I'm worried about you," Bryce said. "I know it's only been six months, but you've almost completely shut down."

"I'm still grieving. Is there an appropriate amount of time one should grieve?"

"No, there's not," Bryce said hesitantly. "But I worry that you're not making progress toward getting healthy. Have you reconsidered Richard's suggestion about therapy?"

"I don't need a shrink... I need time." I blinked back tears that had started to swell in my eyes. "I need him back." I was amazed when the words came out of my mouth.

"I know. We all miss him," Bryce said. He looked at me for a second, and I could tell he was trying to plan what to say next. "I don't know how I would react if Richard died, so I won't presume to tell you how you're supposed to behave. I won't. But I will say I'm worried."

"Thanks..." He meant well. Part of me wanted to come back with a snarky comment, but I held my tongue. "Each day is a little better," I lied.

"Here's your to-go box," Richard said, breezing back into the dining room. He took one look at the serious faces in the room. "Did I miss something?"

"Not at all," I said, using the break in the conversation to my advantage. "Thank you for an amazing meal and lovely company, but I must get to the gym."

Bryce looked like he wanted to say something, but he kept his words to himself, which suited me just fine. I said goodbyes and hugged both men before going home to change and head off to the gym.

* * * *

After hitting the gym, I had run home and grabbed a shower before walking down to the corner supermarket to stock up on boxed meals for the week. I had thrown some pieces of fresh fruit in my basket, but they would spoil before I ate them. Afterward, I had gone home and taken a nap before going in to work at ten p.m.

Overnights on Sundays were quiet most nights. Now that's not saying the random holiday or full moon Sunday didn't bring out the whack jobs, but your average Sunday in early April was nice and quiet. I had seen a couple of panic attacks and a heart attack before one. By six a.m., the ED was quiet, and I hadn't had any interesting cases, just one emergency appendectomy. Then, I helped suture a guy who had sliced open his finger, because I had nothing better to do and the other ED staffers were busy. When Bryce showed up with fresh bagels and coffee, I was mostly bored and catching up on paperwork.

"How's the shift?" Bryce asked, sitting down next to me.

"Relatively uneventful." I ran through the series of cases, and he nodded his head.

"Still awake?"

"Despite the slow night and lack of adrenaline, I'm doing fine. Thank God for coffee. Nature's nectar."

"How much have you had?"

"Depends on which unit of measurement you're using," I said as I suppressed a smile. He's a doctor, so of course he wanted me to respond in ounces or cups, but where's the fun in that?

"Darrin," Bryce said, his exasperation barely contained. "What am I going to do with you?"

I had an answer right on the tip of my tongue, but we were cut off by one of the ED nurses. "Have a pedestrian hit-and-run coming in. Who wants it?"

"I haven't clocked in yet," Bryce said.

"Go, clock in," I told Bryce. "I'll take it." I took another swig of the coffee Bryce had given me and stood to follow the nurse.

I donned some PPE to get ready for the patient and headed outside the ED doors to wait in the ambulance turnaround. I heard the siren thirty seconds later, then the flashing lights created their strobe-light effect off the area buildings as the boxy truck pulled up. Two paramedics jumped out of the back and started rattling off information about the patient. He was a middle-aged man who was nonresponsive but breathing on his own. I sent him to get a CT scan. Bryce joined me outside as a second ambulance pulled up with our next patient...the driver.

The EMT wasn't even out of the truck before he was speaking. "We deployed a breathalyzer, but the results were inconsistent. We got two different readings. In either case, the driver was over the legal limit. NYPD should be here any minute."

Like clockwork, the white car with red and blue lights pulled up. Two officers got out of the car as I headed with the patient into the Emergency Department. Other than finding the patient being drunk, the EMTs had only found a small laceration on the guy's forehead. The drunk patient was docile, so Bryce transferred him into a wheelchair, then wheeled him into the ED.

I followed Bryce and the drunk driver inside. I walked back and took a quick swig of coffee while I waited for the pedestrian victim to finish his CT. Depending on the results, I would determine if he needed to go to ICU or if I would have to scrub in for surgery. I called the operating room and put them on standby, just in case. A nurse wheeled the pedestrian back into the ED after finishing with the CT. I walked over to the patient and spent a minute looking at the chart. The internal trauma wasn't significant. I was getting in my mental space preparing for the inevitable surgery. The shrill sound of beeping cut through my concentration.

"Fuck, he's coding!" I yelled.

Immediately, the code team swung into high gear, and the process of trying to save the man started. I started on chest compressions, and one of the ED nurses began the manual pump CPR bag. I pushed and counted. Then the nurse squeezed the bag twice, forcing oxygen into the man's lungs. As the rest of the code team got there, I handed off compression duties. In less than thirty seconds, we had five nurses and me overseeing the code. One nurse continued the compressions, one handled breathing, one prepped the defibrillator reader, one got the IV ready for drugs and one recorded the code. I looked over the bag of personal effects that had been dropped off with the patient. On top was a smart watch. *I gave Chance that same model for his birthday...his last birthday.*

And I froze. It seemed like an hour, but I stood there, unable to do anything. I'd never frozen in my entire career. The code recorder snapped her fingers in my face.

"Doctor, get your head out of your ass," she barked.

Normally, I would have dressed her down, but I couldn't. Everything was happening around me in fast forward, and I was on pause.

"Dr. Camden-Thompson!" The code recorder yelled across the ED. My friend and mentor got there, shoved me out of the way and took over. I think Bryce may have said something to me, but I honestly don't know. The last thing I heard was, "I knew he was going to crack eventually."

"Get him out of here," Bryce yelled to another nurse.

There was a firm grip on my upper arm, and I was led away from the patient. A single tear crept out of the corner of my eye before I shrugged off the nurse.

"I'm fine," I grumbled.

I headed toward the locker room, aware of all the eyes on me in the ED. For a few more steps, I needed to keep it together. I pushed open the door, then walked over to my locker. I fumbled with the lock and couldn't get my fingers to work properly, so I hit the locker. I split the skin on my knuckles and immediately regretted that decision.

"What the fuck?" came a voice from somewhere else in the room.

"Sorry," I said before leaning against the locker and letting myself collapse to the ground in front of it. There was a wooden bench in front of me, but I didn't feel like getting up to sit on it. A few people entered the locker room and passed me. A couple even asked if I was all right, and I grumbled an answer. I sat there in a daze.

Eventually, someone eased onto the ground next to me. I looked over to see Bryce looking at me. "What happened?" Bryce questioned.

"I don't know," I admitted, almost amazed to hear the words escaping my mouth. "I was handling the code, and I froze."

"Why?"

"I don't know. He…" I tried to remember what had stopped me in my tracks. "The watch." The words escaped my lips almost inaudibly.

"The watch?"

"The victim had the same watch I'd given Chance for his birthday."

"Ahh, fuck," Bryce said. I looked at Bryce's face and the sympathy the man had for me at that moment made me lose it. I started bawling. Honestly, it may have been the first time I'd cried since the funeral. I'd bottled up those emotions for so long. Bryce placed his arm around my shoulder.

I heard the door to the locker room open, and the recording nurse walked in and said, "What the hell is his problem?" I hadn't liked that nurse from the moment I'd met her. She was one of those old-school, no-nonsense-type nurses who have zero humanity. Still, she was very efficient at pushing pencils and doing paperwork. "Is he on drugs?"

"What?" Bryce asked on my behalf. "Why would you say that?"

"Look at him," she groused. "He clearly doesn't have his shit together. I'm going to have to report this. And, for the record, I still think he's on drugs."

"Then test me, you old bat." So, it may not have been my best insult, but it was the only one I had the energy for.

"Great," the nurse said with an evil smile. "I believe that was consent."

Before Bryce could disagree, she hauled me up and motioned for another nurse to come draw my blood. From my seated position, I hadn't even realized another nurse was with her. The nurse who drew the blood at least looked sympathetic as she did her job. I didn't have the energy to care.

"Darrin, you've got to get your shit together," Bryce said after the nurses had left. "Please tell me they won't find anything—?"

"I'm not on drugs," I blurted. "I barely drink. I barely do anything. I go to the gym. I go home. I work. Once in a blue moon, I have sex. That's my life."

"I think you need some time off," Bryce said flatly. "You never took time off after Chance's—"

"I'm fine," I yelled, but I heard myself and winced.

Bryce's eyes bored into me. "You're going to take that vacation you've been meaning to take."

"I don't—"

"That wasn't a suggestion. After what happened in the ED today, I should suspend you pending an investigation." I started to say something, but Bryce waved me off and kept going. "And I'm not going to document a suspension unless you refuse to go on a voluntary vacation to get your act together. You are going to take at least the next three weeks off. No, ifs, ands or buts. Is that understood?"

"Yes," I said flatly.

"Good. Now, pull yourself together and get out of my emergency department."

Bryce looked at my hand, then looked at my locker as I fiddled with the lock again, which immediately opened this time.

"Need me to look at that?" he asked, gesturing to my hand.

"It'll be fine." I flexed all my fingers to show him my hand was fully operational.

Bryce left me in the locker room as I pulled out my street clothes and changed. I didn't say goodbye to anyone and opted to take the back way out of the ED to avoid more pitying stares. I was done with that for the day.

Chapter Two

Jordan

I took a deep breath of fresh air as I stood on a folding ladder investigating a few of the branches that we'd pruned a couple of months ago to ensure fresh growth. Sure enough, the apple trees were looking healthier than ever. I take a lot of pride in my work. Sure, I may be a 'farmhand', but that didn't mean I cared any less than the guy who owned the place. The owner, Dale Devereux, was a few trees over, doing the same thing I was. And his fiancé, Talgat Kudaibergen, was a row over from us, checking on the pruning.

"How are they looking?" Dale asked from atop his ladder.

"So far, so good. The winter pruning sure seems to be doing what it's supposed to."

"I'm still not sure what I'm looking at," Dale admitted. "It still looks like a tree to me."

"Dale," Talgat yelled from where he was perched. "How many times am I going to have to show you?"

There was at least one part love and one part exasperation in Talgat's voice.

Dale wasn't raised on a farm or anywhere near nature. Hell, he hadn't even been on the farm for an entire year, which was one reason he didn't know what he was doing presently. His grandfather owned a series of corporate farms, and our little farm outside Woodstock, NY, was one of them. We were proudly 'Devereux Farms Upstate'. Last year, Dale and Talgat had taken this farm from being perceived as a low-producing farm to one of the highest-grossing operations in the Devereux Farms portfolio. This was a combination of Dale's business smarts and Talgat's genius at farming sciences. Whatever was the magic sauce those two had created, the farm was flourishing.

I climbed down from my ladder and was going to investigate another one, but Dale said, "I think we're done. A flying creature tried to bite me. I swear it had fangs."

I'm sure it was just a baby mosquito or a fly, but I didn't mind calling it a day if Dale did. I looked over to see if Talgat would let his fiancé quit.

"Dale," Talgat said in a tone of voice more appropriate from one's mother than one's fiancé.

"But, Talgat," Dale whined back and pretended to stomp his foot up and down like a kid told he wasn't allowed to buy candy at the drug store.

"I give up," Talgat said, throwing his arms into the air.

"You do?" Dale questioned, almost shocked that he'd gotten away with it. "You're not going to turn me into a farmer?"

"Oh, I will turn you into a farmer if it kills you."

"I thought that was supposed to be '*if it kills me*,'" Dale joked.

"Nope. Trust me, you would most definitely be the one dead. I'll plop you in the forest a half-mile from here and make you hike back to the farm. No one would ever find you."

"That is *so* not funny," Dale chided. "I could have died."

I'd heard both men discuss Dale's little hiking escapade. He'd tried to walk to work through a forest his first day. Let's just say that it didn't exactly end the way Dale had thought it would. Once the horror of what had happened was over, the nonstop joking at Dale's expense had begun.

"Work daddies," I broke in. I'd started using the new nickname a while back to get under their skin. "Can you two stop bickering?"

"Never," Dale said.

He overlapped with Talgat's, "We're not bickering."

I rolled my eyes, folded my ladder and headed to put it in the back of Talgat's truck. Talgat loved his old truck. Sure, the monstrosity looked like it had been pelted by dozens of rotten apples. It had more dings and bumps all over it. The old rust-colored paint was chipping and the inside smelled like an animal may have died in there, but Talgat kept the blasted thing in top running condition. One of Dale's favorite subjects to bitch about was the old truck. I'm amazed Dale hadn't come out in the middle of the night and shot it with a shotgun. *Does Dale even know how to shoot?*

Today, Dale didn't complain about the truck. He folded the ladder before following me to the back of the vehicle and depositing the wooden object on the cargo bed. I made a mental note of the trees Dale had "looked at" and promised to recheck them tomorrow. As much as I loved Dale and Talgat, Dale was often more work than he was help.

"Traitor," Talgat said to me as he brought his ladder over and put it on top of mine.

"When my boss says it's quitting time, who am I to disagree?" I shot Talgat my most innocent-looking smile.

"Yep. Traitor," Talgat replied as he chuckled. "I'm still amazed you haven't caught yourself a husband with that smile of yours."

And there was the topic that we always came back around to...my love life. More specifically, my absolute lack of a love life.

"It's not my fault there are more trolls than princes around these parts."

"They're called hippies," Dale corrected, "not trolls."

"Hardy-har-har," Talgat replied. "How long have you been waiting to use that one?"

And that's how the conversation went all the way back to the corporate office at the front of the farm. In retrospect, I almost wish I had sat in the cargo bed instead of the cabin, listening to them both. Despite their cantankerous bickering, anyone could tell they were in love. It was almost disgusting how in love they were. Personally, I wasn't sure if love was in my cards, and I know that sounds depressing to some people, but that's reality. Many people go through their entire lives without meeting anyone to fall in love with. Others get married to a friend they aren't in love with. Even worse, some marry because the other person loves them, not because they love them back. Despite my personal cynicism toward relationships as a twenty-four-year-old, I'm not anti-love or anti-relationships. I am pro-truth and pro-reality. And my truth was that I was single, and my reality was I probably wasn't going to find Mr. Right living up in Woodstock. There aren't that many guys around my age.

We hit a bump, and I grabbed the 'oh shit' handle to stop myself from landing in Dale's lap, who was sitting in between Talgat and myself.

"Damn," Dale said. "Look at that biceps of yours. You have more definition than I realized."

"It's amazing what years of farm labor can do to the body. Who needs a gym when you work outside lifting things all day? Right, Talgat?"

"Preach!" Talgat replied. Talgat and I were both five-feet-seven-inches-tall. But I had a runner's body, and Talgat looked like a guy who spent hours pumping weights in a gym. Same heights, very different genetics. I could pump iron and get ripped, but I would never have the muscle mass distribution Talgat had. Damn genetics! On the other hand, Dale was six-four, and he could have been a model if he hadn't gotten sucked in by his first job on Wall Street.

We pulled up in front of the corporate office, which had magically appeared one week last summer. From what I gathered from Talgat's siblings, Ayala and Rasul, Dale had pulled out a credit card and ordered the building online. How one orders an office building online is beyond me. Dale was the epitome of privilege. Thankfully, Dale had realized this on his own over the past year and tried to make everyone's lives better. There had been job raises all around. New equipment was procured to replace things that should have been tossed years ago. He'd even purchased us new uniforms to wear when the public showed up for apple picking. *Oh darn.* I'd ripped mine during one of the first weeks I'd had it. I'd 'forgotten' to ask for another one. No one had ever said anything about that. After that first weekend, those shirts slowly disappeared from people's wardrobes. They weren't exactly ugly. They were nice for what they were. But most of us didn't want to run around looking like cookie-cutter copies of each other like we worked for some big-box department store.

I hopped out and grabbed the shovels from the truck bed. "I'm going to take these back to the barn," I said as I headed off.

"Come by my office before you leave," Dale said.

What is that about? Dale usually didn't ask me into the building unless he was apologizing for something. *Unless… Is it someone's birthday?* I ran down the list of birthdays in my head, but I couldn't think of one.

"You heading back up to the mini-castle?" Rasul asked when I entered the barn. Rasul had started calling the corporate office building the mini-castle as a way of poking fun at the house Dale and Talgat lived in, which had a turret for a master bedroom. I've never been in the place, but from how Rasul has described the building, it has a weird castle-like façade.

"Yeah, Dale asked me to stop by," I said. *That was weird.* "Am I missing something?"

"Nah," Rasul lied to my face. Rasul wasn't even a good liar, but I didn't contradict him.

"You coming, too?" I asked. From the look on the man's face, he knew I'd caught on to his untruth.

"Sure," Rasul said with a giant smile. "Let's go. Just give me a second." Rasul put up a few tools, then washed his hands in the sink. "Wanna wash up?" he asked.

Something was going on. I grinned, walked over and washed my hands. Once I'd dried them, I looked at Rasul and said, "After you."

We walked to the corporate office building. "Are you going to tell me what's going on?" I asked Rasul when we were about halfway between the barn and the administration building.

"I d-don't know what you're t-talking about," Rasul stammered.

I stopped walking and faced him. I didn't need to say anything. I raised a single eyebrow. I can control my eyebrows, and I love to use them to an impressive effect. But Rasul didn't budge.

"Out with it," I said.

"I can't. I promised. Just trust me... It's good."

I shot Rasul a distrustful look, but I started walking again. We entered the air-conditioned building. *It's not even that hot outside... Just open a window.* There were streamers, and I wasn't sure what was going on.

Ayala, Talgat's little sister, who was slightly older than I am, was holding a cake. "Did I miss someone's birthday?" I asked without thinking.

"No, silly!" Ayala said. "We're celebrating your graduation early."

"My graduation?" It took my brain a second to catch up with her intention. "Oh, you mean me finally finishing my associate degree at Ulster?"

"Hey, getting your associate degree is the first step in your college career," Talgat said, joining his sister.

"And," Ayala started, "we're also celebrating that Dale and Talgat have *finally* chosen a date."

"It's about time," I said. "I thought you two would stay engaged forever. So, when's the big day?"

"Beginning of August. We wanted it before peak apple-picking season. We'll have it right here on the farm," Dale said as he threw his arm around Talgat. "Dear God, you smell."

"Hey, an honest day's work will do that to ya," Talgat said.

"I hope I don't smell like that. Ayala," Dale said, turning to his future sister-in-law. "Do I smell as bad as he does?"

Ayala took a whiff and said, "You still smell like body wash and shea butter."

"See? You can work outside and not smell," Dale joked.

"You were out there for thirty minutes and called it a day," Talgat said, narrowing his eyes at Dale. "Jordan and I were out there a good eight hours working in the sun."

"Hey, don't bring me into this. I'm sure I smell perfectly fine," I said, trying to extract myself from their conversation.

"Anyway," Dale said, cutting back into the conversation, "we have other news."

At that, everyone turned and stared at me. "What? Do I have something on my face?"

"Sure thing, Pearl," Talgat replied.

"Huh?" I asked.

"*RuPaul's Drag Race*?" Talgat asked. I shrugged. "Are you sure you're gay?"

I had a witty comeback on the tip of my tongue but didn't think it was appropriate in mixed company, so I bit it back.

"Well, Mr. Floyd, we wanted to be the first to congratulate you on being enrolled in the BA in Nutrition and Food Studies at NYU starting this fall."

"I got in?" Without thinking, I sat down on the couch in the waiting room then thought about it for a second. "Wait! How do you know before I do?"

"How do you think?" Ayala asked as she nodded her head in Dale's direction.

"And no," Dale started, "before you ask, I did nothing to help you get in. I mean, I would have if I had known you'd applied. I found out last week."

"Sorry," Rasul said. "That one's on me. I let it slip."

I wanted to respond to Rasul, but Dale didn't give me a chance.

"I reached out to a friend who found out that you'd been accepted. And not only were you accepted, but you've also received a full ride after winning a scholarship created by the Devereux Farm Foundation."

The information was coming at me way too fast to comprehend completely. "I didn't apply for a scholarship." As soon as the words were out of my mouth, the name of the scholarship hit me. "Wait..."

Talgat clearly saw the look of recognition as it washed over my face. "Yep, we created a scholarship for you, applied to it for you then awarded it to you."

"So, you're paying for me to go to NYU?"

"Nope, not at all," Dale said. "The Foundation is paying for you. I am the chair of the foundation, and I appointed Talgat, Ayala and Rasul as the other board members. Granddad and our lawyers thought it was a great idea."

Part of me wanted to balk, but I wasn't about to look a gift horse in the mouth. *Whatever that means.*

Dale got a mischievous grin on his face. "Your room, board, books and a monthly stipend are also part of the scholarship package." I sat there, stupefied by my good fortune. "There is one small caveat, however." *Uh-oh, here it comes.* "You will need to work for Devereux Farms for three years after earning your degree. When you graduate, you'll get to decide whether you want to keep working in the city with Granddad or come back up here and continue working with us."

"Of course, I'll come back here," I blurted.

"There's no need to decide now," Talgat said. "You haven't lived in the city. You have no idea how you'll feel in a couple of years. Finish your degree, then you can decide what the next stage of your life will be."

"I can't believe… It's so much…" I couldn't form a sentence.

"Hopefully, he'll write better than he talks," Rasul chided.

"I'm beyond thankful," I said. "This is so unexpected."

"You've been the backbone of this farm for years." Talgat took a few steps toward me and drew me into a bear hug. "I'm thankful for everything you've done. Honestly, you deserve more than we can possibly give you."

I wrapped my arms around Talgat. There was a time when I thought I had a crush on Talgat when I had first started working here. Over time, that crush went away, and he became the older brother I never had.

"Thanks," I said as I blinked back tears. Then I took a whiff. "Dear God, Dale's right! You smell."

The room erupted into laughter. I nudged Talgat in the gut with my elbow and shot him a half-cocked smile.

Ayala took that opportunity to cut the cake. We sat around the office drinking beer, which had appeared out of nowhere, and eating cake. We talked about life,

Dale and Talgat's wedding plans and my actual graduation.

After a lull in the conversation, I decided now was as good a time as any to pose a question I'd been meaning to ask. "Dale, Talgat, I wondered if I could have a few days off in May? There's a retreat at the Woodstock Esoteric Sanctuary. I've wanted to go every year, but always came up with an excuse not to."

"The *what*?" Dale asked.

"The Woodstock Esoteric Sanctuary," I replied.

"What the hell is that?"

Talgat let out a sigh. "We've driven by it before. It's the retreat center west of town in the Catskills."

"Oh, the hippy-dippy camping ground?" Dale asked.

"It's not a hippy camping ground," Talgat responded. "Not everything in Woodstock revolves around hippies."

"It's more of a spiritual or rejuvenation retreat place. They run different theme weekends all year round," Ayala said, jumping into the conversation. "They had a women's empowerment summit I attended several years back. A bunch of female CEOs from the city were there talking about leadership in corporate America today."

"Anyway," I said, cutting back into the conversation, "there's a big gay camp weekend every year. People from all over New England attend."

"Oh, you mean Namast-Gay?" Talgat asked.

"You're kidding me," Dale said, barely containing himself. "Namast-Gay? You're telling me that ain't some hippy-dippy shit right there?"

"Maybe there is a bit of hippy stuff up there, but it's supposed to be a great weekend. I'm almost amazed none of your crew from the city attended," Talgat said.

"Think about what you just said for a moment. Think about who I ran with down there. Can you really see any of them spending time in the woods playing camper?"

"Yeah...no," Talgat admitted. "Especially not 'he should who should not be named'."

Everyone's head turned my way. Dale had hung out with one guy who had gotten a bit handsy with me when we met. I'd put him in his place, but it had become one of those topics we didn't bring up very often. When we did, he'd basically become Voldemort, which I honestly thought gave the little punk more power than he deserved.

"About the time off?" I asked.

"Not a problem," Dale said.

"Thanks. I've been saving up for it."

"I can totally pay for the retreat," Dale said.

"Work dad number one, I don't need your money. I'm a big boy now. I have a job and my own bills and everything."

"Smartass," Dale said. "You know I didn't mean it like that."

"I know. And thank you for the offer, but I've got this one covered. Besides, I'm about to milk you for a ton of money while at NYU."

Dale threw back his head and laughed.

We hung out for a little longer before we all headed off in our different directions for the evening. When I got into my truck, which was admittedly newer and nicer than Talgat's but still not an older vehicle, I got a whiff of myself for the first time. I needed to go home and take a shower. How Ayala put up with a bunch of smelly guys was beyond me.

Chapter Three

Darrin

Seven of the longest fucking days of my life... I had spent days one and two pissed off at Bryce and the world. I had cleaned everything in Chance's and my brownstone by the end of day four. Chance and I had gotten married before his death, so I had inherited the home we'd lived in. Chance had purchased it back in the nineties, so it was a nice little piece of real estate in the Village in the two-hundred block of West Eleventh Street, which was within walking distance of the ED. His practice had been up on Forty-First, so he had taken either a cab or the train to work, depending on when he was heading in and how much he wanted to mess with the crowd or the funky smell on the subway. Let's face it. The hot and muggy August stench from riding the Metro was not something that easily came out of one's fabric.

By day six I had caught up with everything I hadn't binged on my streaming services. By day seven, I was back to being bored out of my mind. How do other people take vacations? I don't get it. I've never had time for holidays. Sure, I took the random ski excursion up in Vermont with friends or flew down to the Bahamas for a weekend, but that's what they were — weekend getaways. Nothing more.

I had plowed my way through my undergraduate career at Rice University in three years, followed by four years of medical school at Texas Tech. After the first two years at Tech, I entered my last two years of rotations and traveled as much as I could get away with. Want to do emergency in Detroit? Sounded like a plan to me. Want to try family medicine at an out-of-the-way hospital in Alaska? Sure. I learned I didn't want to end up in a small-town hospital for my residency, so I focused all my attention in the last eight months on making inroads at large hospitals. On the day the National Residency Matching Program emails went out, I was thankful my top match choice wanted me, University of Colorado in Denver. I wasn't getting into number one because I hadn't rotated through there. Number one held zero interest for me, so I had gone through Denver twice and tried to make as many connections while I was there as possible so that they'd fall in love with me. I also totally sold the one-fourth of my cultural heritage that was Puerto Rican.

My dad's mother was Puerto Rican, so I milked it for everything it was worth. Thankfully, no one ever asked me to speak Spanish or my attempt at appearing as more than my English, Irish, French ancestry would have been sunk. Sadly, my abuela was Americanized by the time I was born. I think she still spoke Spanish with some of her relatives, but she never spoke it in the family home. And when my grandparents came to live in Dallas to be near us, I don't think I ever heard her speak it with the other Spanish speakers in the Plano area, but that might be because they were all Mexican American. I'd taken Latin in college because I figured it would be more useful for medical school than Spanish would be. In retrospect, I should have added Spanish, because I ended up needing to learn it during my residency out of necessity. It was also a handy language now that I lived in New York.

By day eight, I had wanted to beg Bryce to let me come volunteer as a candy striper. I don't even think we had those in our facility, but I didn't care.

On day nine, I lay in bed all day and slept. I had nothing else to do.

On day ten, my pity party was over. I decided I should clean out Chance's closet. I opened the wardrobe for the first time since the funeral. I looked at the rows of his suits still neat in their cellophane wrappers from the dry cleaner down the street. His shoes were in a row along one side of the wall. Chance was perfect. Everything about him was perfect. He was always in control. The clean lines in his wardrobe were so...so him. On a shelf in the back stood a stack of folded sweaters and sweatshirts. I walked over and grabbed the top one. He'd gone to Johns Hopkins as an undergraduate and for medical school, then to Harvard for his residency, followed by an infectious disease fellowship at Oxford University. He'd grown up in Baltimore and had wanted to practice on the East Coast, but Chance had opted to practice medicine in New York instead of his hometown.

I picked up his old Johns Hopkins sweatshirt. It was thin from years of wear and tear. It was one of the few things Chance had refused to get rid of. The soft fabric was comforting beneath my fingers. I raised it to feel it against my cheek. It smelled like him — a combination of the bodywash he used and the cologne he wore.

I'd forgotten what he'd smelled like.

The tears started running down my face. I looked around the closet. Everything reminded me of him, of all I'd lost and would never get back. I sort of drooped to the floor with tears streaming down my cheeks. I buried my head in the blasted sweatshirt, and my tears threatened to wash away his scent. I curled into a little ball on the floor and cried until I couldn't cry anymore. At some point, I went to sleep, emotionally exhausted.

On day eleven, I pulled myself together. I folded the sweatshirt as neatly as I could. I could practically hear Chance chastising me for not folding it right. The memory made me chuckle. Folding clothes was one of the few continuous arguments we'd had. Chance's folding skills would have put any high-end men's-clothing-store worker to shame. Me? I folded for maximum cramming ability. Half the time, I rolled T-shirts because I could put more T-shirts rolled up tightly into a drawer than if I folded them, which had been an abomination in Chance's view.

I put the sweatshirt back in its place and closed the wardrobe, promising myself that I would deal with it another day. I called Richard around eleven a.m.

"Hey, Darrin," Richard said, answering his cell phone. There was a pause on the other end of the line before he asked, "How are you holding up?"

"My house is spotless."

"That bad, huh?"

"Yep. Any chance you're available for lunch?" I asked.

"You're in luck. I was supposed to have a working luncheon with a client, but their flight was delayed, so they won't be getting into town until late tonight. I'm all yours."

We made plans to meet up at an upscale bistro at one p.m. to avoid the initial rush of office workers looking to get in a quick bite before heading back to their jobs. Richard worked for a large accounting firm in one of those high-rises around Grand Central Station, so I left my place around noon to give myself plenty of time to get there. I could have taken the train or a cab, but the weather was nice, and a long walk could do me some good.

I left the brownstone and traveled east on West Eleventh until I hit Fifth Avenue. Then I headed north for just under two miles. When I was a few blocks away, I called Richard to ensure he was ready.

"Just putting on my coat. Should be at the restaurant in about five minutes," he told me.

The restaurant was slow for a Friday. I had half expected it to be busy at one p.m., but it looked like many people had opted for earlier lunches. I was seated near one of the front windows and handed the seasonal menu. I rarely ventured to Midtown, so it was a pleasant change of scenery.

Richard breezed in, looking totally dashing in a black pinstripe suit with a powder-blue necktie and matching pocket square.

"Nice cufflinks," I said.

"Anniversary present from Bryce last year."

I gestured to my ensemble, which consisted of a pair of jeans, tennis shoes and salmon-colored cashmere sweater. "Sorry. I'm not as dressed up as you are."

"Hush. You're on vacation."

"Oh, that's what we're calling my exile?" Richard had a worried look flash across his face, so I tried to downplay it. "I'm joking." Richard eyed me through his glasses, not very convinced. I needed to keep myself together because as soon as our luncheon was over, he would call and tell Bryce every little detail. "What do you recommend?"

"The seasonal soup and salad are always my go-to."

I read the menu and found the soup was a curried carrot soup with tarragon oil. The salad was mixed greens with goat cheese and balsamic vinegar, maple syrup and cherry tomatoes.

When the waitress came to the table, we both ordered the soup and the salad. The restaurant had a blood-orange wheat beer they got from a Brooklyn microbrewery. I figured if it was good enough for the hipsters, I might as well try it. I was assured by the waitress that it was the best they had, and the beer would pair nicely with my meal.

With our meals ordered, Richard turned his full attention to me. *Lucky me.*

"How has your *vacation* been going?" I hadn't missed the stress he put on the word when asking.

"It's been different," I said in my best noncommittal voice.

He waited for me to say more. He let out a little breath and shook his head. "Tell me more," he finally said, drawing out each word.

I inhaled, then let out a deep sigh before I provided him a blow-by-blow description of the last ten days but left out the more emotional parts.

"Was your house that dirty?" Richard asked.

"No. The cleaning lady comes in twice a week. I didn't know what else to do. I scrubbed everything. I could have eaten off the kitchen floor when I'd gotten done disinfecting it. I may have peeled off a layer of paint from the tiles."

"Well, at least you haven't moped the entire time."

"I've had my moping days." As soon as the words were out of my mouth, I wished I could reach out, grab them and shove them right back in because Richard wouldn't let me get away with not telling him everything.

The waitress chose that time to show up with our meals. I tasted the soup and salad, then tried to start a conversation about how amazing they were, but Richard eyed me...waiting.

"Okay," I said, aiming not to be too exasperated. "I attempted clearing out Chance's wardrobe." I stabbed a piece of lettuce and a cherry tomato and placed them into my mouth as I figured out the best way to explain the experience. After swallowing, I said, "I wasn't ready for that."

"In what way?"

"All of it. When I went inside, it looked like it had the last time Chance had been in there. No one had opened those doors since I'd pulled a suit out for the funeral."

"Oh, honey," Richard said as he reached his hand across the table and put it on top of mine. "I wish you would have called."

"I probably should have, but I think I needed that moment to myself. I needed the cathartic breakdown that followed." I then told him about the sweatshirt and how it still smelled like Chance after all these months. I detailed my minor breakdown and how I cried and fell asleep on the closet floor until the sun rose.

"What made you decide to call me for lunch?" I looked over at Richard as he spooned some of the orange soup into his mouth.

I also spooned in some of the carrot soup. The curry was stronger than I'd expected. Not overpowering, just pretty darn potent. I like curry, but I could see how some palates would be shocked by the heat that accompanied the sweet and savory spices.

"Well, it's not like I have many friends anymore. Basically, I've shut myself off from everyone but you and Bryce since Chance died."

"We'd noticed," Richard said. "We were hoping you'd get around to noticing it, too."

"And I couldn't exactly call Bryce because he's in the awkward position of friend but also Director of Emergency Medicine. And right now, I need a friend and not a boss."

"He can be both, you know?"

"I know that." Richard's face oozed skepticism from the creases on his forehead to the cleft in his chin. "I know that. But sometimes… I don't want someone who thinks he has to solve the problem. It's what we do. We see a problem and we feel the need to fix it. If we can't fix it, we find someone who can. It's what we're trained to do. I needed someone who could listen…objectively, without trying to fix everything."

Richard let out a knowing sigh. "I get what you're saying. He tries to fix my problems all the time. I have to remind him that I'm his husband, not one of his patients."

We spent the rest of lunch just talking. Richard stayed with me long past when he probably should have gone back to work. But I guess being a senior partner affords a few luxuries, like the occasional long lunch break.

"Well, you know I will tell Bryce about our conversation when I see him." I started to say something, but Richard cut me off. "Don't worry. I know how to be judicious with my description. Besides, you look and sound better than I've seen you in months. You sure do look better than how Bryce described your last morning in the ED."

"Yeah, I had a bit of a breakdown that had been long overdue. I had bottled so much shit up from this year and seeing a fucking watch of all things set me off. If it hadn't been a watch that day, it could have been a shoe the next. I'm glad Bryce was the one who stepped in to control the situation. It could have been much, much worse."

"I'll tell him that when I see him this evening."

"Are you two doing something fun?"

"We're heading to an opening of some new Broadway show. Our accounting firm is running the books for the show's general manager, so we got tickets to the opening."

"What's the show?"

"I don't know," Richard said with a shrug. "Bryce is excited. Some Broadway legend has come out of retirement to star in it. Bryce practically squealed when he heard I got tickets."

"Bryce...squealed? Please tell me you recorded that. I would like to use it as my new ringtone."

"You and me both. Maybe I'll pull out my phone and video him meeting her at the opening night party then put it up on TikTok to see if I can get any likes."

"Do people even like things on TikTok?"

"I don't know. I'm an accountant. I don't think there are any accounting TikTok stars."

"Maybe you can be the first one," I suggested.

"Yeah." He drew out the word. "I don't think the other senior partners would find that nearly as entertaining as you would. Anyway, I have something I wanted to talk to you about."

That piqued my attention. "Shoot."

"Bryce and I always go to this little retreat center upstate in May, and I think you should join us this year. It's fun. It's a bunch of gay guys hanging out in little cabins in the woods."

"Gay camping?"

"Gay *glamping* is more like it. There may be nature, but we have resort-quality accommodations. We're just in the trees. There's always fun activities, alcohol and gay men as far as the eye can see."

"I'm not sure if I'm ready for something like that."

"It would be fun. And it's not like you have any better plans. You can only scrub your kitchen tiles so often before you have a problem. Just think about it." He reached into his coat, pulled out a trifold brochure and slid it across the table.

Right on the cover in all its glorious rainbow were the words 'Camp Namast-Gay!'

* * * *

After finishing lunch with Richard, I wasn't in the mood to walk home, so I headed into Grand Central and caught the train to Times Square. I switched to the two-line going south to the Fourteenth Street Station. I exited and pulled out my phone. I had an extra pep in my step and pulled up my favorite app on my phone, Grindr. I opened the app and it let me know anyone close by looking for a casual hookup. No mess. No fuss. I hadn't been inclined to think about dating, but I'm still a thirty-three-year-old with a libido. So occasionally I wanted to have fun with another guy and his libido without complications.

I looked at the guys who were available, and pretty much everyone that was looking was someone I'd already hooked up with or would never in a million years hook up with. I settled on one of my usuals and shot him off a message.

Looking? I asked.

Always.

Your place or mine?

Yours. Your bed is bigger. Just me – or do you want a third?

Just you.

Be there in thirty.

And, like that, I had a fuck date. I walked the two additional blocks home, then quickly dashed through the shower. I'd walked around a lot, so I figured I didn't smell like an Irish spring. On top of that, my hookup would show up nice and clean... He always did.

There was a knock on the door when I stepped out of the shower. I considered opening the door in the buff but wrapped my towel around my waist in case it was a neighbor needing sugar or the postal worker making a delivery.

There was a slight figure standing on the other side of the door. The door was wrought-iron with reeded glass inlays, which let in the light without being transparent. There was one peephole, so I checked and recognized the back of my trick's head. I'd seen that part of his head a lot. I could probably pick it out of a lineup.

I opened the door. "Avery, how nice of you to come."

He turned around and took in my still-damp body with the towel firmly around my waist. He tilted his head, and a grin sprang across his face. "Thanks for dressing up."

I held the door for him as he walked inside. "Only my finest outfit for you, my dear." I leaned in and kissed him as I closed the door. He smelled like a combination of honeysuckle and cherry blossoms. It wasn't overpowering or girlish, just a nice, fresh scent. With the door closed, I let the towel drop to the ground.

I turned and walked away. I took a few steps before turning around to see Avery staring at my backside. "Are you coming?"

He didn't have to be asked twice.

I walked through the house and up the stairs to the master bedroom. Before Avery finished getting into the room, he'd shed all his clothes. I climbed on the bed, lowered myself down and propped my head up on the pillows with my arms folded behind me. My nine-inch uncut cock was standing at full mast, demanding attention. I spread my legs. Avery didn't need any more invitation than that before he bobbed his head up and down on me. We had this act down. He'd blow me for a bit, I'd roll on a condom, then he would straddle me and ride until I flipped him onto his hands and knees before coming. It wasn't romantic. It was barely sexy. But it got the job done…for both of us. In fifteen minutes, my load was inside the condom, and his load coated my duvet. *Time to do some laundry.*

I walked into the master bathroom, grabbed a wet washcloth for Avery and tossed it to him.

"Thanks," he said.

"Not a problem. You're better than takeout, and you come faster," I said.

"From anyone else, I would take that as an insult, but I know how you like it."

"Yes, Mr. Addington, you do. And I know how your ass likes it."

"Yes, Dr. Betancourt, you most definitely do. Your cock hits me in all the right places. We should do this more often." I smiled, and Avery waved me off. "I know. You're a busy doctor and all. I get it. I'm sure you have to get back to work, so I won't keep you."

I probably should have admitted that I was on vacation, but I didn't. "Thanks for understanding."

He started to collect his clothes. I threw on a robe and pulled it snuggly around myself.

"You going?" he asked, gesturing to my pile of dispatched clothes.

"To what?" I followed his gaze and saw a colorful brochure sticking out of the heap.

"Camp Namast-Gay? I've gone for like four years now. It's amazing. I always go by myself and end up meeting the most wonderful people. It's kind of been my secret getaway every spring."

"Honestly, until today, I hadn't even heard of it."

"There is literally dick everywhere. You want morning dick, noon dick or night dick. It's there. Dick in all shapes, sizes and colors."

"Sounds like Dick-topia."

"It is. And there's a bunch of other stuff, too. But last year I fucked my way through camp. It was fabulous. All the cock I could want. Hell, I even topped a few times for the fun of it."

I nodded with a sly grin. I glanced at my cell phone, which I'd plugged into its charger. *I can get dick any time I want now. What I want is Chance back.*

"Well, I best be getting back to what I was doing before this nice late-afternoon reprieve from life," I said.

I walked back downstairs following Avery's mostly naked body to the first floor, where he collected his clothes and put them back on. When he was dressed, I held the door for him, making sure I was out of sight from anyone who walked by. Avery leaned in for one more kiss before heading out.

"I hope to see you at the camp. We would have a total blast and tear that place up!"

"I'll let you know," I said noncommittally. His ass moved smoothly below his jeans as he descended the stairs.

After Avery left, I took another shower, changed the sheets then took a nap. The next thing I knew, I was waking up and it was three in the morning. I turned over, stole a quick glance at the clock and rolled back over to sleep for a couple more hours. At five, I dragged myself to the gym. I thought long and hard about Richard's suggestion that I go up to Camp Namast-Gay with Bryce and him. Then I wondered how much fun it would be to let loose and have a bunch of random sex out in the woods. I headed home after my workout and glanced down at my smartwatch. It was a little after eight a.m., so Richard would be up. I called.

"You're calling me early? Anything wrong?"

"Not at all. Count me in."

"For?" Richard asked.

"Camp Gay."

"Camp Namast-Gay?" Richard double-checked.

"That's right! I'm in."

"Awesome. I'll call you after work. Check out their website and make your reservation. You can do that either by going to the site or calling them directly. The number is on the brochure as well."

"I'll do that now."

As soon as I was home, I grabbed the brochure and found their website, which redirected me to the Woodstock Esoteric Sanctuary. On their site, I found a lot of different retreats, but Camp Namast-Gay was right there on the first page, so I clicked, scanned the information, grabbed my credit card and made my reservation.

"Camp Cock, here I come!"

Chapter Four

I finished packing for my trip. I wasn't sure what I needed for the weekend, so I probably crammed too much into my oversized duffel bag, which was something I have a nasty habit of doing. I had shorts, T-shirts, tank tops, a swimsuit, sweaters, jeans, khakis and more socks and underwear than I could use in a weekend. I'd even thrown in a new box of condoms and a bottle of lube…just in case. I wasn't necessarily planning to get laid, but safety first. After Chance had died and I began having my semi-regular hookups with Avery, I decided to go on PrEP. But even with PrEP, I'd started living by the 'better safe than sorry' motto.

I looked at my luggage and came to a simple realization. "This weekend is about having fun with friends. I'm not Avery. I'm not going to sleep my way through camp. I'm over the random hook." I may have only been telling the couch, but just saying it out loud strengthened my resolve. *I need to be the man Chance would want me to be. The nonsense stops now.*

The sound of sirens filled my apartment cutting into my thoughts just as Bryce's ringtone went off. "Good morning," I said, picking up the phone.

"We're about two minutes from your place," Bryce said. "You haven't backed out on us, have you?"

"No," I said, elongating the word. "I'm packed and ready to go."

"Great! See you soon." With that, Bryce hung up the phone.

I looked around my house and ensured everything was turned off except for one light in the living room. I then slung my duffel bag over my shoulder. *Damn! This is heavy.* I left the house, then locked the door behind me. I turned around in time to see Bryce's SUV pulling up.

Richard got out, went around to the back and lifted the tailgate, then helped me cram my bag inside among the suitcases and rolling bags. I'd worried I had over-packed, but I hadn't seen anything. I wasn't sure if all the stuff belonged to Bryce or Richard, but there was enough luggage for a family of six going on a two-week vacation.

"What all did you bring?" I asked.

"Just a little bit of this, and a little bit of that. You know… We want to make sure we're prepared for any eventuality."

Richard gestured for me to follow him to the passenger side of the SUV. I opened the door as he climbed in the front. A man I didn't know sat behind Bryce.

"Hi," I said as I settled into my seat and buckled in. "I'm Darrin Betancourt."

"Owen Collier," the man said in a Scottish brogue.

I extended my hand and shook the other man's hand. He had calloused palms and fingers.

"Owen's our dog walker," Bryce said. "He came with us last year and couldn't wait to return."

"I'm also the legendary Nessie Loch," the man said.

"Huh?" I blurted without thinking.

"Nessie Loch is my stage name. Maybe you've heard of me?"

"Sorry," I said. "I haven't been in the scene in a long time. I'm sadly and woefully unaware of the drag scene anymore."

Owen, or Nessie, told me all about his life. He'd been on some drag competition show on television, making him an international star. He moved to New York because the scene here was 'legendary'. Of course, it's New York, he needed a day job to make ends meet, so he started walking dogs. I was amazed by the man's stamina, given his day and evening jobs.

"That's my life in a nutshell," Owen said. He'd spoken for the better part of an hour. We were already on I-87 heading north when he paused, took a breath and said, "Tell me about you."

"Not that much to tell, I guess. I work with Bryce in the Emergency Department. Beyond that, I don't have much of a life."

"Dating anyone?" Owen asked.

"Owen!" Richard said. "We talked about that." The intensity in Richard's voice made me grimace internally. What had Bryce and Richard told Owen?

"It's fine," I said, forcing a smile on my face. "I lost my husband in September —"

"Oh shit! I totally forgot about that. I am *so* sorry."

"Thanks," I said, putting on my usual fake demeanor when people gave me condolences. "I'm still grieving, so I haven't dated anyone in years."

Talk about a party killer. The SUV went silent. Bryce turned on his satellite radio, and we listened to show tunes for the next hour. I hadn't heard cast albums in years, so it was a nice escape. Who doesn't want to listen to Bernadette Peter's amazing voice as you drive through the green countryside of upstate New York?

At some point, I closed my eyes and drifted off to sleep.

"We're here!" Bryce's voice cut through my nap, forcing me to wake up.

"Huh?" I instinctively asked as I lifted my hands to my eyes to rub the sleep out of them.

"We're up in Woodstock," Owen said. I had to admit that I could sit and listen to Owen's voice for hours. I'd always been attracted to various English accents that were not American. British, Australian, Irish, Scottish and New Zealand accents could always make me swoon.

I looked down at my watch. It was a little before five p.m. We stepped out into the sun, and I stretched my body. It had been a long time since I'd taken a ride that long. Living in the city, you don't spend much time sitting in a car. Even if I take a cab somewhere, it's not for multiple hours.

A man in an orange vest with the word 'Volunteer' emblazoned across the back walked up to our group. "Welcome to Camp Namast-Gay! Is this your first time joining us?"

"The three of us have been here before," Richard said, gesturing to Bryce, Owen and himself. "But this guy is a total virgin."

The orange vest guy sized me up. "Welcome! We're glad you're able to join us. If you have questions, please ask any of the Camp Namast-Gay volunteers. We'll be in T-shirts that say 'volunteer' all weekend, so we should be easy to find. Now, if you all will head to the building over there"—he pointed to a flat brown building on the other side of the parking lot—"they'll be able to check you in. As for your belongings, please make sure your name is clearly written on your bags." He handed us luggage tags and a marker. "We'll haul everything to your cabin in the next forty-five minutes or so."

We all took the tags and marked our stuff before heading toward the brown building with an extensive array of solar panels on top. There were a bunch of men milling around the place. The organizers appeared on top of things, because everything ran smoothly at check-in.

"Welcome to Camp Namast-Gay," a gorgeous Asian man said. He was wearing a polo with the camp logo on it. "I'm Mano Palakiko, one of the camp organizers. And your name is?"

"Darrin Betancourt."

Mano had a laptop sitting in front of him and clicked a few keys before saying, "We have you in green cabin number two. You must have been one of the late registrants to be up in the nosebleed cabins."

"I made my decision to come last week," I admitted.

"Don't worry," Mano said. "Those cabins may be remote, but they have spectacular views and are great accommodations. I take it you checked your luggage when you got here?"

"Umm…I think so. Some guy in an orange vest said they'd deliver it."

"Perfect," Mano said, pulling out a packet of information and sliding it across the table in front of me. He then flipped through a box and found a small envelope before handing me everything. "This is your key to the cabin. Please do not lose it. There are spares, but there is a twenty-dollar charge for all lost keys."

"Okay."

"Here's the camp map," Mano said, opening the packet. "Here's where we are now." Mano pointed to the building on the map. "And here is where your cabin is located. I'll warn you... It's a bit of an uphill hike. But you look like you're in good shape, so I doubt you'll have any problems. We wouldn't want to put any of our more senior campers up there."

"How are things going?" a bear of a guy said as he sidled up behind Mano before leaning down and kissing him.

"Hey, honey," Mano responded. "Things are smooth here. How is everything going outside?"

"Great." The man looked up at me. "Sorry for the interruption. I wanted to check in with my husband and head off problems, if there were any." He then extended his hand. "Jaxson Richardson." I took the guy's hand for a quick shake while introducing myself.

"It's Darrin's first time with us," Mano said. "He's up in one of the green cabins."

"Ahh," Jaxson said, "one of our late registrants. Well, sorry for the interruption." He leaned down and kissed Mano again.

The stark difference between the two men surprised me. Mano clearly spent a lot of time in the gym, while Jaxson had probably hadn't seen the inside of a gym in years. I guessed Jaxson was at least three-hundred-and-fifty pounds, if not heavier. I learned a long time ago never to underestimate the power of love to draw even the most opposite of people together. *Love is love.*

Once I was finished checking in, I caught up with the rest of my group. We shared where our cabins were located, and Bryce marked our locations on his map, then did the same with Owen's and my maps.

"What's on the agenda for the rest of the evening?" I asked.

Bryce flipped open the folder he'd received and read off the itinerary, "Dinner is at seven-fifteen, followed by 'night activities' at nine."

"Night activities?" Owen said. "That sounds like a euphemism for an orgy."

"You wish," Richard replied with a chuckle. "How many times do I have to tell you? I'm a one-man man."

"I wasn't talking about you. I was hoping to get into this laddie's pants," Owen said, hooking a thumb in my direction. I must have looked very uncomfortable at that suggestion because Owen quickly changed his statement. "Sorry about that. I didn't mean anything by that. I was making a comeback. I hope that didn't make you uncomfortable."

"It's fine," I lied. "Just caught me off guard is all. I guess I have a bit of a hike ahead of me, so I should probably get going."

We left the building and walked across the street before heading in different directions. The camp had signs everywhere letting you know what direction you needed to head, making navigating the place very easy. The camp had six different cabin areas, which were color-coded—blue, green, orange, purple, red and yellow. Signs periodically showed directions to the various cabin areas, so I kept following the signs. They weren't joking about the hike up to the green cabins.

When I crested the hill, I found four cabins standing right on the edge of an extensive forest area.

"Nice," I said. "This should be quite pleasant and quiet."

* * * *

Jordan

I finished the afternoon by packing up the tools I'd been using in the barn before heading to Dale's mini-castle to check in. The May weather was nicer than it had been just a month ago. It could still be a little chilly this weekend, especially in the evenings, but it should be pleasant for camping.

I opened the door to the building and walked inside. Meredith, the older woman Dale had hired to manage the administrative office, greeted me from her desk. "Good afternoon, Mr. Floyd." She always called everyone mister, miss or missus, which was overly formal for a farm, but we all played along. "Here to see Mr. Devereux, Mr. Kudaibergen or Ms. Kudaibergen?"

I had to think about it for a second before I responded, "Mr. Devereux, I guess."

"Give me one second. I'll see if he's available."

The woman picked up her phone and dialed his extension. Watching her manage the office reminded me of how far we'd come since Dale had first arrived on the farm almost a year ago. "Damn, it has been almost a year," I mumbled.

"What was that, Mr. Floyd?" Meredith said, putting down the phone.

"Oh, sorry. I was muttering something to myself."

"I read once that talking to oneself is a sign of genius."

"Or insanity," Dale said, coming down the stairs. "Though I'm sure with Jordan, it's a sign of his genius and not him losing his marbles. Unlike me... I lost my marbles years ago."

She made a *tsk*ing noise. "None of that, Mr. Devereux. Self-deprecating humor can tarnish your image."

"I thought self-deprecating humor made a boss look more relatable and competent," Dale countered.

"That only works until the people around you start believing you."

"So, you think I've lost my marbles?" Dale asked, trying to put on his most innocent smile.

Meredith looked at him and arched a single, well-manicured eyebrow. Her eyebrows would be the envy of any drag queen. And her ability to control each one separately was already taking on mythic proportions around the farm.

"Hey, Dale," I said, cutting in. "Just dropping by real fast to remind you I'm going away for a few days. Need anything from me before I take off?"

Dale and Meredith were now officially locked in a staring contest, Meredith with her arched eyebrow and Dale with his goofy-ass grin.

One afternoon, I had talked to Talgat about the weird relationship Dale and Meredith were developing. Talgat had told me Dale's goal was to get the older woman to break her countenance and laugh at one of his jokes. Meredith clearly had the stronger will.

"Well, I'll leave you to your...whatever the hell you're doing." I turned to walk away, but glanced at Dale and asked, "That is, unless you need me around the farm this weekend?"

"We'll survive without you," Dale said, turning his head toward me and breaking his eye contact with Meredith. Out of the corner of my eye, Meredith upturned the corner of her mouth for a second in triumph. "I promise the farm won't disappear or burn to the ground without you. What's this really about, Jordan?"

"I'm making sure my boss will survive without me. I'm nothing if not a team player."

"And this team will still be here next week. So, are you going to tell me what's running around in your head?"

I hesitated for a second, and Dale gestured to one of the two couches in the reception area. I walked over and sat on one as he sat on the other. Dale stared, waiting for me to talk. I let out a quick breath and began talking. "I'm not sure what to do around gay people."

"You're around gay people every day. You may not realize this yet, so I know this will be hard to hear, but Talgat and I are, in fact…homosexual." He drew out the word like a Southern Baptist televangelist drawing his hand to his chest in mock woe.

I grimaced at the bad joke. "No shit, Sherlock. What's next? You'll tell me you're a pompous, rich ass?"

"I might resemble that remark," he joked. "But, really, what do you mean? You're around gay people all the time."

"I'm around you and Talgat, not actual gay people." As soon as the words flew out of my mouth, I knew that they didn't make sense. "You and Talgat aren't 'normal' gay."

"And what, pray tell, is 'normal' gay?" Dale asked, doing his best not to laugh. "Trust me. Talgat and I did some pretty *normal* gay things to each other last night...and the night before that. Hell, we do some normal gay things to each other every day. When I'm lucky, I can convince Talgat to be *abnormally* gay with me." Meredith let out a chuckle from behind her desk, which caused Dale's head to whip in her direction. But the woman had the countenance of professionalism before Dale's head fully spun. "I heard that."

"Heard what, sir?" Meredith asked.

"You laughed at one of my jokes."

"I'm sure you are mistaken, Mr. Devereux."

Dale narrowed his eyes at her in mock irritation. "I've got your number. I will get you to laugh in my face before I die."

"Why should I do it to your face when I do it behind your back every day?" Meredith asked with so much innocence that it caused me to bust out laughing. "Go on, Mr. Devereux. Finish telling Mr. Floyd about how incredibly and awesomely gay you are." She finished with a little shooing motion with her hand as she went back to staring at her computer screen.

"You saw her laugh?" Dale said, turning his attention back to me.

"I don't know what you're talking about," I said flatly. "So, almighty gay one, are you done telling me about your gayness?"

Dale rolled his eyes. Not a little roll. No, his over-exaggerated gesture rolled his entire face, which caused me to laugh out loud again. "At least someone around here finds me funny."

"He's placating you," Meredith practically sang out. "It's not quite the same."

I could tell Dale wanted to make a comeback, but it wasn't forming in his head fast enough, so he stuck out his tongue. At that moment, the door to the building opened and Talgat walked in.

"Do I even want to know?" Talgat asked.

"Mr. Devereux was explaining how gay you and he are and how you do gay things to each other every day, Mr. Kudaibergen," Meredith said sweetly.

"It's not nearly as bad as it sounds," Dale spat out, his face turning red.

I couldn't help myself. The belly laugh that erupted from me was obnoxious. The more I laughed, the redder Dale turned. There may have been a snort in there, but I can't remember. When I calmed down and regained my composure, I said, "I needed that."

"What's this all about?" Talgat asked, sitting down next to Dale.

"I was trying to explain to Dale that I'm not used to being around gay people."

"I get it," Talgat said.

"You do?" Dale asked.

"Of course I do. Being around gay guys up here differs from being around gay guys from the city. Up here, people are people first and gay second. Jordan's about to go somewhere where everyone is gay first and people second. There's a fundamental difference. And, let's face it, some of the city-gays are barely people."

"What's that supposed to mean?" Dale questioned, a look of seriousness overtaking his countenance.

"You know what I mean," Talgat said. "Don't give me that look. We've had this conversation before. Citidiots are just different. Even those from rural areas originally become so jaded and warped by the city. It's not intentional, and they're not malicious, but they are different. And the ones who can afford to come up here regularly tend to be the 'A-gays,' which adds a whole other layer of 'otherness' to Jordan." Talgat turned to me and said, "Right?" I nodded my head, so he continued. "As for being nervous around them, they may be shiny, have perfect bodies and expensive wardrobes, but they're still the same scared little gay boys we all are inside. We're all still worried about being picked last for kickball. Keep that in mind, and you'll be able to deal with any of those city-gays."

"Thanks for the pep talk, coach," I joked. "I think I'm ready to get in there and take one for the team."

"Just use protection, Mr. Floyd," Meredith said. Dale's jaw dropped as I snickered at the older woman's advice.

"Well, I guess it's time to head out to the sanctuary. I'll tell you all about it when I return."

With that, I stood up and Dale and Talgat did the same. We hugged before I turned and left the building. I was afraid I'd lose my nerve if I didn't head up there right then. I climbed into my truck and got on the road. Within ten minutes, I pulled into the parking lot. I had no sooner parked than a guy in an orange vest was at my window.

"Can I help you?" he asked.

"I don't know," I replied. I wasn't sure what the right thing was to say. "I'm supposed to be checking in for Camp Namast-Gay. The email said just to come to the Woodstock Esoteric Sanctuary, and I'd be directed where to go next."

"Oh, okay. I wanted to make sure you were in the right place." He glanced at my pickup. He didn't come right out and say, 'I didn't think gays drove ugly trucks like that,' but that was the vibe rolling off the guy. "Do you have luggage?"

"Why?" I asked, not sure what the purpose of the question was.

"We'll have it taken up to your cabin for you."

"I can carry it." I reached in, grabbed my bag and slung it over my shoulder. "See? No need for any help."

The poor guy appeared confused. His look changed from confusion to something else, but I couldn't decipher it. "I take it this is your first time here. Here's how this works," he said. The tone in his voice was like a teacher talking to a kindergartener. "We tag your bag here with your name. We'll deliver your stuff to your cabin in about thirty minutes. Don't worry. We don't go through your belongings. It's a hike, and for insurance purposes, it's safer for everyone this way."

I looked at the poor guy, who was clearly just doing his job. I slumped the bag off my shoulder and onto the ground.

The orange-vested guy smiled in triumph before handing me a luggage tag and a marker. I wrote my name in big, blocky letters. When that was done, he directed me to the registration area.

I felt like a fish out of water. The surrounding people stared at me. I was still in my plaid shirt, blue jeans and work boots. *Before heading out here, I should have gone home, showered and changed into something more…gay. Do I even own a gay outfit?* I planned on showering and changing, but I'd figured I'd do that once I got here. I hadn't thought I'd need to get all gussied up before heading to the camp. I regretted that decision. Around me, everyone was wearing designer clothes and looked like they had stepped out of the pages of magazines. I looked like I had stepped out of a farmer's online dating advertisement—and not one of the good ones, one of the backwoods generic farmer dating apps.

Once I had flown through check-in, I made my way through the camp up to my cabin. I was following the signs. "Excuse me, sir," a voice said.

I spun my head, my eyes pinging to the guy. He was a Californian wet dream, perfectly tanned. His buttoned-down shirt was completely unbuttoned, showing his developed chest and abs.

"Yes?" I asked.

"I'm trying to find the pool. Am I near it?"

I pulled out my map. "From what I can tell, if you take that path over there, you should be able to find it."

"Thanks," the guy said with a smile that practically blinded me.

He turned and started walking away with another guy.

"I totally assumed he was a gardener," I heard the other guy say when they thought they were out of earshot.

"Do you think he's even gay?" the gorgeous guy asked.

I sighed. I wanted to scream, 'Yes, I'm gay!' I turned back to the path and almost ran into a guy in a wheelchair.

"I'm so sorry," I blurted.

"No problem," the guy said, looking up at me. "And pay those guys no mind. They're asses."

"You saw that?" I asked, feeling embarrassed.

"I'm a paraplegic. I'm used to guys looking past me. I'm Isaac Robinson."

He extended his hand, and I shook it. "Jordan Floyd."

"Nice to meet you, Jordan. Remember, when you see those assholes again...fuck 'em." Without waiting for a response, Isaac rolled away.

Holy fuck! I just shook Isaac Robinson's hand. Part of me wanted to fawn after Isaac and totally fan boy, but I kept it together. I'd followed his football career since he'd been in high school, long before he'd gone pro. A goofy grin expanded over my face. *I touched Isaac Robinson.*

The rest of the trek was a haze. And the people at registration were right. Getting to my cabin was a hike. I was glad I didn't have to haul my stupid suitcase up the hill. By the time I got there, I could see my suitcase sitting on the porch. I pulled out the key and let myself into the cabin before returning to grab my bag.

The cabin was nicer than my apartment. I quickly unpacked, then stepped into the bathroom to take a quick shower. It was nice to feel the warm water running over my naked body as I scrubbed off the dirt and grime from the farm. It wasn't like working in an apple orchard was filthy work, but I was in nature, and getting dirty was part of the job. Once I was done, I toweled dry and put on a pair of khaki shorts and a polo shirt with a pair of tennis shoes. I stared at myself in the mirror while I ran a comb through my hair. I went for a natural, outdoorsy style that was popular up here. I may not have looked like one of the cover model gays I'd seen around camp, but I wasn't unattractive by any stretch of the imagination.

Once I was happy with my appearance, I grabbed my wallet and key and headed out to the front porch. I figured I'd go explore the camp before dinner.

"Hey, Jordan," a familiar voice said as I stepped on the porch. "Fancy meeting you here."

I turned my head in the voice's direction. Chad Powell waved from his porch. Chad was a local UPS driver. He was fucking gorgeous, which is why almost every guy in Woodstock had slept with him at one point or another. I was one of the few guys who had refused his advances. Not because I didn't think Chad was hot, he was. It was just everyone I knew had fucked or been fucked by Chad, so even thinking about having sex with him would be weird.

"Hey, Chad," I yelled back with a smile.

A guy in his late twenties suddenly walked out onto the porch between Chad and me. He was fucking gorgeous and looked like he had stepped off the pages of *GQ*. He nodded his head at me before looking at Chad and doing the same.

"Who's that?" a voice said from the porch on the other side of Chad.

I recognized that voice. The muscles in my stomach clenched as the blood in my veins boiled at the memory from last summer. The other man leaned forward, and my worst nightmare came true. The one guy in the world I never wanted to see again, Avery Addington.

"Oh, hell no!" I exploded, balling my hands into fists at my side. "I'm fucking out of here."

Apparently, my voice carried a bit because one guy from registration came around the corner on a golf cart. The built Asian guy stopped and asked, "Everything good here?"

I stared at the guy. His name tag read 'Mano'. I took a breath before saying, "The guy in the last cabin and I have history."

"He assaulted me," Avery said, leaning over the railing on the front porch of his cabin. "I want him removed."

"I barely shoved you," I spat back. "If you hadn't been trying to grab my dick, it never would have happened. I believe that's called sexual assault, asshole."

"Well, for the sakes of everyone around here, please keep your distance. I'd gladly move you if we had room somewhere else, but we don't. If either of you wants to take off, I'll refund your money instantly and you can leave. If not, stay out of each other's way." Mano looked at me, waiting for a reaction.

"As long as that little prick can keep his hands to himself, I promise not to finish what I started last time." I wasn't even sure now if I wanted to be here, but I sure as hell wouldn't let Avery drive me away. Fuck that! I wasn't going to let him win.

Mano swiveled toward Avery. "I'll stay clear of him. But if something happens to me, remember he threatened me. We all heard it."

"Fuck you!" I yelled back. I know it was making me look like some deranged madman, but I didn't fucking care.

Mano's gaze bounced between Chad and me. "Are you with them?"

Chad said, "I know both of them."

The *GQ* model shook his head. "I'm here with friends elsewhere on the property. Just minding my own damn business."

Mano appeared satisfied. He dropped off Chad's bag. *So that's what he's doing up here.* The electric whir of the golf cart could be heard as it left the four cabins and headed down the paved road.

Chad was now sitting on his porch stairs. Avery was standing in front of him. I half expected him to whip it out right there and let Chad have a go. "Besides, it's not like I would be interested in some two-bit hick from Tennessee."

I leaped off my porch and started toward Avery. Suddenly, there was a mound of muscle in my way. I was about to sidestep the guy when the *GQ* model extended his hand. "I'm Darrin."

I took a step back and eyed the guy. *What's his deal?* I extended my hand and said, "Jordan."

"Wanna go for a hike?"

I took another step back wearily. Was 'hike' euphemism up here for sex? I glanced to the man's right. Avery was digging for ear wax in Chad with his tongue.

"I think we both could use a hike. I've been stuck in a car. And, well" — the guy gestured to me before turning his head to see Avery and Chad's public display of affection — "I think you could probably use some time away from up here to cool off."

"You don't know me," I spat.

"True enough. But we'll be here for a few days, so I might as well meet my neighbor."

"Fine, whatever. I need to get out of here."

I looked over at Chad to see him drag Avery into his cabin. I think I threw up a little.

"Great. Let's go."

Darrin

Drama! That's what exploded around me when I stepped onto my front porch. The guy next to me looked like he was ready to leap over and take a shot at Avery. Whatever Avery had done, this kid was pissed. Sadly, it's hardly the first time I've heard of Avery pissing someone off enough that they'd want to punch his lights out. Avery may be fun in bed, but he didn't exactly have a clear moral compass. I had fucked around with him after Chance had died, but Avery had hit on me many times before his passing.

I had watched as Mano from registration pulled up and stepped between both men. I'd been afraid I would have to be the one to step in. Chad hadn't seemed very keen on getting involved. In fact, I caught him licking his lips in Avery's direction when Mano was talking to my neighbor.

After Mano left, I could tell my neighbor needed to get away from Avery and cool the fuck off. I was about to say something when Avery ran his fucking mouth again. I threw myself off the porch and stood in front of my neighbor. I extended my hand and said, "I'm Darrin." I hoped I wouldn't be a casualty between warring parties. The guy took a step back and glowered at me before shaking my hand.

"Jordan."

Immediately, I could tell that Jordan was not a white-collar worker. His hands were calloused. He also had an incredible grip. I don't know if his grip was usually that strong or if it was because of the adrenaline running through his system, but damn. "Wanna go for a hike?" I asked. I could tell he wasn't sure what to make of me, and he put up a brief resistance, but he eventually caved in, thanks to my dazzling smile and sparkling personality. He probably wanted to get out of there when he realized Chad had taken Avery into his cabin. I didn't even want to stick around long enough to know what was about to happen.

"Great. Let's go," Jordan said before turning around and heading down the path away from our cabins.

I jogged a few steps to catch up and did my best to match Jordan's stride.

Once we were no longer near the cabin, I casually asked, "What was that all about?"

We took a few more steps before Jordan answered. "I met him last summer when he came up here to visit my boss. Avery tried to grope me. I politely asked him to keep his hands to himself. He didn't. I shoved him, and he went tits over ass over a bar stool before landing on the ground."

"I wish I could say I was surprised," I admitted.

"What? You know that asshole?" Jordan stopped in the middle of the path and looked at me accusatorily.

"A lot of people know Avery. And he's definitely…special. He has a reputation for causing trouble."

"Oh fuck. You've totally slept with him," Jordan accused. He spun around and headed back down the path. "Has everyone fucking slept with that asshole?"

I stared after Jordan, not sure what I wanted to do. Part of me was like, 'Fuck you, you don't know me,' but I could see things from his perspective. "Hey, wait up," I yelled after him. I jogged again to catch up with him. "I won't lie. I've fucked around with Avery…on more than one occasion. But —"

"But?"

"But I wouldn't call us friends. Hell, I know more about the back dimples above his ass than I do about him as a person." Jordan stopped again in the middle of the path before looking at me. "Wow, that *so* didn't come out right. I mean… Ah, hell… I don't know what I mean. Avery has been a hookup — nothing less, nothing more."

Apparently mollified, Jordan turned around and headed back down the path. I quickly matched his stride. "So, what's your story? And why Avery?"

It was my turn to stop in the middle of the path. Jordan noticed a few steps later. He gave me a quizzical look, tilting his head sideways. It reminded me of how the golden retriever we had growing up would tilt its head when listening. I half expected an encouraging bark for me to continue.

"Let's just say I lost my husband last September. And Avery...? Well, he gave me the physical outlet I needed."

"So, you've been using Avery for sex while grieving?"

The bluntness of his question took me by surprise. I stammered out a simple, "That about sums it up."

"I can get that...even if it is with Avery. But why did you fuck that asshole?"

"It was a readily available asshole?"

"But how can you fuck an asshole?"

"Well, when two gay men like each other..." I started, trying my best not to snicker.

"I walked right into that one, didn't I?"

We continued our walk. "But honestly, he lives near me in the city. And he's on Grindr twenty-four-seven. Any time I need a booty call, he's generally up for it. He delivers his ass to me faster than the Chinese takeout place around the corner."

"Does he know you've just used him for sex?" Jordan asked.

"I assume so. We don't exactly talk. He shows up. I fuck him. He leaves. Then I shower, change the sheets and take a nap."

"Wow, that's blunt."

"I know. It makes me sound like an asshole, too. But I promise, I'm not normally like that. It's just... After Chance's death, I sometimes want to be with another man. And Avery is always willing, ready and lubed up." I looked at Jordan. It was my turn to ask a few questions. "What about you? How did you not fall for Avery's charm offensive? It's been my experience that he gets what he wants."

He walked for a few steps before he spoke. "I don't have much experience with guys. And when Avery laid a hand on me without asking, I sort of flipped the fuck out. Call it internalized homophobia or whatever, but I didn't want a strange guy touching me in public. Maybe *you* city-gays are used to public displays of affection, but that shit is still a problem up here."

"I thought you were in a gay bar when this happened?"

"It's not really a gay bar. Sure, it's where a bunch of gays hang out. And it's run by this cantankerous lesbian, but it's still just a bar. And I like to keep my personal life and my private life separate."

"I can get that," I admitted. "I was raised outside Dallas, Texas. I understand what it's like to be gay in a conservative environment."

"Woodstock's not conservative," Jordan said. "We're just not as open about everything as people down in New York City. In the city, everything is so 'in your face'. Up here, we're a little more chill. I don't want to see straight people groping each other in public, either. I find it socially uncouth."

"Uncouth?"

"Lacking manners or good judgment."

"I know what the word means. I was just surprised to hear it—"

"What? Come out of my mouth? You think I'm some kind of two-bit hick who doesn't know how to pick up a dictionary?"

"Down, boy," I said. "I didn't say that. Clearly, you're articulate and have a good head on your shoulders. You proved that by seeing through Avery's bullshit. 'Uncouth' just sounds like a word my grandmother would say."

He laughed, and we walked in silence for a few minutes. "Sorry about jumping down your throat back there. Avery has me tense. I feel like a spring wound tightly. One tiny thing could cause me to explode."

"I've worked with many people who are victims of sex crimes. I can't imagine what it's like seeing the guy who did that to you."

"He groped me, which I know is technically a form of sexual battery. I looked it up after it happened."

"Did you think about filing charges?" I asked.

"It would be a 'his story' against 'my story' kind of situation. Besides, he left the next day, and my boss promised Avery would never be allowed on the farm again, so I did my best to put it out of my mind."

"You work on a farm?"

"Apple orchard, technically. But, yeah, it's basically a farm."

"That explains your physique," I said, without pausing for a second to filter.

He twisted his head and gave me a sly smile. "You've noticed my *physique*, have you?"

"I'm a thirty-three-year-old gay man. And you're a well-put-together younger twenty-something. I'm not blind."

A loud gong broke through the evening mountain air. *Thank God!*

"What was that?" Jordan asked.

"Not sure. Maybe we're being invaded?"

"Yep, the Canadians have had enough of our shit," a built bodybuilder type said, walking past us in a distinctly non-US accent. "Just kidding. It's the bell telling us it's time for the opening meeting. They also ring the blasted thing for meals."

"The *what?*" I asked. The man said it so fast, and I didn't recognize it through his accent.

He stopped on the path and took us in. "Sorry... I'm a fast talker and my New Zealand accent throws people. I'm taking it you've never been to Namast-Gay before?"

"Yep," Jordan said. "Both this stranger who has been staring at my physique and me are new here."

"Cheeky little bastard, isn't he?" the Kiwi said, shooting a grin in my direction.

"Darrin Betancourt," I said, extending a hand.

"Kieran Ashley." Kieran was a blond guy around my age. His tanned body made the tribal tattoo on his shoulder and arm pop underneath his red tank top. When he turned, I could see his pecs in all their perky glory. A small horizontal scar ran below his pectoral muscles. *Implants?* But I immediately dismissed the idea.

"What part of New Zealand?" I asked.

"Grew up in Auckland. You been?"

"I spent a semester abroad in Wellington when I was an undergraduate. I flew in and out of Auckland but didn't get to spend nearly enough time there to explore the city."

"Wellington's nice. Have most of the American creature comforts down there," Kieran said. "And who is your traveling companion?"

"Jordan Floyd." Kieran extended his other hand to Jordan, exchanging a handshake.

"Nice to meet both of ya."

"So, where are we going?" Jordan asked.

"Do you have any idea where you are?" Kieran asked.

"Not a clue. We just started walking," I admitted.

"Ahh... It's easy to get lost up here with all the hills. Until you know the layout, keep a copy of the camp map on you. It should take you a day or so to get your footing."

"Thanks," I said. "I'll grab a map when we're done."

"Follow me," Kieran said. We fell into step with Kieran. "So, how long have you been together?"

"Oh, we're not... We just met," Jordan stammered.

"Our cabins are next to each other," I added. Kieran turned his head and eyed me with a questioning look. "Really. I'm one-hundred-percent completely single."

"Me too," Jordan added.

"Let's see how long that lasts for two hot guys like yourselves." Kieran said it as a statement and not really a question.

We walked for a few minutes. Before long, we started seeing a throng of campers all heading in one direction.

The loud gong rang out over the hills again. I asked Kieran, "Do they ring that bell for every meal?"

"Don't worry. They don't ring the blasted thing for breakfast. But for lunch and dinner, it's like the fucking Wild, Wild West up in here. Now, we're going to the kickoff meeting. Dinner will be right afterward."

Chapter Five

Jordan

Darrin and I started following the New Zealand guy. He told us a little about himself as we walked.

"I saw someone I had hoped never to see again. Darrin was nice enough to come with me while I calmed the fuck down. Why? What direction were we heading?"

"Well, if you two had traveled another twenty feet, you would have ended up on a nice hiking trail, but that hike is at least a two-hour trek, so it's a good thing I found you before you started that sucker. Once you're on the path, you don't want to venture off, because you can easily find yourself lost in the forest."

"I'm not worried about that," I said. "I grew up in these forests, so hiking in them is second nature."

"Besides," Darrin cut in, "moss grows thickest on the north side of a tree. You can always use that to figure out your direction."

"Sure," I said, "if your goal is to get lost. That's a survivor myth. Moss doesn't care if it's north, south, east or west. If it's moist on the tree, moss will grow."

"Someone spun that yarn generations ago," Kieran said. "Too many people are gullible and have gotten themselves lost because of that bad piece of information."

"Well, consider me chastised," Darrin said. "We didn't exactly have forests like this where I grew up in Texas."

"Ah, you're from Texas, mate?" Kieran asked Darrin.

"I am originally. But I came to NYC after I finished my surgical residency to complete my Surgical Critical Care Fellowship at NYU."

"You're a surgeon then?"

"I am," Darrin replied.

"What do you do, Jordan?" Kieran asked, bringing me back to the conversation.

"I'm finishing up my associate's degree at a local community college, then heading down to finish my bachelor's at NYU starting this fall. I also work for an apple orchard."

"Congratulations," Darrin said, looking at me. "We should totally hang out when you move to the city in the fall—assuming you don't tire of me after this weekend."

"Good on ya for finishing your education," Kieran said.

"What do you do?" I asked Kieran.

"Currently, I'm a model. I'm not sure how long I'll be able to do that, but I was also in the New Zealand military before moving to the States."

"What brought you to the US?" Darrin asked.

A large brown building stood before us, and people piled in and out of it. Thankfully, the event didn't look very formal. I hadn't even considered what I should wear when I'd left the cabin.

"So, how long have you lived up here?" Kieran asked me. It took me a second to realize he was talking to me.

"Sorry... I was people watching for a second."

"I get it. So many hot men in one place can do that to a gay guy. Gay people live up here...on purpose?"

I shrugged. "I grew up here. But we get quite a few older gay guys and lesbians moving in up here after they tire of the city."

"Define older?" Kieran asked.

Fuck! "I don't mean old as in really old... You know, like guys in their fifties. But I've known a few older guys in their thirties and forties who have moved up. My boss is in his thirties. He's not that old."

"Keep digging that hole," Darrin joked. "You're but a wee whipper snapper."

Kieran laughed. "It's okay. I know what you meant. Anyone over thirty is practically ancient to a guy in his early twenties. When you hit your early forties like I have, trust me, you'll see that thirty was still very, very young."

"That's what my husband used to say," Darrin added. "We met when I was in my mid-twenties, and he was in his mid-fifties. At first, he was surprised I was interested in him. Admittedly, I was surprised myself. But love is a weird thing."

"That it is," Kieran said. "Well, I hope you two have a great rest of your weekend. I see the people I came with. I'm sure we'll see each other around."

When Kieran walked away, Darrin cut his eyes to me. "Know anyone here?"

"Not at all. Hell, I talked to a few gay guys up here and they didn't even know the WES existed."

"Who's Wes?"

"Sorry, the Woodstock Esoteric Sanctuary. Us locals call this place WES because the full name doesn't roll off the tongue easily."

"Have you been to WES before?" Darrin asked me.

"I've driven by but never ventured onto the property. I've heard good things."

"You looking forward to going to NYU in the fall?"

I opened my mouth but wasn't sure what I should say. "I don't know," I admitted. "My boss set me up with a full-ride, and all my basic needs are taken care of."

"Sounds like an amazing boss."

"He is. Well, he means well. He's one of those crazy-rich types who throw money at things and forget what that does to people who don't have it. I mean, I'm very thankful he's willing to pay my way through college. And I plan on working for the corporation if they'll have me — it's a great organization, and I feel like we're family. But we live in different worlds."

"How so?"

"Like this weekend. He told me out of nowhere I should have asked him to pay for my vacation because he would have. I was like...'*I earn money. I can pay my own way.*' Maybe it's my macho pride getting in the way, but I don't want him to feel like he needs to take care of me."

"You two lovers?"

"Oh God, no. He's engaged to my other boss. I call them my work daddies, but they're more like the older gay brothers I always needed. And I was the one who sort of pushed them together."

"There's a story in there somewhere," Darrin said.

"You're right. Basically, everyone on the farm knew they were making googly eyes at each other. So, one day, I was like, '*You want to date him*' and '*He wants to date you,*' so '*Go on a fucking date already.*' And the rest was history."

Darrin

Bryce and Richard walked in. I raised my arm and waved it like a mad person trying to get their attention.

"Well, I see my friends, too. I'm sure I'll see you around later," I said to Jordan. I felt terrible leaving him alone, but he slipped into a row and started talking to a couple of guys before I'd even made it halfway across the room.

Walking over to my friends, I took a minute to take in the Central Sanctuary. There was a large glass dome over the room's center with dark wood lattice work connecting the pieces of glass. The main room was a decagon and every wall had at least one window. Natural light filled the room. Someone had opened a few of the windows, letting in the cool mountain air. Metal folding chairs had been erected in rows looking toward a small, raised dais where a lectern and microphone sat. Off to the dais's left, a sound guy sat in a little makeshift cubicle.

"Thanks for saving me a seat," I said as I joined Bryce and Richard.

"Not a problem," Richard said. "I take it you got settled in up in the North Pole?"

"It's not that far out there. Sure, it's a bit of a hike, but it's not an unpleasant walk."

"Who were you talking to?" Bryce asked.

"That would be my neighbor, Jordan. He's a local. I have two other neighbors up there. Some other local guy named Chad. From what Jordan's told me, Chad is sort of the town slut. And right on the other side of him is the New York City slut." Richard cocked his head, and I could tell he was trying to guess who I meant, so I let him off the hook. "Avery's here."

"Your fuck buddy?" Bryce asked.

"Bryce!" Richard chastised. "Do you think you could have yelled that a little louder?"

I don't think anyone had turned their heads to look at us, so it didn't bother me. "Yes, *that* Avery. And I think the two town sluts may already be hooking up."

"That's like two stars colliding and making a black hole," Bryce said.

"I wonder if these two will suck everything close by into them?" Richard asked, giving me an evil eye.

"I'm not planning on having sex with Avery this weekend or with this Chad fellow — or my new friends, Jordan and Kieran. I'm here to relax. Nothing else."

"You met Kieran?" Bryce asked.

"Yep. Always been a sucker for a Kiwi accent, so it was fun to talk to him for a while. I take it you two know him?" A quick glance shifted between Bryce and Richard. They weren't telling me something. "Did you two have a threesome with Kieran?" I asked, tossing out the first idea that ran through my head.

"Oh God, no!" Richard said. "Not that I wouldn't be happy to have sex with someone like Kieran."

Bryce reached out and put a hand on his husband's knee. "If you keep talking, you're going to say something you shouldn't say."

"What are you two going on about?"

"Nothing," Bryce said. He narrowed his focus at me and said, "You know our job. There are some things we don't talk about."

So, Kieran has some kind of medical condition? He looked perfectly healthy to me. Then it hit me. The horizontal scarring under the pectoral muscle. I started running through Kieran's anatomy and quickly understood he was a trans man. "Oh, like I'd fucking care," I whispered. "He's still fucking gorgeous."

"I didn't say a word," Bryce said. "And neither should Richard."

"I'd already noticed the scar under the pec muscle. I hadn't put too much thought into it until you forced me. No wonder he's a model. He is fucking gorgeous. Is he pretty open about it?"

"I think so," Richard said. "But it's not our place to say anything."

Of course, you didn't say anything. You just alluded to it and let me put the pieces together myself.

Someone tapped on a microphone, and the sound reverberated around the room. The room grew quiet as Mano stood up next to the microphone with his partner, Jaxson.

"Good evening, everyone, and welcome to our fifth annual Camp Namast-Gay!" There were whoops and applause from the hundred-plus guys in the room. "We are so glad to see so many old faces, and new faces—and old faces with new faces this year. It's nice to know some of you won't need a flotation device in the pool or lake with the amount of new filler you have." There were polite chuckles, and I'm sure a few queens with a bit too much filler in the room wondered if they were the ones being called out. "As you know, my husband Jaxson and I are the Namast-Gay coordinators." He gestured to Jaxson, who was standing beside him. "To help us get this weekend off to a fun start, Jaxson will lead us in a fun get-to-know-you ice-breaker."

There were a few groans from around the room, but most of the guys were ready for whatever Jaxson threw our way.

"We're going to play 'The Queen Says.' It's like 'Simon Says', but I don't know that bitch Simon or why he feels the need to be such a bossy bottom."

For the next ten minutes, we played what had to have been the gayest icebreaker game in the history of icebreakers. We had "The Queen says, 'Perform *YMCA.*'" "The Queen says, 'Stomp the runway,'" and "The Queen says, 'Do your makeup.'"

Periodically, Jaxson would say, "Stop doing your makeup." And, invariably, someone would stop, and he'd point them out and yell, "I didn't say '*The Queen says.*'"

At one point, he had said, "The Queen says, 'Touch your toes.'"

Mano had laughed next to him before grabbing the microphone and saying, "I now know who the tops in the crowd are. Some of you clearly haven't needed to touch your toes in years." That got a good rise out of everyone.

As the game progressed, the things the Queen said to do became more and more risqué. I purposefully took myself out of the game when the queen said to hump your neighbor. I was officially done with that game. I didn't even bother. I started making my way back to where Bryce and Richard were sitting. They'd also taken themselves out of the game at some point. I looked to see if Jordan was still in the room and found him in a back corner, holding up a wall. I was kind of envious of him. I'd happily join Jordan standing in the back if Bryce and Richard would let me get away with it.

A sharp pain suddenly shot up from my foot as something crushed over it.

"Fuck!" I let out over the game.

I looked down to find a guy in a wheelchair on top of my foot. He looked up at me suddenly, "Oh, my God! I'm so sorry. Are you okay?" the guy said in rapid succession as he rolled off my foot.

I gritted through my teeth. "I'm sure I'm fine. I'm going to go sit down." I was about to hobble over to where Bryce and Richard sat. Someone slid an arm under me, and I looked to see Bryce standing next to me. A second later, someone was under my other arm. I turned to thank Richard. And words failed me as Jordan stood beside me, helping me back to my chair.

"Are you all right?" Jordan asked. "I saw you scream and ran over."

Bryce looked at Jordan and said, "Let's get him out of here."

We headed for the main entrance.

Mano was in front of us, clearing the way. They ushered me into a side room off the foyer where they could more easily prop me up. Frankly, all the fuss wasn't necessary.

When I was seated, Bryce said, "I'm going to take off your shoes."

"Is that necessary?" I asked.

"You know as well as I do that having something heavy roll over your foot is no laughing matter. How many people have we treated with a broken foot or crush injury compartment syndrome?"

"And you are?" an unknown voice asked, coming into the room.

"Dr. Darrin Betancourt," I said, swiveling to look at the hot Latino who'd walked in.

"Great," the guy said, "a doctor. You people always make the worst patients. And you?" the guy asked, looking at Bryce.

"I'm Dr. Bryce Camden-Thompson, an emergency medicine physician and this guy's boss."

"Just my luck, two doctors." The exaggerated eye-roll made it clear he was already over both of us. "I'm Cody Benton, the camp nurse. What happened?"

"I'm fine," I said. "See? My toes are all wiggling." I pointed to my now shoeless foot and wiggled my toes for emphasis. I had to admit that the bruise developing across the top part of my foot didn't look good.

"I've seen enough. We need to call the EMTs. You're going to the hospital for X-rays or a CT scan...*Doctor.*"

"I'm fine," I tried to reassure the room.

"Can we get some ice in here?" Bryce asked.

"Does he need crutches?" Mano asked. "I'll go see if we have crutches."

Cody brought his fingers up to his lips and whistled a deafening whistle. "Now that I have everyone's attention. Unless you are my patient or me, please back the fuck off. That goes the same for you, Doctor," he said, staring down at Bryce.

"But he's—"

"You're here on vacation. I'm here working. You may be a surgeon, but you're not *his* surgeon. And at this moment I need to get my patient into an ambulance and down the mountain to make sure he's safe to be up here."

"Do we really need an ambulance?" I asked.

"I can take him to the hospital," Bryce said.

"One, do you even know where the nearest hospital is?" Cody asked.

"Well, no—"

"I didn't think so, Doctor. And two, you wouldn't have admitting privileges even if you did, so you're going to be sitting there twiddling your thumbs and probably driving the nurses crazy."

"I could take him," a soft voice said.

I turned my head to watch Cody turn on the unfamiliar voice. "Oh, hey, baby," Cody said. "You know this man?"

"His cabin's next to mine. I have my truck up here. I can get him to the hospital faster than an EMT could."

"Where are you planning on taking him?" Cody asked.

"Probably Kingston Urgent Care. I know they have an X-ray and CT machine there. Trust me. I've hurt myself enough between high-school sports and the farm. I was going to get frequent flyer miles with all the injuries I've had."

"The local Urgent Care is closer than Kingston. Makes sense to me."

Mano showed up in the doorway. "They didn't have crutches, but they had an old wheelchair."

I eyed the wheelchair skeptically. The machine had seen better days. "I'm sure I can walk," I said, standing.

A hand on my shoulder shoved me back down into the chair. "Don't even think about it, Doctor," Cody informed me in no uncertain terms.

"Jordan, go bring your truck up to the main entrance. I'll have the good doctor there shortly."

With that, Jordan set out. Over the next five minutes, I was forced through a completely unnecessary humiliation. I was lifted and helped into the wheelchair, then Nurse Cody wheeled me out of the room. Everyone at camp was rubbernecking when I was hauled out of the building. I caught the look of the poor guy who had run over my foot by accident. He looked worse than I did. I tried to shoot him a smile, but someone got between us before he could see.

Outside, Cody headed down the path toward the parking lot. Jordan had pulled up already and stood waiting for me next to a beaten-up old truck with a propped open door.

"Okay, people," Cody said. "We're going to lift the good doctor here and put him comfortably into the truck's back seat."

"Why not put him on the front seat with me?"

"He needs to keep his foot elevated as much as possible," Cody said.

"He can sit with his back to me and his foot up on the seat?" Jordan asked.

Cody looked at me, the truck then Jordan before saying, "That will work."

The group of men helped me into the truck. I sat with my back next to Jordan. He provided me with enough support.

"No way in hell am I sitting on that death trap again," I muttered, looking at the dilapidated wheelchair as Cody closed the truck door. I was almost amazed that none of the wheels had fallen off. Someone had gotten me a bag of ice for my foot, so it was already feeling better. But I needed to get it X-rayed at the very least.

"You ready?" Jordan asked.

"As ready as I'll ever be."

Jordan released the brake and threw the truck into drive as we drifted away from the curb and headed back toward Woodstock.

Chapter Six

The trip down the mountain and into Woodstock had been faster than expected. Jordan knew every bumpy, dirty road to get into the city. At least twice, he'd thrown his arm over me like a mother, making sure her child wouldn't fly off the passenger seat into the dashboard. I had to admit, Jordan's desire to make sure I was safe was cute.

We pulled up to a free-standing building in a large shopping center with the words 'Woodstock Urgent Care' above the white brick box. From the outside, the building didn't look like much.

"You sure they have an X-ray in that place?"

"X-ray and a CT scan. Trust me. I've broken my fair share of bones, and I always got those things done here. They'd splint me and send me down to Kingston Hospital if I needed a cast. But the doc-in-the-box works for most things."

I let out a laugh at the joke. "I was just thinking this place looks like a big white box."

"The last time I joked about a big white box, I lost my virginity to Carly Canary," Jordan replied.

"Was that a drag queen?" I asked.

"Nope. Just the poor unfortunate girl's real name. We were in high school together. I thought I was straight, and she thought she was sexual. It wasn't good for either of us. I figured out I was gay, and she realized she was asexual. Neither of us got what we needed out of that encounter." He turned and looked at me. "You ready to go in?"

"As ready as I will be." Without waiting, I scooched over, opened the door and hauled myself out of the cab. I was almost on the sidewalk when Jordan caught up with me and threw his body under my arm to help take the weight off my foot. "I'm fine," I said.

"Maybe," Jordan said, opening the door to the Urgent Care. "But let's wait until we get the X-ray back before doing anything that could make it worse. Deal?"

I let out an exasperated sigh but said, "Deal."

The Urgent Care was empty, so we were ushered into the back area quickly. Jordan said he'd be in the waiting room if I needed him after getting me situated in an exam room.

I had my shoes off and my foot propped up as soon as I was on the examination table. The nurse came in and took my vitals and medical history. Soon, the doctor on call walked in.

"Good evening, I'm Dr. Scott Crandall."

"Nice to meet you, Dr. Crandall. I'm Dr. Darrin Betancourt. I'm visiting for the weekend and had a wheelchair run over my foot. I think it's perfectly fine, but the *nurse* at the Woodstock Esoteric Sanctuary wanted me to get an X-ray just to make sure I didn't break anything." I then ran through the events and explained why I was sure it was nothing.

"Well, Dr. Betancourt, let's get that X-ray and see if we can't get you out of here."

"Perfect."

The nurse came and got me while Dr. Crandall went and attended to a different patient. I was wheeled into the back and helped atop a bed while the radiology tech took a series of images. I was then wheeled back.

I sat there in the room, bored out of my mind. I pulled out my phone and texted Bryce and Richard to let them know I was okay. Dr. Crandall's diagnosis was unnecessary. I could tell I was already doing better. While I waited, I put on my shoe and paced around the room.

The door opened and Dr. Crandall met my eyes over the rims of his glasses. "Would you like to take a seat? I just got the images." He gestured at me with the iPad, and it took everything not to roll my eyes and snatch the thing out of his hands.

"Well," Dr. Crandall said, "I'm not seeing anything broken or compressed. You may have some minor tissue bruising, but nothing that taking it easy for a day or two wouldn't help. I can prescribe you an anti-inflammatory and something non-narcotic for the pain."

"No thanks. I have ibuprofen and acetaminophen in my toiletry bag, so I think I'm good."

"If it gets worse —"

"I promise I'll head right to the Emergency Room. Don't worry. I won't do anything that puts my foot at risk."

Dr. Crandall sighed and left the room. I was checked out and back in the truck in ten minutes.

"How are you feeling?" Jordan asked.

"I'll be fine. Nothing a good night's rest won't fix. What time is it?"

"A little after eight. Why?"

"Well, that sucks. We've officially missed dinner up at camp. Any chance you know somewhere we can go grab something to eat, my treat."

"You don't need to pay for my meal," Jordan said.

"Just let me. It's the least I can do after you carted me off the mountain and got me to the Urgent Care. Let me repay you for being my personal hero tonight."

"Whatever. I know a coffee shop that has decent sandwiches. It'll still be open and quick, but it won't be fast food."

"Sounds perfect."

"So, were you nice to Dr. Crandall?"

"I was professional."

"That's not what I asked," Jordan said. "I've always heard doctors make the worst patients."

"It's true. It's hard to sit there and let others care for you when you think you could do it better."

"You realize that makes you sound a bit like a dick?"

"Tell me how you really feel."

"Think about it from their vantage point. Some 'big city' doctor hurts himself, then orders people around like he owns the place."

"I wasn't *that* bad."

Jordan didn't respond. I sat there for a few moments, replaying what happened. So, I hadn't been that bad, but I hadn't been that nice, either. "I suck at being a patient."

"Why did you become a doctor in the first place?"

"I like puzzles." It was my traditional response when people asked me this question because I get asked it a lot. We pulled up in front of a coffee shop. I could see a handful of customers inside through the glass windows. I turned and looked at Jordan. "Every day I get dozens of puzzles that come in. Some are harder to solve than others. My job is to get people either fixed so they can leave or stable so I can turf them to someone else who will provide the standard of care they need to get better. Tonight, I was the puzzle. I knew the signs to look for, and I trusted my judgment more than others. Was the scan the right step to take? Yes. I would have required one for any of my patients, but I wasn't convinced it was necessary, based on the other sources of information I had."

"Hmm... That's gotta be a hard way to live."

Jordan

I opened my door and watched Darrin struggle out of the truck. I could tell his macho bravado wasn't matching the actual pain in his foot. Sure, the foot may not have been broken, but it was hurting him.

"Need a hand?" I asked.

"I'm fine. Just need to get the blood flowing down there is all."

I hopped up on the curb and strolled over to Java Junkie Café & Roastery entrance. I'd been hanging out at Java Junkie since the French owner, Stefan, started roasting his own beans at the place. I'm not one of those guys who needs an IV bag filled with coffee to get out of their beds, but I always enjoy a good cup of joe. The corner of the street was octagonal-shaped, and the café was built with the harsh angles in mind. Soon, the tall glass panes would be open in the evening, making the place an open-air café in the summer. I held open the door for Darrin, who finally got there. I wanted to help, but he'd shoot me down if I tried.

Inside, several two- and four-top tables peppered the interior. Off to the right was a glassed-in roastery. The lights in the glass box were off, but I knew Stefan would be here before dawn to roast their daily reserve of fresh coffee.

"The menu's up there," I said to Darrin, motioning to the chalkboards above the cash register. "Why don't you decide what you want, and I'll go order."

"Not going to happen," Darrin said, walking past me as he headed to the counter. "Besides, I'm buying, remember?"

"Welcome to Java Junkie Café & Roastery," a bubbly young woman said. "Oh, hey, Jordan. What has you out and about this evening?"

"Hey, Autumn. This is my new friend Darrin. I had to take him to Urgent Care to get his foot checked out."

"Oh, my!" Autumn gasped. "Are you okay?" Autumn was the type who was slightly dramatic but genuinely cared.

"I'll be fine," Darrin said. "I need to make sure I keep walking so my foot doesn't stiffen, which would make things worse."

"How did you hurt yourself?" Autumn asked.

"Guy in a wheelchair accidentally ran over it."

"Ouch!"

"Autumn, do we need any more paper cups out front?" a voice called from the back. A young blond guy stuck his head out.

"Hey, Wes," I said with a quick wave. "How's Roger?"

"Roger's amazing, as always. He's picking me up in a little while. What brings you in tonight?"

"Darrin, this is Wes. Wes, this is Darrin." They nodded at each other after I introduced them. "Darrin needed to have an X-ray taken to make sure his foot wasn't broken."

"I guess, since you're up and walking, everything is hunky-dory," Wes said.

"Yep. But we missed dinner up at camp, so I brought him here for a quick bite."

"What would you recommend?" Darrin asked.

"I would recommend the grilled chicken breast, portobello mushrooms, caramelized onions, mozzarella cheese with the balsamic glaze. It's served on a panini bread roll with chips. Everything but the chips is locally sourced," Autumn rattled off.

"She takes classes over at the Culinary Institute of America, so she's a bit of a foodie," Wes cut in.

"That sounds great to me," Darrin said.

"Make that two," I added.

"Anything to drink?" Autumn inquired after ringing in the two sandwiches.

"Just coffee for me," I said. "They roast their beans here daily. The owner may be stiff, but he knows how to roast coffee." Wes cackled. I looked at him oddly before saying, "What?"

"You said Stefan was stiff," Wes said again.

"Get your mind out of the gutter, Wes," Autumn chastised. "Sorry about him. Pay him no attention. He's in the honeymoon period with his boyfriend and still driving all of us around him crazy. All he thinks about is sex."

"And that's different from how he was before he met Roger?" I asked.

"No. But at least then he wasn't getting any, like the rest of us."

"I guess I'll try the coffee," Darrin said, cutting into the conversation. He reached into his pocket, pulled out his wallet and placed a fifty-dollar bill on the counter. "Keep the change." He looked at me. "I think I should sit down."

Without asking, I nuzzled beside him and helped him distribute some of his weight across my shoulders as I helped him over to a table. Sliding out one of the other chairs, I motioned for him to prop up his foot.

"Want me to see if I can get you some ice for it?"

Darrin looked down before saying, "Probably not a bad idea…if it's no trouble for your friends."

"Oh, I wouldn't exactly call them friends. It's more like Woodstock is a small town, and the gay community is even smaller, so we all know each other. Wes and Autumn are good people, from what I can tell. I haven't socialized with them outside of Java Junkie. I'm a bit of a regular."

With Darrin situated, I walked back to the counter and found Wes standing behind it now. "What can I get you, Jordan?"

"Yeah, can I get a bag of ice for my friend's foot?"

"Sure. Give me a minute. I'll be right back." Wes headed through the swinging door into the kitchen. The door flapped open. Autumn stood in the kitchen making our sandwiches. Just looking at the food made my mouth water.

A few seconds later, the door swung open, and Wes came out with a Ziploc bag full of ice. "Here you go," he said, handing it to me. "So, are you two —?"

"No," I said. "I met him today. This weekend, I'm hanging out at the Woodstock Esoteric Sanctuary. His cabin is next to mine. When he got hurt, I volunteered to bring him into town."

"What's going on at WES this weekend?"

"You're going to laugh," I said. "Camp Namast-Gay."

"That's a thing?"

"Yep. Bunch of gay guys camping for the weekend."

"I wonder if Roger knows about that."

"Apparently, a lot of the city-gays come up for it every year. That's what Darrin is," I said, cocking my head in his direction. He was sitting at the table staring at his cell phone. His fingers dashed over the screen. "He's an ER doc down in the city and a bit of a handful as a patient. Gave poor old Dr. Crandall a run for his money."

Autumn came out from the back with two plates. "Did Wes get your coffees yet?"

"Oh geez," Wes said. "Sorry about that. I got distracted by the bag of ice."

"Go. Sit down," Autumn said, shooing me away from the counter. "I'll follow you with the food, and Wes will get those coffees out to you in a second."

I did as Autumn said. When I got to the table, Darrin put his phone back in his pocket and accepted the bag of ice from me before gently lowering it to the top of his foot. Autumn slid his plate in around his other side before placing mine. True to her word, Wes was seconds behind us with two cups of coffee.

"Do you need anything for your coffee?" Wes asked.

"Just cream for me," Darrin said.

"Nothing for me," I added.

"Be right back."

Darrin had his cream in less than a minute, and we were both digging into our meals. We were halfway through them when the door opened, and Wes' boyfriend Roger came in. I watched as he scanned the room. I nodded a single nod when we locked eyes.

"Any chance you know him?" I asked, gesturing to Roger with my sandwich between bites.

Darrin turned his head and took in the other guy. "Can't say that I do. Why?"

"That's Wes' boyfriend. There's almost a twenty-year age gap between them."

"Hey, I'm the last one to talk about May–December romances. Remember, Chance and I had a thirty-year age gap. Love is love. When I was your age, I don't think I would have guessed I'd end up in a relationship with someone more than twice my age, but it happened." Darrin took a deep breath before taking another bite of his sandwich. "This is fantastic."

We took our time eating. It got closer and closer to nine, and I could tell Autumn and Wes wanted to get out of there. Roger hovered over Wes as he finished up.

"I guess we should go. I can tell they're ready to go home," Darrin said. "I used to hate it when I had customers lingering past closing time when I waited tables."

"You were a waiter?"

"Yep. I waited tables throughout college. I was good at it. Don't get me wrong, if I never have to do it again for the rest of my life, I'll be perfectly happy. But it was a good job when I was younger. You?"

"Me? No," I said, drawing out the word. "I've never had to work in the food service industry. When I was in high school, I was lucky to land a job at the orchard. I've been there ever since. I've kind of grown to love it. And my one boss, Talgat—he's kind of the brains behind the farming side of things—he's the one who convinced me to pursue my degree in Nutrition and

Food Studies at NYU. They don't have a traditional farming sciences program, but this program is supposed to be amazing."

Darrin took the last swig of coffee before putting the mug down. "Finished?" he asked.

"I am." I waved over to Autumn. "We're getting out of your hair. Thanks for everything."

"See you next time. And have fun gay camping this weekend," she said.

Looking around the café, I noticed we were the only ones left. I grinned and gave her two huge thumbs up. "I'll do my best to gay it up as much as possible."

This time, when Darrin stood, he let me help him out to the truck with no complaints. I could already tell he was walking better, but at least he allowed me to give him a hand.

Chapter Seven

The drive back to WES was short and uneventful. No four-legged furry things jumped in front of my truck. I kept one eye on the road and another eye on Darrin, who was lost in thought.

"Penny for your thoughts?" I finally asked.

"Just remembering a time when Chance and I went camping. It was more glamping than camping. Heck, it makes what we're doing this weekend look completely rugged. We went on a backpacking trip up in Ottawa. We would hike through nature for five hours to arrive at our destination. We had yurts—"

"Yurts?"

"Big round tents that originated in Mongolia. They were amazing. It had a full king-sized bed about a foot off the ground. The inside was completely carpeted. We didn't even have to carry our backpacks because they delivered that stuff each night. They even had these giant bronze wash bins filled with a bubble bath for us each evening. There were also shower facilities at each place we stopped for those that preferred showering.

Still, we enjoyed the individual bubble baths as we drank champagne and listened to the night sounds. Other than the fact we walked through nature every day, it was one of the nicest resorts I ever stayed at."

"How did that work, exactly?"

"I didn't even ask. I enjoyed the experience and let the camping fairies figure it out. But they had a team. So, I guess while we traipsed through the woods, the team packed up our stuff, carted it off to the next location and had it set up before we even got there."

"Wow, and I thought kicking it old school in a sleeping bag on the ground staring up at the stars was the way to camp."

"I've done that, too," Darrin said. "Admittedly, I was a young Boy Scout and not worried about my back, so sleeping on the ground was fun."

"You were in Boy Scouts?"

"Yep. I's been a decade since I did any of that stuff. But it was fun when I was younger."

I pulled into the parking lot. A couple of lights provided just enough lighting to make it easy to navigate. When I parked, I realized I didn't have a way to get Darrin up to the cabin.

"Stay here," I said. "I'm going to see if I can find Mano and his golf cart."

"I can walk," Darrin said immediately.

"Are you sure? I don't want to end up having to carry you up the hill."

"I don't think you could," Darrin replied.

"I'm a lot stronger than I look."

"I can tell that."

"Fine. But you must keep your arm around me."

"Are you flirting with me, Mr. Floyd?"

"You wish," I said with a wink that I'm sure he couldn't even see in the darkened interior of the truck cab. "Trust me. If I was flirting with you, you'd know it. I'm not exactly known for my subtlety."

Darrin barked out a laugh. "That makes two of us. I hate the 'does he like me?' game so many gays play when they're dating. I've found it much easier to be direct. That's how I landed Chance. I undressed him with my eyes one night when we were sitting at a Cantina in Mexico and said, '*I kind of think I want you to kiss me now.*' I was young and ballsy, but I also think it may have been the tequila that gave me the guts to put it right out there like that."

"And did he?"

"Kiss me? Nope. Not that night. He didn't want to do anything with me while I was even the slightest bit inebriated. Instead, he took me out to dinner two nights later, then back to his hotel room. And let's just say, the rest of was history."

"It's almost like a fairytale."

"Yeah, except we were surrounded by the devastation of an earthquake in between bouts of passionate sex."

"On that note," I said dryly, "let's get you up to your cabin."

I walked around to his side of the truck and helped him out. Sure to his word, he leaned on me the whole time. We didn't run into anyone while we hiked up to the green cabins. It was as if everyone had disappeared while we were down in the town.

"Where is everyone?" I remarked when we were a little more than halfway to the cabin.

"Weren't there more fun and games going on this evening?" Darrin asked.

I tried to remember what we had been told during the opening meeting, but my mind was drawing a blank. So, I lied, "Oh yeah. I totally forgot about that."

"If you wanted to find the games..." Darrin let the sentence hang in the mountain air for a second.

"Nah...I'm fine. I'm not much of a games person."

"But you played all those sports in high school?"

"I did," I admitted. "But I also played them because I thought I had to. Had to keep up the pretense that I was straight. Over time, I learned I'm much more of a builder or gardener type of guy than someone who plays games. I don't have the patience for them."

"Must make dating difficult. Gays always seem to want to play games."

"You're telling me. Did you want to find the games?"

"It's been a long day. Besides, with the bum foot, I'm not sure what use I will be to anyone's team tonight."

"Are you sure?"

"I promise. Right now, I just want a good night's sleep."

We continued our trek up the hill. Over time, I could tell he was getting more and more tired and his pace slowed a bit, but he didn't complain.

Darrin

My foot hurt. Thankfully, it wasn't broken. I'd need to massage it then stretch it out tonight and again first thing in the morning to get the muscles relaxed. In all honesty, the best thing for the foot at that moment was to walk on it lightly and down a few ibuprofen to help with the inflammation. I'd had worse.

"So, did you live on a ranch in Texas?" Jordan asked. I hadn't been following the conversation, so it took me a second to respond.

"I lived in a large city by East Coast standards. Do you know much about Texas?"

"Not really."

"Basically, Plano is a town of almost three-hundred-thousand people that is north of Dallas. How do I explain this?" I considered it for a second. "There's a city called Fort Worth and to its east is another big city called Dallas. Combined, the two make up the Dallas-Fort Worth Metropolitan area, which has about seven million people. That makes this area the fourth largest city in the US. Plano is north of Dallas, but part of that general area. Make sense?"

"Sure," Jordan said. "So, it's like the five boroughs down in the city?"

"Except that it's about ten-thousand square miles of land compared to the three-hundred square miles that are NYC."

"You're shitting me?"

"I shit you not. For comparison purposes, the Dallas Metro area is larger than the entire state of New Jersey."

Jordan let out a low whistle. "Damn."

"But I visited a ranch once." I had some cousins who lived out in West Texas, and we went to their ranch on vacation. I had the whole ranch experience. We got to fire shotguns at tin cans sitting on a wooden fence. We rode around on a tractor. The ranch had a water tower that we swam in. In retrospect, it's kind of amazing I didn't die from any diseases after swimming in that water tank. It had green slime growing on the sides and live fish lived in there.

"Yeah, I've definitely swam in some pretty sketchy places when I was a kid, too," Jordan said after my water tower of doom story. "Mostly creeks and ponds, but once I was swimming out at Lake Minnewaska and ended up with leeches. They ended up closing the lake to treat it with copper sulfate to manage the leech problem."

"Eww," Darrin said. "I can handle many things, but finding a parasite attached to me is not my idea of fun."

When we got back to the cabin, the area was noisy. "What is that noise?"

"What?" Jordan asked.

"All the peep, peep. It's so loud."

"Oh, the peepers?" He must have seen my incredulous expression. "No, really, the peepers. That's what we call them. Every year, it's how we know spring is finally with us. One night there will be dead silence. The next night you'll hear one of them singing. Before the end of the week, it's like a full-blown peeping orchestra blasting its way through your house."

"How do you sleep with all that noise?"

"How do you sleep with all the traffic and constant police and fire alarms wailing through the night in the city? I spent one weekend down there and had the damnedest time trying to sleep because everything was so…loud."

I had to think about it. I'd lived in a large city for so long that I'd forgotten what it was like to be out in nature. But those damn peepers were crazy loud. *Thank God, I brought earplugs.*

"Thanks for everything tonight," I said, looking at Jordan in the single lamp light that illuminated the area.

"Any time... Well, that sounds awkward. Please, let's not do that again. I don't feel like taking you to another urgent care before you leave."

"I will do my best," I said between chuckles. "Trust me. It wasn't on my itinerary for the weekend, either."

He helped me up the stairs, and I pulled out my keys. Once I had opened the door, Jordan said, "Good night," and bounded back down. I walked into my cabin and flipped on the lights. I heard the door shut next door.

After walking in, I went to the bathroom and pulled out ibuprofen from my toiletry bag. I medicated myself with the same dose I would have prescribed a patient and added acetaminophen for the pain. I then sat on the edge of my bed and massaged my foot. It wasn't going to be fun, but doing it now, and again first thing in the morning, should make my foot feel better. And the last thing I wanted was to be off my feet for the next day.

After finishing my exercises, I climbed out of my clothes, leaving on only my boxer briefs. I slipped into the bed, turned off the lights and lay there in the darkness. A glow came in from the single outside lamp, providing a tiny glimmer of illumination in the cabin. I listened to the sounds of nature around me.

"Take it, take it, take it!" sounded from the cabin to the north, followed by a wailing sound.

"Fuck me, Daddy!" The voice screeched when it stopped wailing.

"Well, I recognize that voice," I said to myself as I put the pillow over my head.

Suddenly, there was a loud pounding on the door north of me.

"Will you two keep it down!" Jordan's voice cut through the night. "I got back with Darrin from Urgent

Care. He needs his rest. And your loud sexcapades aren't going to let that happen."

I then heard the stomping of feet down Chad's steps as they crossed in front of my cabin, then back to Jordan's. I heard his door open and close.

Jordan's brief outburst caused the other two men to stop screaming and wailing. I could still hear them occasionally as I tried to go to bed, but it was quiet enough to fit in with the ambient noise of nature as I drifted to sleep.

Chapter Eight

Daylight crept into my room. I hadn't even noticed my front window faced east. The sliver of light hit right where my head lay on the pillow, blinding me when I opened my eyes for a second. I readjusted to get out of the sunlight's path. I was so not ready to be awake. I looked over at my watch and found that it was only six-thirty a.m. I let out a low groan. I'd been in bed for seven-plus hours, so it was time to start the day.

I rolled over and massaged my foot. It was a little tender but felt a whole lot better than it had right after it had gotten run over. If anything, my foot was a little stiff and walking on it would be the best treatment for that. I realized I shouldn't go out and run a marathon, but anything else would be okay. I got out of bed tentatively, putting only a little weight on my foot, and it took my weight with no problems. The muscles were a bit sore, but they would loosen up quickly and be back to normal.

I ran through the shower and threw on a pair of khaki shorts and a polo shirt. I slipped the room key back into my wallet and put it into my back pocket along with a folded-up copy of the camp map. Before leaving my cabin, I took a last look at myself to make sure I was presentable. The crisp, clean, cool mountain air made me excited to feel alive.

"Morning, neighbor."

"Good morning," I said as I turned to look in Chad's direction. "Oh, wow!" I said, averting my eyes from the completely nude guy standing on his porch with a mug of coffee in his hand.

"Don't worry about it. The camp is completely clothing optional. Hang out as the Good Lord made you. Besides, if I didn't expect people to look, I would cover myself. But why cover up what you're born with when you look like this?" Chad made a gesture to himself, which I tried not to pay attention to.

"That's good to know," I said noncommittally.

"Sorry to hear about your foot. How's it feeling today?"

"Thanks," I said, looking at the single light pole that stood in the distance. I was doing my best not to look at Chad's swinging manhood out of the corner of my eye, but there it was for all the camp to see. "As for the foot, it's doing much better." I took a deep breath of air before saying, "Well, I'm going to head down into the heart of camp. I'm sure I'll see you later." *Preferably clothed.*

I bounded off my porch and took off at a brisk pace. It wasn't that I minded seeing my neighbor naked. Objectively speaking, he was very hot. But I think there needed to be boundaries, and this guy apparently didn't seem to know where they should exist. I've been skinny dipping...once. I was hiking up in the Rocky Mountains with some friends. We'd found a nice mountain pond and had gone for a dip. The water was so fucking cold that I worried my balls would retreat inside my body and hang out around my throat. *Talk about shrinkage.*

I made my way through the camp and found the main dining hall, but they didn't open until eight. I glanced down at my watch. I still had a good forty minutes before breakfast. I pulled the map out of my pocket. It had a café listed. *I wonder if it opens earlier.* I figured I could meander around the campgrounds for another hour, if nothing else. I started following the map.

"Hey there, mate," a voice with a Kiwi accent said through the morning air. I looked up to see Kieran walking toward me.

"Good morning," I said, covering my eyes from the sun to make out Kieran's face.

"What has you out and about so early?" Kieran said, but then he added, "Actually, kind of amazed you're up and about. How's the foot?"

"A little sore, but nothing a little more exercise and some stretching won't fix. It wasn't as bad as people made out last night. Nothing was broken."

"Glad to hear, mate. Where ya heading?"

"Was going to see if" — I looked down at the map to remember the name of the place — "the Mug Slug Café is open. I already found out I'm too early for the dining hall."

"Ahh yea, the café opens at six-thirty. That's where I'm heading. I need my morning coffee."

"You and me both, brother. You and me both." I then made a sweeping gesture and said, "After you."

"What time did you get back last night?"

"Jordan and I got back probably around nine-forty-five or ten o'clock."

"Ahh," Kieran said in that uniquely New Zealand-sounding way, "you should have joined us for games last night. We had a load of fun."

"I was just tired when we got back."

"Did ya at least get some dinner in ya?"

"Jordan took me to a restaurant he likes in town?"

"Jordan? That's the guy in the cabin next to you who hauled you to the ER?"

I wanted to correct him, but said, "That's the one."

We chitchatted for the next two minutes before approaching a large wooden building with two floors. The first floor contained a large clothing and bookstore. Kieran walked around the corner to a large set of stairs. On the side of the building was a giant arrow pointing up the stairs with the words Mug Slug Café painted on it.

The café had both large outdoor and indoor seating areas. We opened the glass door and walked in. There were a bunch of tables scattered around the interior. On the far wall was a counter with an espresso machine, an industrial blender and an array of colorful bottles with pumps sticking out of the tops. On the opposite wall was a toaster and some kind of oven. There was also a smattering of boxes with various types of teas. They had a sign next to the cash register that read, '*We are proud to serve coffee from Woodstock's own Java Junkie Café & Roastery.*'

"Huh," I said, gesturing at the sign to Kieran. "That's where I had dinner last night. Apparently, the owner roasts their coffee every day."

"Sadly, we don't serve their daily roasts here. The owner roasts for us on Sundays," the barista said, cutting into the conversation. "What can I get for the two of you?"

"Medium flat white," Kieran said without hesitation.

"And for you?" the barista asked.

"Just a large coffee with cream."

"I'll have that flat white out in a minute," the barista said. "Let me get you your coffee first." He turned around and grabbed a large porcelain mug, filled it and handed it to me. "The cream is over there," he said, pointing at a table next to a side wall.

"Thanks. What do I owe?" I asked.

"It's an all-inclusive weekend, so regular coffee and tea are part of the package. Fancier drinks are half-priced."

I pulled out a five and tossed it in the tip jar. The barista said, "Thanks," as he started working on Kieran's flat white.

"Morning, Kieran," a voice cut through the quiet. I turned to see a young white guy with brown hair, brown eyes and a boyish smile walking into the café. He was wearing a pair of pea-green-colored shorts with a 'Namast-Gay' tank top and what looked like a yoga mat flung over his shoulder.

"Kia Ora," Kieran said as the other man approached. "No takers this morning?"

"Nope. The seven a.m. yoga session at this camp is usually empty. But I got in a quick sequence to get me started before my more intense sessions later this morning."

As both men hugged, I took a swig of my coffee. I hated being the third wheel in a conversation. I was about to separate myself from the conversation when Kieran asked, "Have you two met yet?"

I shook my head as the other guy said, "Nope." He thrust his hand in my direction with enthusiasm. "I'm Finlay Winslow. I'm a yoga instructor. Maybe you've seen my DVDs and books?"

"I'm more of a gym guy," I admitted as I offered him my hand. "I'm Darrin Betancourt. It's nice to meet you."

"Yoga is a perfect addition to anyone's physical fitness and wellness routine. I've worked with tons of top-tier athletes at my studio down in the city, Rainbow Flow."

"Flat white," the barista said.

Kieran grabbed his cup and saucer before turning back to Finlay. "Leave the poor man alone. Get your coffee. We're going to take a seat outside."

Okay then, thanks for asking, I thought, but I still followed Kieran out of the door. The deck was still a little cool in the morning air, but it wasn't horrible. Kieran found a nice table away from the café entrance that looked like a very sturdy picnic table, complete with benches instead of chairs. I straddled a bench and angled myself to overlook the camp while still able to chat with Kieran. We sat there for almost an entire minute in silence, drinking our coffee.

"So, Darrin, what's on your agenda for the day?" Finlay asked, his voice cutting through the silence as he opened the door with his own cup and saucer in hand.

"I have no agenda. Just plan on seeing what the day brings, I guess."

"Is he joking?" Finlay asked, sitting at the table and turning to look at Kieran. Kieran shrugged and took a sip. Finlay turned back to me. "Are you joking?"

"No…am I missing something?"

"You should have a camp itinerary," Kieran said.

"Well, what sessions did you pick?" Finlay asked.

"Sessions? I don't think I picked any sessions."

"After you registered, you should have received a list of offerings to choose from," Finlay stated.

"Yeah… I don't know what you're talking about. I registered last week. They didn't ask me about anything like that."

"Give me a second," Finlay said. "Mano and Jaxson walked into the café when I finished my order. I'll find out what's going on for you?"

And with that, hurricane Finlay was off.

"Is he always like that?" I asked.

"Like what?" Kieran asked.

I thought about my words for a second before I said, "Forceful?"

"I would have gone with 'pushy', but 'forceful' works," Kieran said with a wink. "And yeah, Finlay is a force to be reckoned with. When he decides he's going to do something or that something needs to be done, he doesn't let anything get in his way. He's a great guy to have in your corner, and one you don't want working against you."

I drank more of my coffee. Mano and Jaxson walked outside. Mano had an attaché case flung over his shoulder. "Let me put our stuff down and I'll check," I heard Mano saying to Finlay. Jaxson put their coffees on the table, and Mano placed the case on the table before he started rummaging through it. "Who am I looking for again?"

"What's your name?" Finlay yelled.

I grimaced internally while plastering on a smile. "Darrin, Darrin Betancourt."

"Oh right," Jaxson said. "You were one of the last-minute guys."

"That would be me," I said as I lifted my cup in his direction.

"Sorry about that," Mano said a second later as he approached the table. "You should have gotten this when you checked in yesterday, but they hadn't gotten in the latest batch of registrations."

He handed me a small stack of papers stapled together. My name was scrawled at the top with the word 'Itinerary' in blocky letters in the center.

"How's the foot?" Mano asked. "Jaxson and I were worried about you when we didn't see you again last night."

"It's fine. Jordan and I got back kind of late, so we went right up to our cabins. Thanks for asking, though."

"I'm glad to hear it's okay. Well, let me know if you have questions," Mano said with a smile before turning around and hurrying back to sit with Jaxson.

"So, what's on your agenda?" Finlay asked as I sat down.

Instead of answering, I handed him the packet.

He looked at it and visibly grimaced.

"What?" I questioned.

"Huh?" Finlay said absently, still reading my itinerary.

"You made a face," I said, narrowing my eyes at the other man, waiting for him to look up again.

"Oh, that... It's nothing."

"Don't be like that, Fin," Kieran said.

Finlay let out a sigh. "He has 'finding your inner gay orgasm' and 'tree whispering' with Roodra Rahim."

Kieran made the unfortunate mistake of taking a sip of his flat white right before Finlay responded, then spat it across the table. Thankfully, no one was in the projectile's path.

"Who's Roodra Rahim?" I asked. "And I'm finding my inner gay *what*? And whispering to trees? Are you fucking with me?"

"It's 'finding your inner gay orgasm' then 'tree whispering'. Those are two of Rahim's workshops," Kieran said with zero mirth in his voice.

"Those are actual things?"

"Yep," Finlay said.

"What's with this guy?" I asked, my obvious concern penetrating through the question.

"I don't want to speak ill of him," Finlay said. "I wouldn't want to taint your perception of the man before you form your own opinion."

"Let's say that Fin and Rahim have...history."

"But you also have hiking and partner massages, so that should be fun," Finlay said, changing the topic.

"Don't I need to have a partner for the partner massage?"

"Don't worry about it," Finlay replied. "That's one of my sessions. If you don't have a partner already, I'll either work with you or find someone."

Admittedly, the idea of a bendy Finlay could be interesting, assuming I could find something better for his mouth to do.

"And don't worry. The partner massages are totally nonsexual...mostly."

Jordan

I slept through the night and finally rolled out of bed a little after seven-fifteen. I heard Darrin talking to Chad outside but couldn't make out their words. I got out of bed and headed into the bathroom for a quick piss. I then threw on my running shorts and laced up my tennis shoes. I'd started long-distance running as my primary sport when I was in high school. Even after school, I'd kept it up. I put my wireless earphones in and strapped my phone to my upper arm before taking a step into the morning mountain air. Thankfully, no one was around, so I took off in the direction of the trailhead that I'd found when I'd consulted the camp map. About one-hundred yards down from my cabin was a turnoff for a hiking slash running path. I took off running. The map said the trail was only about five miles, so it would be a nice morning jog and take me maybe thirty to thirty-five minutes. I was on vacation, so I didn't want to do anything too strenuous.

It took about twelve minutes before I broke a sweat in the cool air. I looked down at my pale white chest. I had just a little chest hair around each nipple and a smattering of hair that created the treasure trail into the top of my shorts. The sides of my blue shorts were six-inch slits that went to my waistband to give me more comfort running. The internal lining kept my junk from wobbling, but I probably should have packed a jockstrap to keep it more secure.

I kept listening to my music and running. Just past the three-mile mark, I saw the tops of the three cabins more in the east, so I figured the path had taken me north, then back around to the west. Now, I was heading more south. I figured eventually I'd start going east before going north again to make the entire loop of the trail.

Mostly, the trail was flat. Sure, there were a few little hills, but nothing that caused me to strain even a little bit. It was quite pleasant. I had trees on both sides of me. A squirrel ran in front of me on the path and a few birds flew away as I approached, but I saw no other wildlife to speak of. The trail opened up ahead on a straightaway. In the distance, there were a few picnic tables scattering a giant open field. I remember seeing a picnic spot on the map, which gave me a pretty good idea of where I was in my morning run. I drew up short before leaving the tree cover. On one of the picnic tables up ahead were two muscle-bound studs fucking.

I'm generally not a voyeur, but if you're fucking out in public on a picnic table, you're just asking to be watched. I got off the path, stood behind a tree and watched the guys. These were not the guys I found around Woodstock. These were the types of guys I see when I watch porn online.

Without even consciously doing it, I slipped my hand into my shorts and my dick started sticking out of the bottom. My shorts were not designed to hide any part of an erection. I'm not what I would call huge. I'm slightly above average, but these shorts would show any hint of sexual excitement. And right then, I might as well have been standing butt-ass naked myself because my dick was poking out of my shorts in the early morning air.

Thump...thump. I heard the telltale sound of someone else running up behind me on the path. *Fuck! What do I do?* I did the only thing I could think to do. I hopped onto the path, coughed, ran by the fucking duo and hoped they couldn't see my dick sticking straight out in front of me as I darted past them.

"Hey, don't run away. You could come over and play," I heard as I sped past.

"Don't mind if I do," another voice said behind me.

I kept wondering if they were talking to the jogger behind me or me. Either way, I kept running. I didn't stop until I bounded up the steps and headed into my cabin. I was still running with a raging hard-on, so I was glad I hadn't bumped into anyone else along the path.

I threw myself out of my shorts and shoes and into the shower. I turned the water to a cold setting, hoping to calm down. "What the fuck? Might as well." I reached down, grabbed my dick and stroked myself as I turned up the water's temperature. I leaned against the back of the shower so the water could pour over me as I daydreamed about the gorgeous men on the picnic table. I wasn't sure who I wanted to be more – the guy fucking or the guy getting fucked. I imagined being in the middle of that sandwich for my personal fantasy. I imagined the one muscle-bound stud taking me from behind as I lowered myself into the other guy. My stomach muscles tensed seconds before I exploded and hit the front wall of the shower. I pumped myself repeatedly until the last drop of cum rinsed down the shower drain. Part of me wanted to collapse, but I had to clean up. I grabbed the bar of soap and started washing myself.

A few minutes later, I was out of the shower and dressed in a pair of gym shorts and a T-shirt before grabbing my room key. I locked my cabin and headed down the hill to breakfast. This time, I had memorized the path to the dining hall, so I knew where I was going. It took me a few minutes, but I joined the throngs of people heading there.

Breakfast was served buffet style, which was great because I was starved. I was looking forward to all the delicious food, then I looked at what was available. *Ahh fuck, it's all vegetarian.* I should have known that. I've grown up with enough hippies that love their plants. Still, I hadn't even considered that this place didn't serve meat. They had eggs, but that was the only protein source. There was no bacon or sausage to be found. There was faux sausage, but that looked like a charcoal briquet. I was sure it constituted food to someone, but not me. I scooped a hefty helping of eggs onto my plate, then headed over to the bread area. There were a lot of different loaves. I kept hoping to find something that said 'bread-bread', but nope. There was pumpernickel, rye, seven-grain, whole-grain, challah, sprouted, potato and a bunch of other words I didn't recognize and didn't know how to pronounce. I grabbed a bagel. *Can't fuck up a bagel*, I hoped.

With breakfast—or at least a plate full of food that allegedly resembled breakfast—in tow, I looked out over the room and had my high-school nightmare come rushing back to me. I stood with my tray, but I didn't know where to sit or whom to sit with. *This isn't high school*, I told myself, trying to avoid a panic attack. I was on the verge of finding an empty table and sitting by myself when I looked across the space, and Darrin waved at me. *Thank you, Jesus.*

I worked my way through the room. When I approached, there was an empty seat next to Darrin, so I looked at him and asked, "Is this seat taken?"

"Good morning, Jordan," Darrin said. He smiled and pushed the chair out for me. "Take a load off."

"Thanks," I said. "I'm glad I saw you. I had a brief flash of lunchroom hell from high school."

"I think we all know how that goes," Darrin said as he took a bite of his eggs. "You were looking around the room, and I could tell you weren't sure who to sit with or where to sit. I'm glad I noticed you before you sat by yourself."

I laughed, hoping I sounded like I was joking and would never in a million years have done something like that. I checked in with Darrin about his foot and was glad to hear that it was just fine.

"So, let me introduce you to everyone." Darrin formally introduced me to his friends, Bryce and Richard. He also reintroduced me to Kieran, who then introduced me to a handsome guy he was sitting with named Finlay.

"So, did you know about your itinerary for the day?" Darrin asked.

"My *what*?" I replied as I shoveled a bit of egg into my mouth.

Darrin proceeded to tell me about the schedule he'd received from Mano that morning. Since Darrin was already finished with his breakfast, he hopped up and meandered across the room to where Mano and Jaxson were sitting.

"So, I hear you're a local boy," Finlay said, drawing me back into the table's discussion.

"Guilty as charged. Born and raised in this area."

"You must come out here often?" either Bryce or Richard asked me, I couldn't remember which.

"Actually, this is my first time. Sure, I knew where it was, but it's not a place where many locals spend time."

"Why's that?" Kieran asked.

Because we get enough hippy-dippy shit just living in Woodstock. Thankfully, I kept my internal monologue from leaving my mouth. "I can't say. A lot of locals probably don't even know this place exists. It's off the beaten path enough…" I let the idea kind of float off on its own.

"Here's your itinerary," Darrin said, leaving a stapled stack of papers in front of me on the table. "Our schedules are identical."

"Guess you both got the leftovers," Finlay said. "Sorry about that."

"Huh?" I asked, looking at Darrin, who slid in beside me.

"Don't worry about it. Apparently, our activities for the day will be interesting, according to Finlay and Kieran. They wouldn't tell me why because they didn't want to bias me."

I cocked my head in confusion but didn't ask anything else.

"Good morning, slags," a slender guy said, sitting down. It took me a second to decipher what he was saying through his thick Scottish brogue. "You'll never guess what I was just up to."

"More like who he was up to," either Bryce or Richard said. I was meeting too many people too quickly for my brain to keep them all straight in my head.

"So, I went for a morning jog," the Scottish guy said, "and I came across a couple of guys shagging on a picnic table. They yelled at me to join them, so I said sure. The guys had been yelling after another guy who had hightailed it outta there. Some guy stood in the trees, jerking off, watching them going at it. He must have come and taken off when he heard me running by."

"I didn't come," I mumbled. Darrin shot me a sideways glance but didn't say anything. I stared intently at my schedule.

"I jumped right in between those two and rode them both for all they were worth. I love this place!"

I must have turned beet red because one of Darrin's friends looked my way and said, "Is he all right?"

Darrin patted me on the back and said, "Something went down the wrong pipe."

"Speaking of pipes," the Scottish gay cut in, clearly oblivious to anyone else, "whose pipe are you most interested in sharing while we're here?" He swiveled his fork between the married couple Darrin was friends with.

The two men looked at each other and said, "Each other's."

"Ahh, feck that! You gotta add a little spice up in there this weekend. I'm sure I could get one of my new friends..." The Scottish guy stood up and looked around the place before pointing to a pair of guys on the other side of the room who were casually clothed. He waved, and they waved back. "I'm sure I can get one or both of them to join ya."

"Owen," one of the other men said, "we don't need anyone else in our relationship. Trust us. We're perfectly fulfilled with each other."

"Whatever. Just let me know if ya change your minds." He turned and looked at me then. "Do I know you? I don't think we've met yet."

"Owen," Darrin said, cutting in and saving me, "this is Jordan. He's in the cabin next to mine. He's also the gentleman who drove me to the Urgent Care last night. Jordan, this is Owen, also known by his alter drag ego Nessie Loch."

"And, before ya ask, I am actually Scottish."

I smiled and nodded, before shoving a piece of bagel into my mouth. Owen turned and glanced at Darrin. "Don't bother asking," Darrin said. "I know what's going on in that head of yours. I'm not looking."

"Ahh, you all are no fun. We're surrounded by hot, horny gay men and you're all celibate as priests. Fuck that." His eyes bounced between the four of us as he shook his head. Then he turned to Kieran. "What about you?"

"I'll let you know who I haven't had sex with on Sunday." With that, Kieran stood, grabbed his tray and headed off to give the dirty dishes to the kitchen staff.

Chapter Nine

I flipped through the schedule and honestly had no idea what to make of it. *Inner gay orgasm? Tree whispering? Couple's massage? WTF!* I was glad to know that Darrin's and my schedules were virtually identical, so at least I wouldn't be alone.

I flipped the page to see what was on my agenda tomorrow. "What is remote viewing?"

Finlay barked out a laugh, so I got an uneasy feeling in my stomach. "Don't worry about it. Trust me. You'll find it a highly entertaining experience, if nothing else." His answer didn't exactly reassure me.

"Well," Darrin said, looking at me, "I guess we should make our way to get our inner gay orgasms on."

I looked from side to side, eyeing the other men at the table to see if they would give us a reaction to what Darrin had said. Unfortunately, everyone was doing a great job of keeping their poker faces on.

"Okay then," I said, doing my best to keep the reluctance out of my voice but failing.

I picked up my breakfast tray and walked through the dining hall to an open window area where we could deposit our trays. I thanked the people in the kitchen and followed Darrin out through a side door.

"Where are we heading?" I asked.

"Our first event of the day is being held in the Central Sanctuary. If I remember correctly, that's where we had the opening ceremony last night."

I reached into my back pocket, pulled out my camp map. I glanced at Darrin, who had done the same thing. I couldn't help but chuckle. Darrin looked at me and let out his own laugh.

"Great minds think alike," he said.

We figured out where we were heading and started on our short hike. Our quick jaunt through the campground led us through the flower gardens, which were just blooming. I was impressed with the groundkeeper's work. "From what I can tell," I said, gesturing to the flowers, "these are all native wildflowers."

"Really? They're so well organized." I cocked my head, not sure what to make of this statement. "From the look on your face, 'organized' may not have been the best word." Darrin grimaced, thinking of what he'd said.

"These right here," I said, pointing to a yellow flower that looked like it was staring at the ground, "are called a trout lily. These purple ones over here are wild blue phlox."

"But they're purple."

"The name is a bit of a misnomer. They come in blue, purple and white. This gorgeous bad boy over here" — I pointed to a red perennial — "is a lobelia cardinalis. As the summer hits its peak, they become much more brilliant in color."

"Wow, you know a lot about flowers?"

"I spent a lot of time in the forests with my father growing up. He was a bit of a horticulturist, so he taught me a lot about nature and plants. I can honestly say, I think it was those early discussions about flowers that led me to work on the apple orchard."

We approached the Central Sanctuary, and Darrin reached out and grabbed the door, saying, "After you."

"Thanks."

I walked in and took in the hodgepodge of people in the room. Off to the left, Chad and Avery talked, so I made a beeline to the opposite side. I immediately found a quasi-friendly face, so I dragged Darrin in his direction.

"Hey, Phil," I said, sitting down next to him. "How are you? Kind of surprised to see you here."

Phil Tucker was a pharmacist at a local grocery store. We'd also hooked up when I was younger. He was a nice guy, but I didn't feel any chemistry with him. Unfortunately, when you're young, dumb and full of cum, you don't always think about the ramifications of having sex with someone you know.

"Hello, Jordan," Phil said. There wasn't any hint of malice, but he also didn't show any trace of fondness. "Who's your friend?"

"Darrin Betancourt," he said as he extended his hand. Phil eyed the hand for a second before grasping it.

"Phil Tucker. It's nice to meet you, Darrin."

"Why are you over here alone?" I asked.

"I'm avoiding someone." His eyes darted in Avery and Chad's direction.

"Me too. Are you avoiding Chad or Avery?"

"Avery? Is that the younger guy?"

"Yep. I had a bit of a run-in with him last year. It wasn't my finest moment. But," I said, drawing out the word, "he did something he shouldn't have."

"I'm avoiding Chad. He broke something when he delivered it to my house a while back. He swears it wasn't him, but I think it's a revenge thing. He's still pissed I wouldn't have a threesome with him a few years ago."

"Wow," Darrin said. "He really gets around."

"You have no idea," I responded.

"I was looking for a genuine connection, and Chad was looking for what Chad always looks for. He's not relationship mat—"

Phil was cut off by the sound of a gong from the back of the room. I spun my head to see a guy in his late twenties walking down the row. As he walked by, I heard him chanting something under his breath in a language I didn't recognize. He wore a long white toga that had rainbow embroidery. His long brown hair was pulled back in a ponytail. He looked like a cross between Gandhi and Jesus. Behind him were two other men dressed in similar outfits. One held the gong and the other had teeny-tiny cymbals on his thumb and pointer fingers. Periodically, the gong would get rung, followed by the metallic resonance of the cymbals.

"What the fuck?" Darrin said.

When the group of three reached the front, the two acolytes sat down on the floor and stared up at the man in the white toga. I caught a glimpse at one of the men on the ground. *Holy shit. He was on a picnic table this morning.* Sure enough, when I saw the other one's face, I recognized him from the picnic table also.

"Am I late?" Finlay said as he sat down behind us. He leaned between Darrin and me before saying, "Let the shit show begin."

Darrin

"Who the fuck is that?" I asked, looking at Finlay.

"That's Roodra Rahim in all his glory."

The toga guy and his followers made their way to the front of the sanctuary. I was about to ask Finlay for more details when the room suddenly became silent. I turned back to see what the hell was going on. The man had pulled out what looked like a wooden recorder.

"This is the best part," Finlay said before he leaned back, clasped his arms behind his head and stretched out his legs in front of him, crossed at the ankles.

"Good morning, my children," Roodra said. He chanted in some language that seemed a poor imitation hovering between Latin and gibberish. It reminded me of the crazy people who would speak in tongues in the mega-churches when I was growing up. I half expected one of his followers to stand up and act as his interpreter. *What's next? Do we bring out the serpents?* When Roodra finished chanting, he raised the recorder to his lips and played…badly. It sounded like a group of kindergarteners with their first plastic recorders. I sat in stunned silence. My ears begged me to raise my hands and plug them to keep out the infernal sound of damnation.

One group of guys toward the front apparently snapped out of their shock and started snickering. The acolyte dudes shot death daggers with their eyes in the group's direction. The snickering came to a sudden halt.

"Am I missing something? What the fuck is this?" Jordan asked. "I may not be the most worldly or spiritual guy, but what is this shit?"

I looked over at Jordan and responded, "I haven't the foggiest idea."

"This, my new friends, is my ex," Finlay said with zero emotion.

"You dated him?" Jordan questioned. The look that crossed his face was a combination of amazement and horror.

"He wasn't like that when we dated. The guru façade came after. When I met him, he was just plain Jeremy Smith. Back then, he didn't have a spiritual bone in his body."

I wanted to ask for more details, but the playing stopped. I clapped my best polite golf clap. Roodra bowed like he was a rock-n-roll idol.

"Thank you for indulging me as I blessed you with my music this morning. For those I have not had the pleasure of meeting, I am Roodra Rahim. I'm sure you've all read my book or seen my popular YouTube channel."

"His book was self-published, and his channel has, like, five-hundred followers," Finlay said quietly.

Roodra shot Finlay a look. I don't think the guru could have heard what Finlay said, but Roodra was obviously not happy that Finlay was in the audience.

"Today, we are going to discuss finding the inner gay orgasm. For those who have not had an inner or spiritual orgasm, let me demonstrate." He looked down at one of his acolytes and nodded. The man jumped up and went to the side of the sanctuary where a lone chair had been sitting. He dragged the chair center stage, and Roodra sat down without saying a word. Then there was more chanting.

"What's happening?" Jordan asked.

"I…yeah… You got me," I said with a shrug.

Suddenly, there was the sound of terrible porn sex. I snapped my head back and found Roodra gyrating in his chair. His acolytes were doing the same thing on the ground before him.

"Holy shit," Jordan said. "Is he?"

Roodra gripped the sides of the chair as he suddenly exploded in front of the entire room. His muscles spasmed and ejaculate coated the underside of his toga, causing a large visible wet spot. I couldn't see the guys on the floor, but from the reactions of some closer in the room, I'm betting they had a similar response.

"Well, that takes all the fun out of a circle jerk," Finlay joked.

I sat there in stunned silence. I didn't know what I had just watched. Medically, I've heard of cerebral ejaculation. That's basically what a wet dream is. And I know it's possible to do what Roodra just did, but it's not something most men try or experiment with.

Roodra let out a loud breath and slowly opened his eyes. "As you can see," he said, looking down at the wet space on his toga, "it is completely possible to have a full orgasm without touching oneself. I call this the inner gay orgasm. Others call it a spiritual orgasm. And it's possible to do alone" — he then glanced at the men in front of him who had sat up while he was speaking — "or with friends." Roodra grinned at his acolytes.

I sat there trying to parcel out the physiology of what I'd just witnessed. *Group hallucination? Maybe actual hallucinogens are involved?* I was so fascinated by the medical question that I had half stopped listening to Roodra completely. Something snapped my attention back to him.

"I would recommend refraining from sex — and that includes masturbating — for at least a week before attempting to have an inner orgasm. Having that kind of pent-up sexual energy helps you find your inner gay orgasm easier the first time."

"Well, that's not likely to happen around here," Jordan whispered. "I think I've seen half these guys fucking already. We may be the only four guys who haven't gotten laid yet."

"Well, don't count me in that group," Finlay joked. "I definitely had a hot piece of ass last night." I turned to look at him. Finlay was staring at Phil, the pharmacist, who was sitting on the other side of Jordan.

"Well, yes, I think we both had a mutually enjoyable evening," Phil said, turning a shade of red akin to a fire engine.

"And he may look like he's a little uptight," Finlay said, looking at Phil. His tongue licked the top of his lip seductively. "But, trust me, he's almost as flexible as I am. I put him through his paces. The positions we explored…" Finlay looked almost like he would have his own inner gay orgasm remembering whatever had happened.

"Excuse me, Mr. Winslow. If you're going to distract my followers from finding enlightenment, please leave." I looked to the front of the sanctuary to find Roodra looking highly perturbed.

"Sure thing, Jeremy," he said, deliberately drawing out Roodra's name. "I'll stop talking to your followers."

"That's a dead name, Mr. Winslow. I've asked you several times to stop calling me that. I am no longer the man you —"

"I *what*? Fucked? Dated? Loved?" The entire room was darting their eyes between both men, like watching hot tennis players volleying. Finlay didn't wait for a response. He stood and strolled out of the building.

"What just happened?" Jordan asked.

"Drama," Phil said. "Lots of gay drama. Let's just say Fin gave me an earful last night when I told him I'd signed up for Roodra's classes this weekend."

You signed up for this on purpose? I wanted to question Phil about his life choices, but there was another loud gong.

"I'm sorry, my children, for that interruption."

The 'my children' thing was irking me. I could tell that Roodra was older than me, but maybe by one or two years. "I need everyone to lie on the ground. I will walk you through a meditative exercise to help you find your inner gay orgasm." He then clapped his hands twice.

People slowly spread out over the room, lying down. *When in Rome?* I moved over to the side of the room before lowering myself. Jordan had followed me and was just an arm's length away. I fidgeted until I found a somewhat comfortable position. I wondered how some of the older guys' backs would fare, lying on the hard surface.

"I want you to close your eyes and listen to the flute," and the duck mating call started again.

"How is this supposed to be soothing?" Jordan asked.

"Beats me." The flute stopped, and Roodra started chanting in the room's front in a voice barely louder than a whisper.

Jordan

Jeremy Smith? I kept running Roodra's dead name repeatedly in my head as I listened to the man chanting. Periodically, there would be a light chime. If nothing else, lying on the floor brought me back to nap time as a child. I listened to Darrin's breathing, and it slowly changed to a gentle snoring. *How can he sleep with that nonsense in the background?*

I twisted my head and got a look at Darrin's jawline. He had what my mother would call a strong jaw. I could see the line of the bone from his ear through his chin. He was clearly chiseled. And from the way his pecs looked under his shirt, he was chiseled all over. I almost gasped when I watched his shirt ride up slightly and his underwear peeked up from beneath his shorts. He was tanned and had a treasure trail that led underneath. I absently licked my lip. *Don't even go there. He's a citidiot. You know better than to ponder his type.* I turned my head and closed my eyes again.

My mind was a whirlwind of thoughts. Half of them included me ripping off Darrin's clothes and mounting him right then. The idea of taking him inside me caused me to get rock hard.

"Good, you're getting closer," Roodra said right above me. "Now, become one with your manhood. Force him to release."

I opened my eyes, but Roodra had moved past me. "I see pre-cum. You're getting there," he said to someone else.

As if on cue, my hard-on decided it was done for the day and deflated. We stayed on the ground like that for what seemed like forever. Finally, there was a loud gong.

"You may sit up and go with your inner gay goddess."

My inner gay goddess? I sat up and shook my head. Darrin hadn't moved.

I crawled over to him and nudged him gently. "Time to get up, sleepyhead." He reached out and tried to bring me down to him.

"Just five more minutes."

"Umm...Darrin. Wake up," I said louder as I disentangled myself from him.

He opened his eyes and looked into my face. "Sorry. I was dreaming. I didn't mean to touch you."

"It's cool. No harm, no foul."

"What happened?" he asked, rubbing the sleep from his eyes as he got into a sitting position.

"You found your inner gay orgasm. Then, like most guys, you passed out and took a nap," I said, trying my best at levity.

He looked at me like I'd grown a second head or something before realization of what I had said flashed across his face. "Oh fuck, I fell asleep. Guess I wasn't meant to have an inner gay orgasm today."

"Me neither. I guess I'll have to go back to the good old hand method." I stood up and offered my hand to Darrin. He accepted it, and I helped him to his feet. "What now?" I asked.

"I think we have couple's massages." He scrunched up his face before revising his answer. "No, I think we have a hike now. That sounds right."

"Couple's massages?"

"It's on our agenda for some time today."

"Isn't that for couples?" I asked. We headed toward the exit and passed between Roodra's acolytes. I nodded my head politely as we exited into the air.

"It's one of Finlay's classes. He said single guys will be coupled with other single guys. He also said it's nonsexual."

"Well, there goes my sex life," I joked. "With my luck, I'll get stuck with Roodra, and he'll try to massage my inner gay orgasm out of me. Or, worse, I'd get stuck with Avery." I involuntarily shuddered. "On second thought, I could see the joy of getting my hands on him." I must have sounded like a Bond villain, because Darrin looked at me oddly. "I'm joking. I don't condone violence. Avery, he just… He brings out the worst in me."

"We all have those people who know how to push our buttons. I guess Avery is that for you." He stopped on the path and looked me in the eyes. "I'm not one to judge. I wasn't there when Avery laid his hands on you. And, sadly, I can completely see Avery being an ass. He is what he is. And if you know that going into your interactions with him, you'll never expect anything more or anything less."

We started walking again before I asked, "Shouldn't we expect more from people? I mean, I get the excuse of '*he is what he is*.' Doesn't that just let someone off the hook for inappropriate behavior?"

Darrin thought about it for a moment. We passed a few guys on the trail walking this way and that. "I'm not saying to excuse his behavior or even condone it. Just don't be surprised by it. It's like the old Aesop fable of the scorpion and the frog. Only you're the frog and Avery's the scorpion. Don't be surprised when you're swimming across the river with him on your back and he stings you. It's his nature. Hopefully, he'll grow up. But I know a lot of guys in the city that have a Peter Pan complex, so it may never happen."

We approached the mark on the trail where we were to meet up with the rest of the hiking group. And, of course, there were Phil, Chad and Avery. I chiseled on a thin smile before saying, "Great...the gang's all here."

Chapter Ten

Darrin

I stared between Avery and Jordan and noticed their tense jaws. *Great, this is going to be a fun hike. I wonder which one will make it back alive.*

"Good morning, hikers," Mano said, approaching the group wholly decked out in hiking gear. He had one of those floppy hats you see on wilderness survivor television shows, a 'Camp Namast-Gay' T-shirt and a pair of cargo shorts. He had on brown hiking shorts and carried trekking poles. This man looked like we were going to go climb Mount Everest.

"Whoa, I think I'm a little overdressed," Phil said, gesturing down to his long-sleeved button-down dress shirt, khaki pants and shiny brown loafers.

"That makes two of us," Avery said. "I don't think sandals will be the best from the looks of you, Mano."

"Didn't you all sign up for the wilderness hiking excursion?" Mano asked. We all looked at him for a second before he smacked himself in the forehead.

"That's right. None of you knew what you were doing before breakfast. Why don't we meet back here in, say, fifteen minutes? In twenty minutes, we'll head out with or without you. Here's what you need to bring with you." He then rattled off a list of items from sunscreen to bug spray.

The green cabins were only one-hundred yards away from the trail end.

"Do you think we have time for a quickie?" Avery asked Chad.

I glanced over in time to watch Chad shake his head. "Nah. Besides, I'm not a huge fan of quickies. Much rather take things long and —"

Before I heard the end of that sentence, I escaped into my cabin. I looked down at my outfit and didn't know what else to wear. I pulled my trail hiking shoes from my duffle bag and put them on. I threw on a T-shirt with the logo of a musical I'd seen on Broadway the previous year. *Gotta prove I deserve my gay card around here somehow.* I also had a ballcap I'd thrown in my bag. I put on some SPF fifteen and my Oakley's and was as ready to go on a hike as I could be. I did a quick internal check of my foot to make sure it was ready for this. I twisted it from side to side and front to back. *Good to go.*

I stepped out on the porch, walked down the three steps and started walking back toward where Mano stood by himself.

"Wait up," I heard from behind me. Jordan shut his door and bounded down the stairs. He was wearing a pair of green tactical shorts and one of those moisture-wicking T-shirts that kept sweat away from your skin. He wore a pair of shades and a ballcap for what I assumed was a minor league sports team. As he got closer, the smell of coconut wafted off his body. I wasn't sure how much he put on, but the scent was overpowering. I kept my thoughts to myself.

"Do you think Chad and Avery will show back up?" Jordan asked.

"I think Chad wants to go on the hike while Avery wants to explore Chad's tent pole some more," I said, rolling my eyes.

"Welcome back, guys," Mano said as we approached. "Did you remember a water bottle?"

I lifted mine out of a pocket in my shorts. It was only a twelve-ounce bottle, but it should be good.

"If that's not enough, you can always borrow some from me," Jordan said. He turned his back to me. He was wearing one of those water backpack things for hiking.

"Wow, you are prepared," I said.

"I grew up hiking in these mountains. I know how to go for a hike and not hurt myself. What about you? Are you sure you can handle this? I mean, your foot and all."

"It's fine." He threw me a skeptical look. "I promise. I wouldn't go on this hike if I was at all worried it would be bad for my foot. Trust me. I need my feet. I stand on my feet for hours at a time in operating rooms, so I wouldn't take a risky chance."

Laughing voices from behind let me know Avery and Chad had joined us for the hike, after all. Chad was ready for a hike, but Avery looked like he was prepared for a White Party in Miami. He wore a white linen shirt unbuttoned to his navel over the top of white linen cargo shorts that barely covered the lower part of his body. When he stepped out of the shadow of a tree, I quickly learned Avery wasn't wearing underwear beneath those shorts. He topped off the look with a pair of white boat shoes and large designer sunglasses covering much of his face.

After getting that eyeful, I turned away and caught Mano taking in Avery's newer outfit. "Are you sure that's what you want to wear?" Mano asked. "I mean. We're going to be in nature. Your outfit…might get dirty."

"Trust me. This outfit has seen plenty of stains. I have a great dry cleaner who can get out anything," Avery responded.

"Oh, hey, Phil," Mano said, looking in a different direction. In all the commotion of Avery's outfit, I hadn't seen Phil get back. I turned to look at Phil, who was now dressed somewhere between Mano and me — sturdy shoes, khaki pants, hat, sunglasses and a 'Camp Namast-Gay' T-shirt. "Just a few quick words of warning. We are going into nature. Please stay on the path. There are a few places where the path is hard to see. If you fall behind, yell at the rest of us and we'll let you catch up. This hike should only take a couple of hours. We'll be a little late for lunch, but no biggie. I have snacks for when we hit the midway point."

We all nodded along with his announcements, then he turned and started walking. It took me a couple of seconds to get moving. Soon, Jordan and I were immediately behind Mano, Phil was behind us and Avery and Chad were bringing up the rear. *How long will it be before those two slip off into the woods to fuck?*

The path was nice and flat as we started out. Mano walked at a quick clip. He was a couple of inches shorter than me, but he was a man on a mission, and my long legs had to move to keep up with him.

I sidled up beside Mano with Jordan on my right. "So," I started, trying to start a conversation, "what do you do when you're not running things around here?"

"I work at a tech firm. I have a Master's in electrical engineering from the University of Hawaii. That's where I'm from originally. Born in Hilo on the Big Island, then moved to Honolulu for college and stayed for my Master's."

"How'd you end up in New York?" Jordan asked.

"After my Master's degree, I headed off to Silicon Valley to make my fortune. I did well for myself, but the cost of living was getting ridiculous, so I kept looking for other opportunities. A headhunter found my resume on LinkedIn and contacted me about a job with the firm I work for now, down in the city."

"How long have you been on this coast?" I asked.

"Almost five years."

"And you've been with Jaxson for how long?" I sounded like I was a radio interviewer.

"We met about three years ago and got married last summer in a small, traditional Hawaiian ceremony on the Kona side of the Big Island."

If I hadn't been to Hawaii a few times over the years, I don't think I would have known what Mano was talking about. I glanced at Jordan, but he nodded like he knew Hawaiian geography, so I didn't say anything.

We hiked in silence after that. I was about to strike up another conversation with Mano when he stopped in the middle of the trail and waited for Phil, Avery and Chad to catch up. "If you look off to the left about one-hundred feet in front of us. You'll see a large red maple tree. A little down from the top, you should see a bald eagle's nest."

I looked in the direction Mano pointed and all I could see were trees — lots and lots of trees. Admittedly, I couldn't tell one tree from the next, so I couldn't tell which tree Mano was talking about. I leaned over to Jordan. "Which one is the red maple?"

"If you look through the green trees, you'll find one with splotches of red balls on it. That's the red maple. It's still red this time of the year, but the full extent of its leaves' unfurling hasn't happened."

I followed his directions and found the tree. Sure enough, about halfway up the tree was an eagle sitting in a nest. "Is the eagle waiting for its chicks to hatch?" I asked.

"Nah," Jordan replied. "Bald eagles hatch their eggs in January and February. Occasionally, you'll hear of one hatching in May, but that's rare. Takes the chicks another ten to twelve weeks before they leave the nest, and another one to two months after that, the eagle has an empty nest."

"You know a lot about eagles," Mano said. I hadn't noticed everyone listening in on our conversation.

"My grandfather was an ornithologist," Jordan said.

"I have to go see mine every year for a new prescription," Avery said. I inclined my head to the left and scrunched my face in confusion. "You know, for new glasses."

"Oh, you meant ophthalmologist," I said.

"Yeah, an ornithologist is another term for 'bird watcher'. My grandfather loved to watch birds. Their kitchen table was right next to a large bay window, and he kept three different bird books and his binoculars on that table until the day he died. Some of that knowledge rubbed off on me over the years."

"No offense, but that sounds excruciatingly dull," Avery replied.

Jordan's shoulders tensed, so I leaned in and whispered, "Remember, he's a scorpion." Jordan took a breath through his nose and let it out before turning away from Avery.

"Okay, people. Let's keep moving." And with that, Mano started hiking away again.

The hike became increasingly more difficult as the incline increased. Before long, a slight river of sweat was running down my back. I wasn't huffing and puffing like poor Phil behind us. I almost wanted to go back and see if he needed a piggyback ride. The poor pharmacist may have been thin, but he was clearly not in the greatest shape.

Finally, the trail opened, and a meadow stretched out in front of us with a medium-sized pond.

"If we're quiet and lucky, sometimes various animals that live up here come out and visit on their way to the pond," Mano informed the group.

"What types of animals are up here?" I asked.

"White-tailed deer, foxes, coyotes," Jordan started.

"There's also raccoons and fishers, turtles, frogs and various birds," Mano added.

"There's also the occasional bobcat, but they aren't that common," Jordan said. "In fact, I've never seen one in all my years trekking around the woods."

"I think I'm going to take a sit," Phil said before plopping down in a patch of grass on the side of the path.

"I need to piss," I said. "Be right back."

"Don't stray too far," Mano yelled at my back.

"Don't worry, just going behind a tree."

I found a tree I could pee behind and made sure I was out of sight before unzipping my shorts then relieving myself. I was tucking myself back inside when a blood-curdling scream pierced the air.

I raced back to the path and found the men huddled near Phil, but they were all keeping their distance from him.

"What's going on?" I asked as I approached.

"Rattlesnake," Jordan said.

I moved to see past Phil. There was a coiled snake five feet away from him. *Still within striking distance.* I could see why the other men weren't approaching. The little slithery guy's tail was making a lot of noise as it watched us.

"Phil," I said quietly, trying to get the man's attention, "where were you bit?"

"Leg," the man said, looking into my eyes. I could see tears forming there.

"I know you're scared now, but please make no sudden moves. The snake is still within striking distance." Phil's eyes practically jumped out of his head as he swiveled and stared at his attacker lying nearby. *Not the right thing to say.* "He's more scared of you. If you don't make any sudden moves, he will move on. I don't want you to freak out. Freaking out will increase your blood pressure and speed up the venom dispersion. Take a deep breath." Phil took a deep breath and let it out. I pulled out my phone and took a couple of pictures of the snake. My phone had a pretty good camera, so I zoomed in on the snake and got some good shots so the Emergency Room would have a record of the snake that had bitten Phil.

"I'm going to come help you stand. Don't make any sudden movements. Remember, the snake isn't your enemy. It's scared of you and doing what it thinks is necessary to protect itself. If you don't give it any more reason to snap at you, it will leave you alone."

"Are you sure about that?" Mano asked. "I mean, rattlesnakes are aggressive."

"They can be. But that's just a timber rattler. They are territorial, but not assholes. Trust me. I dealt with asshole rattlers in Texas. Both diamondbacks and pygmy rattlers can be quite aggressive. Timber rattlers rarely bite."

"Lucky me," Phil said. The sweat beaded on his forehead.

"We need to move him, then get him to an emergency room for antivenom," I said matter-of-factly.

"We don't have cell service out here," Chad said, holding up his phone. "I already tried to call nine-one-one, but zero bars."

"Avery, do you think you can run back to camp and get help?"

"Sure, but I'm not exactly a runner. Maybe if I was being chased by a bear—and I'm not talking about the kind that I see in Speedos at Fire Island during the summer. I spend some time on a stair climber, but that's just to get my ass looking like this."

I didn't bother following up that response. "Jordan, you were a long-distance runner. How fast do you think you can make it back?"

"Full tilt..." Jordan looked up like he was doing some mental math. "Maybe twenty minutes."

"Do you have your phone on you?"

"I left it in the cabin. Didn't think I would need it."

"Here," I said, handing him my phone. "Take mine. As soon as you get a signal, call nine-one-one and let them know what we're dealing with here. You can also send them the pictures of the rattler."

"Got it." Jordan didn't hesitate. He took off running. His long legs kicked into hyper-drive as he sped away.

I let out a breath from my nose and turned back to Phil. The rattler had uncoiled and slithered away into the underbrush. *Thank God for small mercies.*

"You'll be glad to know, Phil, that your friend has just left. I'm going to get you out of that tall grass, though...just in case he has friends."

I walked over and squatted down next to Phil, cautious of my surroundings.

"Mano, can you clear the area in front of that tree?" I pointed to a tree that sat just off the road. There wasn't much near it but a few twigs and fallen leaves.

"Sure thing," Mano said.

"On three," I said. I looped my arm under Phil's arm and counted down. On three, I lifted him off the ground. "Don't put any weight on that leg. Lean on me."

We moved slowly until we got to the tree, and I could prop his back against its trunk. "I need to examine the bite. Mano, do you have a first-aid kit on you by chance?"

"Fuck no, man. I didn't even —"

"No worries. What about a pocketknife?"

"I have one," Chad said, whipping out a six-inch knife. I swear Avery practically swooned when the guy pulled out the blade. "You gonna cut open the wound and suck out the poisoned blood?" Chad asked as he handed me the knife.

"No. That's a horrible idea. I want to cut into the pants and check out the damaged area — and wash it real fast." I reached into my pant pockets, pulled out my unopened water bottle and set it on the ground next to me. I took the pocketknife, cut away the lower part of Phil's pants and took them off so I could get a better look at the bite. There was some blood on the area. I screwed off the top of my water bottle and poured it over the wound to irrigate it. Phil let out a yip. "Sorry about that. I know it stings." Once the area was cleaned, I looked at what was going on. Sure enough, right on the exterior side of his left calf muscle were two puncture wounds.

"I'm going to die, aren't I?" Phil asked.

"Less than five people die every year from snake bites. I'm not going to let you be one of them. But we need to get your belt, class ring and watch off. If there is any swelling, we don't want to make it worse by you having tight jewelry on."

Phil took off his watch, but the ring was more challenging for him to remove. I wasn't sure if the venom was already spreading or the ring was a little small. I helped him with the belt. "Mano, can you put these in your pack?" I asked.

"Sure," Mano said. He grabbed the items from me and stored them.

"You have a marker or pen in there?" I asked. Mano searched in his bag before pulling out a black marker. "Perfect," I said as he handed it to me. I turned back to Phil and said, "This will hurt, but I need to do it." I drew a circle around the puncture marks. Phil let out a breath when I lifted the felt tip off his skin.

"Who would have known that a felt-tip marker could feel like Satan was stabbing you with a pitchfork?" Phil said.

"Now comes the hard part." I looked at Chad and Mano. "We need to get him out of here as gently as humanly possible. This is too remote, and the path is too narrow in places to get an all-terrain vehicle up here, so we need to carry him. We'll take turns."

"What can I do?" Avery asked. From the shocked look on his face, he may have been equally surprised by his willingness to help.

"Carry Mano's bag and poles. The less weight any of us has will make it easier to carry Phil."

And that's precisely what we did. Mano and I lifted Phil off the ground and handed him first to Chad. After a bit, Mano took over. Then it was my turn. I witnessed a rippling of the muscles north of the puncture wounds. *Minor myokymia. That's not good but not uncommon.* It took us almost an hour to get back before we rounded a bend in the trail. Nurse Cody stood ahead in a utility task vehicle waiting for us.

"Sorry. This was as close as I could get," Cody said, running to help me load Phil up on the cart's back end.

"I'm coming with you," I said, sitting in the passenger seat.

"Let's go," Cody replied before turning on the gas and moving. A whimper escaped Phil's mouth with every bounce the vehicle made. "Is it really that bad?" Cody yelled over the engine.

"It looks like minor to moderate venomization. It could have been worse, but he'll be holed up in a hospital for a couple of days."

"Unlike my patient yesterday," Cody yelled back, giving me a wink.

"As you can see, I'm perfectly fine."

We met up with the EMTs a couple of minutes later. The EMTs ran with a stretcher to get Phil from the UTV. The two EMTs, Cody and I lifted him off the back and placed him atop the stretcher. "There is minor tissue inflammation, minor coagulopathy, and I witnessed mild myokymia when we were carrying him out of the woods. Did my friend already get you the pictures?" I asked. I looked around to see if Jordan was there, but he wasn't.

"Yeah, he texted us the pics when we got here. We'll get them to the ER docs when we get the patient into Kingston," the EMT told me as he shut the driver's-side door. And just like that, the truck pulled away, its blue and red lights flashing in the distance.

About that time, Avery, Chad and Mano finally caught back up with us. "They just left," I said as they approached. "I think he's going to be fine. Has a rough couple of days ahead of him, but he should be okay."

Cody's cell phone chirped, and he answered it. "It's for you." He held out his phone to Mano, who listened. Mano mouthed 'it's Jaxson' in our direction in between his "Yes, honeys" and "I'm okays." When he hung up the phone, he looked at the rest of us and said, "They held lunch for us, so we should get down there. Jordan's already eating."

"He wanted to come back with me on the UTV," Cody said. "I told him to sit that one out. That run he'd just taken is not an easy one…even for a young, fit guy like he is."

We piled on the UTV, and Cody slowly drove us to the dining hall, where food awaited. Only then did I realize that the four of us looked ragged. Yet somehow, Avery's shorts and shirt had maintained their pristine white. *Maybe he made a deal with a crossroads demon?*

Jordan

I was a bit of a sweaty mess when Jaxson ushered me into the now-empty dining hall. I'd waited for the

EMTs to get to camp so I could share the images Darrin had taken of the rattler that had bitten Phil. I had tried to convince Cody to take me on the ATV to meet up with the guys when they hiked out with Phil, but Cody told me he wanted to make sure he had plenty of room on his vehicle. I was also quickly informed that it was a UTV and not an ATV. Apparently, ATVs are only for recreation, and UTVs are for work.

"The model WES picked up last year was an old fire and rescue vehicle. We bought it at a surplus auction online," Cody had explained while we waited for the EMTs.

I smiled and nodded my head. Other than the ample cargo space on the back, it looked like the ATVs we rode around the farm. *Guess I'll do some googling next week when I have time. We need one of these bad boys on the farm.*

For now, I looked down at the veggie burger option for lunch. I don't mind veggie burgers, but can we not call them burgers? If there wasn't a cow involved in the patty's making, it's not a burger. It's a sandwich. This specific sandwich was a black bean patty. I was hungry, so I grabbed two buns and made up two black-bean-patty sandwiches, complete with all the trimmings. They also had fries, and they're kind of hard to fuck up. These had the perfect balance between crisp on the outside and mushy potato goodness on the inside.

I sat down at a table and Jaxson joined me. "How are you holding up?" Jaxson asked me.

"I'm fine," I said as I bit into my sandwich. "You?"

"I'm nervous," Jaxson said. He wrung his hands. I didn't think I'd ever seen someone actually wring their hands outside of a movie villain before. "I know Mano is smart and even-tempered, but I don't know how he will handle this crisis. He can be melodramatic."

"He seemed in better shape than Phil did." I threw a ketchup-covered fry into my mouth.

"Did you see the bite?"

I chewed for a second before answering. "Darrin hadn't looked at the bite yet when I started to run back to camp. I'm sure he has things under control."

"Thank God Darrin was with Mano out there. I can't imagine Mano doing this on his own without an ER doctor there to guide him. Sure, we've both read the manuals on wilderness safety, but we've never had a problem like this. Usually, we go the whole weekend with only a couple of minor scrapes but nothing bad. Here we are on day two, and we're already sending our second camper to the hospital."

Jaxson stood and started pacing. I finished my first sandwich and started on my second one. The door to the dining hall opened and the rest of my hiking group walked in. They were sweatier than when I'd left them, but they looked no more haggard than I did. Avery was the last to walk in, and he somehow had managed to neither sweat nor spoil his white outfit. I'm sure he didn't help much. I wanted to get mad, but Darrin's words about Avery being a scorpion rang in my head. *He is what he is.*

Darrin grabbed his food and joined me at the table. He gave me a brief rundown of what had happened while I was running back to camp. I then filled him in on what had transpired in the camp. I popped the last fry on my plate into my mouth.

"I want more fries," I said. "Need anything else?"

"Nah, I'm good. I'll keep the table from running off while you're gone," Darrin said with a grin.

I walked up to the buffet line and grabbed a new plate.

"Thank God Chad and I were there to save the day," Avery told Jaxson. "Sure, the other guys helped, but Chad did the lion's share of carrying poor Peter back to camp."

"Phil," Chad corrected.

"That's right, poor Phil."

Mano appeared beside me and whispered, "Don't worry. Jaxson takes anything Avery says with a grain of salt. Jaxson will know who the true heroes of the day are."

"Thanks."

With fries in hand, I walked back to the table. "You won't believe the tale Avery is spinning."

"Do tell," Darrin said as I sat down.

"In his version, Chad is cast as Zeus, who came down from on high to single-handedly carry Phil back to camp."

Darrin chuckled. "That sounds like Avery. Drama queen as usual."

"Doesn't it irk you that he's lying?"

"Not really. I think I would be more surprised if he told the truth."

"I still don't understand what you see in him." Darrin started to say something, but I held my hand up to stop him. "I know. Avery is who he is. And I'm trying to internalize that idea, but it's infuriating. *He's* infuriating."

Darrin took a bite of his sandwich and chewed. When he'd swallowed, he answered, "I don't necessarily like Avery. I don't have ill will toward him, either. He's been a convenient release during my pity party this year. And I know you're not going to want to hear this, but Avery can do some things with his mouth and ass that are pretty fucking amazing." Darrin winked at me before taking another bite.

"Eww… I *so* didn't need to hear that over lunch." I made a barfing sound for emphasis. Darrin chuckled around his bite. "I could have gone my whole life without knowing that."

The sound of the screen door opening in the dining hall squeaked. I turned my head to see Darrin's friend Bryce walking into the room.

"Thank God," Bryce said as he slid into a seat opposite Darrin. "What happened? You were supposed to go on a pleasant hike, not cause a national emergency." Darrin filled in Bryce on what had happened. "Well, I'm glad to see that both of you are all right. And you're sure there was muscle fluttering?"

"Yes, Dad," Darrin said in an exaggerated tone. "I think I know what muscle fluttering looks like. And pray tell, Bryce, how many rattlesnake bites have you treated down in the city?"

Bryce rolled his eyes. "Maybe one. And that was because some jackass had an illegal snake in an aquarium. The moron thought it was a pet."

"Exactly. Between growing up in Texas and treating them in Denver, I've seen more than a few rattlesnake bites."

"You know what I mean. Surgeons don't generally handle snake-bite care."

"True, but I've treated a few during my residency. I'm hardly an expert, but I know how to stabilize and turf a patient to someone who is. He'll be fine. Hopefully, the area hospital has antivenom on hand. Since the Catskills have timber rattlers, I can't imagine they wouldn't."

"Wow," Bryce said. "The way you said *'rattlers'* made you sound like a Texan."

"Well, that's because I *am* a Texan."

"You know what I mean. You may have grown up in Texas, but you don't sound like a Texan."

"I think that's supposed to be a compliment," Darrin said before taking a swig of lemonade. "My dad and mother sound very Texan, but I lost any accent I had during college and medical school. But, like you pointed out, I have a few words that still slip out with my drawl attached."

"I thought it was cute," I said, then immediately wished I could put those words back in my mouth.

Bryce raised his eyebrows. "You think Darrin is cute, ehh?" There was a mischievous glint in his eyes.

I could feel the blush coming on. I stammered, "I said, '*I thought the Texas twang was cute.*'"

"So, you don't find Darrin attractive?" Bryce countered.

"Bryce," Darrin stepped in, "stop interrogating Jordan." He turned and looked at me. "Don't worry. He's trying to get a rise out of both of us. It's what he does." He turned and locked eyes with Bryce. "Where's Richard? Don't you have a husband you can terrorize?"

"He's no fun. He calls me on my bullshit before I even get it out of my mouth." Bryce glanced down at his watch. "Well, I should get back to him. We're in the pottery class all afternoon."

With that, Bryce left the building. The rest of lunch was uneventful. Afterward, we made our way to the session we were signed up for — tree whispering — but we were already late. We walked up the hill to where there was a clearing with a dozen or so trees and found

Roodra Rahim in a very compromising position with a tree.

"Dear God," I said as we walked toward him. "That tree is getting more action than I've had in the past year."

"I wonder if the tree consented before being attacked like that."

Roodra was practically gyrating on the poor tree. I waited for him to spank the bark and bellow out, 'Who's your daddy?' He was at least fully clothed.

When we entered the clearing, Roodra stopped what he was doing and turned to address Darrin and me.

"Why, if it isn't the heroes of the hour?"

Everyone turned to look at us. I curved my lips upward. Another blush heated my skin. One of the things about being whiter than a lot of guys—besides the kick-ass farmer tan—was my tendency to flush easily. I could go from white to cherry tomato in ten seconds flat.

"Well, don't dilly-dally," Roodra said. "Find a tree. We were becoming one with our trees."

A couple of unmolested trees stood in the back of the field, so we went and stood next to our new timber friends.

"Talk to your tree," Roodra said. "Make friends with your tree."

"Well, hello, Mr. Tree. Or is it Mrs. Tree?" I said, offering my hand for a handshake. Darrin laughed.

"I believe trees are nonbinary," Darrin said. "What's that?" Darrin said as if talking to his tree. "Oh, you prefer to go by Charly...with a y."

Roodra's acolytes shot us a look. "Uh-oh, the good kids aren't happy with us," I said.

"Charly says...'*fuck 'em*.'"

Darrin and I sat there cutting jokes for the rest of the session. I think the point of tree whispering was to become one with nature or some shit like that.

Afterward, Darrin and I headed back to our cabins to get cleaned up since we hadn't done so after lunch.

Chapter Eleven

Darrin

I didn't realize how much of a mess I was until I had stripped out of my clothes. They had been stained with sweat and mud. Honestly, I had no idea how I had gotten that much mud on them. I discarded my dirty wardrobe in a corner of the room before taking a quick shower, the second of the day. Once I was squeaky clean, I collapsed naked atop the bed for a minute and lay there.

I grabbed my schedule and looked to see what session we missed by sneaking off to clean up. 'The Angelic Path to Self-Love.' *Angel fucking?* We already had self-fucking and tree fucking, so nothing much would surprise me at this point. I flipped to the back, where longer descriptions of the programs were written. I found the one I was looking for and read, "*In this short intensive, you will learn how to use angelic oracle cards to find self-fulfillment. This process aims to tap into the ethereal plane and learn how to engage in self-love from your angel spirit guide."* I read the description twice.

Thankfully, this one wasn't taught by Roodra. *Maybe that's a little too out there even for him.* Perhaps it's because I grew up in conservative Christian Texas, but I have difficulty grasping anything labeled as 'New Age'. I never went out of my way to belittle or degrade someone's beliefs openly. Still, I'm no longer as open to religious or spiritual things as I once had been. The church had screwed with my head about the 'demons of homosexuality' when I was coming to terms with my sexuality.

When I came out as an undergraduate, the campus minister had sent me to a conversion therapy specialist, who told me not to masturbate and to 'pray away the gay'. The same minister hit on me at a local gay bar about six months later. After that, I decided God had made me this way, and fuck anyone else who thought otherwise. Their ignorance wasn't my problem. After attending Rice, I went to Texas Tech for medical school, and it was worse than Rice for gay people. Half the reason I had wanted to be in Denver for my residency was that Colorado was a liberal bastille by comparison to West Texas. I had enjoyed my time in medical school, but I had needed to escape the conservative oppression.

I looked at the clock and groaned. I needed to get moving if we would make it to couple's massage.

I threw on a pair of workout shorts and a tank top. I put my tennis shoes back on, even though my feet weren't exactly thrilled by the prospect of wearing them again so soon.

I exited my cabin and walked over to Jordan's and knocked. "Wakey, wakey. We need to head down."

"Be right out," he called from inside the room. A second later, Jordan opened the door. He had a white towel hanging right on his hips. "Come on in. I'll be ready shortly." I walked in and sat in the guest chair inside the cabin. Jordan went back to his bathroom. "Sorry I'm running behind. I came in and passed out for a few minutes."

I looked toward his voice and caught a nude glimpse of him in the mirror. The chair was at the right angle with the mirror to give me a fantastic view of Jordan's perfectly sculpted runner's ass. He bent over to pull up his shorts — *hmm, no underwear* — and it took all my self-control not to run into the bathroom and take him from behind. My little Darrin stirred in my pants, wanting to come out and play. And in my current attire there'd be no way to hide an erection. I stopped staring at the mirror and refocused my attention on a spot on the wall.

He walked out a few seconds later, wearing practically the same outfit I was wearing, just in a different color. *We almost look like a couple who coordinated our outfits.*

"Ready?" Jordan asked.

"Yes," I said. I pushed back the chair, stood and angled my leg in front of my semi to prevent Jordan from seeing it. I walked out through the door.

In a second, Jordan was standing beside me. I could smell the scent of his body wash on his skin. *I wonder if it tastes as good as it smells.*

"Snake!" I heard Chad yell through the closed door of his cabin. I turned to move, but then a second voice filled the air.

"Hmm…and what an enormous snake it is," Avery said. "Here… Let me suck the venom out of you." The sounds that followed were clearly not those of someone in pain.

Jordan burst out laughing. "The look on your face is priceless."

They must hear us. I stood there a bit shocked, shaking my head. "Those two..."

"I know," Jordan responded. "Let's get out of here. The last thing we want is to have Chad's trouser snake come after us, too." He turned away from our cabins and started heading down the path into the central part of the camp.

"I could have gone my entire life without that mental picture," I said as I caught up to Jordan.

"I guess they're trying to make little snake babies. I wonder if they realize that's not how it works."

We hiked back into camp and made it to Finlay's couple massage workshop with plenty of time.

"Hey, guys," Finlay said as we walked in. "I know you two just met. Did you sign up for this workshop together?"

"No, we were both kind of assigned this workshop," I said. Images of Jordan's naked body flooded my mind, and my brain told my mouth to shut up.

"I don't know if we have any other singles signed up," Finlay said. He looked down at a clipboard and said, "I take that back. Three other singles are supposed to be here, Avery, Chad and Phil. Well, I guess Phil is out. Maybe you could pair up with—"

"I doubt Avery and Chad will make it," Jordan said. "They seemed to need a break after their harrowing rescue of Phil." The sarcasm dripped out of his mouth, more potent than the venom running through Phil's veins.

"I see…" Finlay said with a knowing smirk. "I ran into Mano." He let that acknowledgment hang in the air. "I guess that leaves the two of you paired…if you're okay with that?"

"Sure," we both said simultaneously. If I didn't know better, I would have assumed Jordan's response was just as welcoming of that idea as I was.

"Perfect," Finlay said. "You two can grab any spot on the floor that's still open."

There were small mats with sheets and a pillow scattered around the room. Each station had a small bottle with a pump on top. *Guess that's the massage oil.* Jordan and I found one in the farthest corner from everyone else. We sat down on the mattress and waited. As Bryce and Richard entered, I waved, and Bryce shot me a knowing look when he noticed I was sitting with Jordan. Mano and Jaxson came in. A few minutes later, the guy in the wheelchair rolled in with Owen. Owen saw us and immediately wheeled his friend over.

"Hey, Darrin, isn't it?" the guy said. "I'm Isaac. I wanted to apologize for last night again. Your foot feeling better?"

"Accidents happen," I reassured him. "And I'm fine. Went on a hike today and everything."

"Wait! Were you part of the hike from hell? It's been all over camp."

"Yep, Jordan ran back to get help, and I helped carry Phil out."

"He's an ER doctor," Owen added. "I'm sure the victim was glad to have you there."

"I definitely made sure he was handled with care," I said.

"Is this mat taken?" Isaac asked, pointing to the nearest one to us.

"Nope. Have at it."

Owen bent over and helped Isaac out of his chair and onto the mat before moving the chair to a spot behind us — out of the way.

Finlay cleared his throat a few minutes later, and the group quieted.

"Good afternoon, everyone. Welcome to couple's massage. As you know, this session is an hour and a half long. We'll spend forty-five minutes on each partner. Whoever the first partner to receive the massage is, you can take off your clothes. Partners, you can use the towel under the pillow for modesty."

"I didn't know this involved nudity." Jordan looked at me with wide eyes. "We can back out."

"Nah, I'm a doctor. I can handle a little nudity. That is, if you're all right with me touching your body. I don't want to do anything that would make you uncomfortable." Part of me hoped he'd bow out, but another part hoped he'd be up for it.

Jordan let out a breath, looked at the ceiling and removed his tank top. He folded it and placed it beside the mat before getting out of his socks and shoes. I looked under the pillow, grabbed the towel and handed it to Jordan. He stood and wrapped the towel around his waist before dropping his shorts. He was free-balling, so I didn't wait for underwear to drop. I grabbed his shorts before he could, folded them neatly and placed them on his tank top. I motioned for Jordan to lie down on his stomach like Finlay was demonstrating on Kieran in the room's front.

We spent the first twenty minutes massaging our partner's back, arms and legs. It was nice to touch another guy in a nonsexual way. I'd forgotten how nice it was to feel another guy's skin under my fingertips.

"Okay," Finlay started. "If you're using a towel, please raise one side and tuck it between your partner's leg, exposing one buttock."

I hesitated before gently lifting Jordan's towel and placing it between his ass cheeks without touching anything. Finlay then had us massage our partner's butt on one side then the other. *Keep it professional,* I kept reminding myself. There would be no hiding it if I sprang a hard-on. I glanced over as Owen massaged Isaac. Owen was wearing only a jockstrap and his dick was on full display, barely contained by the jock itself. I averted my eyes back to Jordan as I finished up the rest of the massage on his backside.

"We're now going to have our partners roll over. To help with modesty, lift the towel up and let them roll beneath the towel." I turned my head to watch Finlay demonstrate this technique on Kieran. Finlay's movement was smooth, and nothing of Kieran showed. When Finlay lowered the towel back, you could see Kieran's bulge in the white towel, but he was perfectly covered.

"Ready for this?" I said to Jordan.

"Umm…not really."

"What's wrong?" There was a long silence. "Are you hurt? Did I hurt you?"

"No, no. Nothing like that. I… I'm having a problem that will stand on its own if I roll over, if you know what I mean."

"Oh," I chuckled. "Trust me. You're hardly the only erection in here. It's quite common among men who get a massage." I didn't know if it was or not, but I thought it was the right thing to say.

"Okay then, let's do this. Just don't look at me."

"I won't," I promised. I held the towel up and he turned beneath it. When the turning stopped, I looked back and lowered the towel. Jordan's erection was fully on display beneath the towel. He had the type of erection that laid flat against his stomach instead of creating a circus tent out of the towel. I glanced over at Isaac and Owen and saw Isaac had a circus tent. *Holy fuck, that thing looks huge. He can fit a full three-ring circus under that.* Owen caught me looking and humor touched his lips as he grinned. I gave him a thumbs-up. *Why did I give him a thumbs-up?*

I focused back on Jordan and asked, "How are you doing?"

"I'm fine. Again, sorry about my friend down there."

"It's fine."

"How are you doing this without getting hard? I know this isn't sexual and all, but still."

"You're assuming I don't have an erection," I reassured him.

Jordan

Did he just say that? I wanted to move my arm to see if I could 'accidentally' brush into him to see if he was hard. *That would be totally uncool.* I focused on my deep breathing like Finlay kept telling us to do.

Down, boy! I tried to will my dick down.

"You're going to maneuver to the top of your partner and start by putting your hands on his shoulders, like this."

I heard Darrin shift around until he was right above me. I opened my eyes for a second and gazed right up his tank top. *Holy shit, he's cut.* I hadn't imagined what he had under that shirt. I could see his six-pack as he massaged the fronts of my shoulders. All that did was send more blood to my cock. I closed my eyes and took a deep breath in through my nose. He smelled amazing. The combination of his recently washed body with whatever laundry detergent he used smelled outstanding. *Who the fuck needs Christmas? He's the present I want to unwrap!* I took in another breath as he started massaging my chest muscles. My skin sang under his touch. Every tiny hair follicle on my body stood straight up. The sensation of goosebumps flashed over my body, causing me to shudder.

"Are you okay?" Darrin asked. "Too cold?"

"I'm fine," I somehow squeaked out of my mouth.

Darrin then moved down to my feet. And he moved his way up to my quad muscles. "Just like we did on the calves and hamstrings. I want you to form a 'v' with both hands on your partner's quadriceps and effleurage all the way up in one smooth motion."

Before Darrin did, I heard the squirting of the oil bottle as he dribbled it down on the front of my leg. He touched me right above my left knee and moved to my… *Dear God!* His forearm hit my erection.

"Sorry about that. I wasn't trying to get fresh with you. Just trying to maneuver around you. I'll be more careful on the other side."

"Uh-huh," was all I could say. I was afraid to open my eyes and look at the man. I was on the verge of having one of Roodra's inner gay orgasms if this kept up too much longer. I wanted him to touch me, lick me and do all kinds of things with and to my body.

"Let's switch." Finlay's voice rang in my head. "The partner who received a massage, roll to your side and take your time sitting up. I'll be going around handing out bottles of water. You must drink lots of water for the rest of the day."

Darrin patted me on the shoulder. "Hope that was goodish. Massage isn't necessarily a skill set I've developed."

"It was incredible," I admitted as I rolled to my side, looking away from him. I wanted to make sure my dick didn't point at him — or give Owen and Isaac an eyeful — when I sat up. Pushing myself into a seated position with the towel firmly around me, I opened my eyes and circled my neck, stretching my muscles slightly. Isaac sat on his mat across from me. Unlike me, his cock was pointing straight at me. "Holy shit," I stammered as my eyes bugged out of my head. I blushed and quickly turned away.

"It's okay," Isaac reassured me. "We're all men. It's not like we haven't seen dangly and hard bits before."

"True... I just wasn't expecting to see you... All of that, I mean... Dear God, it's huge."

"Thanks," Isaac responded. I didn't need my eyes open to hear the mirth in Isaac's voice.

I reached out my hands and searched for my pile of clothes, keeping my eyes closed to avoid any other accidental peeks. *That thing is freaking amazing.*

"What are you looking for?" Darrin asked.

"My clothes?"

"I had to move them out of the way while working on you. Let me grab them."

A second later, Darrin placed his hand on my shoulder as he reached down and put the stack of clothes in my lap. I grabbed my tank top, slipping it over my head. With my tank top on, I made sure the towel was secured around my waist before standing, and I shimmied into my shorts. *Why didn't I wear underwear? What was I thinking?* Mr. Man Down South was still standing at attention, and he was going to be for the foreseeable future.

"Partners, it's time to get your man on the mat."

I stood and found Darrin had already taken my spot on the mat. He lay there on his stomach, and his ass was facing up from the ground. I threw the towel over him.

"Sorry that took so long," I said.

"No worries. I've been in enough locker rooms over the years. A little nudity doesn't scare me. I just don't flaunt it like some of the other guys around here."

I reached under my shorts and caught the top part of my dick under the waistband to keep it pinned against my abs. *Be professional, just like Darrin.* Finlay started walking us through the same sequence of steps that we'd had used on us. I tentatively spread massage oil on my hands and kneeled next to Darrin's head. Thank God I tucked my dick in my waistband or it would have flung out and smacked Darrin across the back of his head. I put my hands on his shoulders and glided down the length of his back. I've had sex before, quite a few times, but nothing had felt this intimate before as my white hands effleuraged the hell out of Darrin's skin.

We went through the whole routine. When we got to the turning-over point, I held out the towel to ensure Darrin didn't expose himself. Unlike me, when I released the towel back down to his torso, he hadn't pitched a tent. I glanced around. Quite a few tents were pitched, so I was glad to know I wasn't the only guy who'd had that problem. I focused back on Darrin and finished the routine. At some point, my dick started cooperating and deflated. Maybe it was the exercise or my desire to concentrate on making Darrin's body sing the way mine had.

"Again, make sure you drink plenty of water. Some of you will want to shower off the oil, which is perfectly fine. It shouldn't stain your clothes, so you can keep wearing it if you want to let the natural healing properties of the oil continue to do its job—or you can go touch your partner a little more. You know, now that you're both oiled up."

A laugh went around the room. I averted my gaze from Darrin. If I locked eyes with him, I was afraid my dick would want that hot, oiled man-on-man action.

"Heading back to shower?" Darrin asked me.

"Yep," I said without thinking.

"Let's go."

We hiked back to our lodgings. From the sounds coming out of Chad's cabin, they had a few more people who had joined them next door.

"Why do they have to be so loud?" I asked.

"Yeah, it's absurd." Darrin then turned toward Chad's. "We're back! Can you keep the noise down for a while?"

A murmur of voices was heard from Chad's, but no one said anything. Darrin walked up the three steps into his cabin and shut the door behind him.

I practically ran into my room. After lying down on the bed, I grabbed my dick and headed to town. Images of Darrin's chest, arms, legs and ass... *Oh God, that ass!* I pictured myself licking it and shoving my tongue deep inside him before slipping in one of my fingers. I imagined myself like he had been on the mat, face down and ass up. I switched vantage points and imagined lowering my cock in between his ass cheeks before thrusting deep inside him—and I exploded. The first shot hit me in the forehead. The second caught my chin. I kept pumping my cock until I'd milked out every last drop.

I opened my eyes and looked down at my cum-covered torso. My stomach muscles were moving in and out as my breathing slowed.

I let out a low whistle. "I needed that." I lay there for a few more seconds before sliding myself to the edge of the bed, doing my best not to get any cum on the bed cover before I stood and headed to take my shower.

* * * *

The rest of the evening was uneventful. It had been an utterly exhausting day. When Darrin and I hiked back up the mountain to our rooms, I was ready to crash. As we rounded the corner to our cabins, the orgy had moved over to Avery's. "How the hell am I going to sleep with that?" I asked under my breath.

"Come into my cabin for a minute," Darrin said.

I followed him. Part of me hoped he was about to recommend we fight fire with fire and make a shit ton of noise ourselves. That clearly wasn't Darrin's style, but a man could dream.

He walked through his room, which was much neater than mine was. Everything was very organized, just like him. In the corner was a small stack of discarded clothes. *He's human after all*. I followed him to the mouth of his bathroom. He opened his large toiletry bag, pulled out a small cardboard box and handed it to me.

"Thanks," I said as I accepted the small package. "What are these?"

"Earplugs. After Chance and I flew in a military cargo jet, I started traveling with them. Those fuckers are beyond loud. They don't insulate them like commercial airliners, so it was hard to hear ourselves think, let alone sleep. They're not perfect, but they cancel a lot of noise and should help you."

"Thanks again," I said. I walked out of the cabin, and he followed me to his front porch. I hoped he would reach out, grab me and swing me around in his arms for a deep embrace, but that shit only happens in romance novels.

"Good night," Darrin said before he closed his cabin door.

I looked down and found I had tented again. *What is up with my hormones today?* Thankfully, there was no one out and about in the night air.

"Who wants to play *pin their dick in my ass*?" I heard Avery's voice pierce through the night.

Unfortunately, several guys voiced their desire to help him out as I walked up the steps into my cabin. Half of me wanted to go knock on Avery's door and ask him to keep it down again. But I was afraid if I touched the door, I'd be hauled in, stripped and wind up in a sling before I could land the second knock. Instead, I jerked off again before bed.

Things had died down a bit, but I could still hear sounds from the sex shack a few doors down. I opened the rectangle box and slid the rubbery earplugs into my ears. I was surprised at how quiet the world became. *Almost eerily quiet.* I was used to some noise while I slept, but these really did a fantastic job of blocking any noise from the sex shanty. I lay down on my bed wearing a pair of nylon shorts and let myself fall to sleep.

Chapter Twelve

Darrin

A gap in the blinds let in enough sun for me to know it was daylight. I'd had a decent night's rest. Sadly, I could still hear orgy town through my earplugs. And if my body hadn't been so tired after the day, I may have gone over there and yelled at them. I hoped the earplugs I'd given Jordan had allowed him to sleep better than I had. I wanted to roll over and hit the snooze button on life, but I dragged my ass out of bed instead.

I had buried myself under the comforter during the night, so I pulled it back and lay there in my boxer briefs, willing the rest of my body to move. I heard the door next to me open and shut. *Jordan must be taking off for his morning run.* I wish I had that level of dedication. I didn't mind running but preferred it on a treadmill with a television to watch. Thoughts of yesterday afternoon swarmed my head. Jordan had the stereotypical farm tan I'd grown up loving on guys.

The tan arms with the pale white torso. I had traced the parts of the tan line when I'd massaged him. I could do a lot of things to his body under the pretense of massage. I'd touched almost every inch of him, from his delectable toes to the cute, slightly turned-up nose. And when he'd rolled over and was sporting an erection. Dear God, it took every ounce of self-control not to massage it and give him a happy ending.

My cock throbbed just thinking about his body the day before. I wasn't sure which I wanted more, to shove my dick inside that tight ass of his or to ride his amazingly shaped cock that had just the right curvature to hit my prostate. And I had admittedly let my forearm brush against it. It hadn't been on purpose, but I probably let it happen longer than it should have, once it had happened. Oh well, he hadn't freaked out, so I guess that was good. When he started rubbing his hands on my body, it was a battle of wills with my dick to keep it down. I don't even remember much of the massage because I was trying to control myself. It's easy to put on an air of professionalism when performing the massage. Still, as soon as his calloused fingers had touched my shoulders, I wanted to curl into his lap for days.

I looked down at my cock. The only thing I could do was jack off. I spit in my hand and imagined Jordan fucking me, then me fucking him as I drove myself into a frenzied conclusion. My orgasm was probably a little louder than I had expected, but I collapsed back on the bed when I finished. My abs were covered in cum.

I let out a sigh. "Now that that's taken care of, I guess I can get ready for the day."

I cupped my balls as I stood to make sure no cum fell on the floor as I dashed into the bathroom. I grabbed a washcloth and wiped myself clean. Once my typical shit, shower and shave were finished, I was raring to go. I threw on a maroon polo and pair of navy cargo shorts. I had ankle socks and my tennis shoes. I picked up my wallet to throw in my pocket. I lost my grip, and it slipped out of my fingers and hit the ground. When I picked it up, a photo from my wallet slipped out. I knew it was a picture of Chance before I turned it over. Sighing, I sat on the corner of the bed.

"What am I doing?" I looked at Chance's face. "I miss you. God, I miss you." I talked to his picture occasionally, when I didn't know what to do. Today was one of those days. "There's a guy I think I may like. If given a chance, I'd hop into bed with him. But unlike my fuck buddy, Avery, I don't think I could have emotionless sex with this guy. He's younger. Who'd have guessed I'd be the one chasing after a younger guy? His name is Jordan, and I think you would like him. He's a little rough around the edges, but that's because he grew up in the Catskills and hasn't had many experiences outside of here. I want to get close to him and watch the man he's going to grow into." I caressed Chance's cheek. Part of me felt like I was cheating on his memory, even thinking about Jordan. Another part of me knew Chance would be the first one to tell me to grab life by the balls and go for it. That's what Chance was like. He had never been the type to let an opportunity pass him by.

I decided then and there that I was going to pursue Jordan. I wasn't sure if he was interested in me, but it could work. Images of him moving into my townhouse while he was in college in the fall flooded my mind. "Whoa there, don't put the cart before the horse," I warned myself. *Need to find out if he even likes you first.*

I grabbed my wallet and slipped the photo back inside. "I love you," I said to Chance's image as I closed the wallet. I stood from the bed and slipped it into my pocket. Just knowing his picture was with me gave me a certain amount of strength.

I left the cabin, stepped down the stairs and started hiking toward the café. I needed coffee. I glanced down at my wrist to see what time it was. I'd forgotten to put on my watch. I reached for my cell and realized I hadn't unplugged it from its charger on the nightstand. *I really am a mess before I get my morning caffeine injection.*

I heard laughing up ahead. I looked up and found a shirtless Jordan riding in Isaac's lap on his wheelchair. I froze. Jordan got off the man's lap and stood next to him. Jordan leaned in, Isaac turned his head and they kissed.

Well, fuck, guess that answers that question.

Jordan

The earplugs Darrin had given me worked like a charm. I'd slept through the whole night. At one point, I got up to pee and took them out and could still hear the orgy going on three cabins down. How Darrin was sleeping through that was beyond me. Once I put the earplugs back in, the world went silent again. Sure, I missed the natural sounds of the peepers and owls, but I didn't miss the squealing, yelling and other sounds that came from Avery's cabin.

I woke up early feeling refreshed. The previous day's adventures had exhausted me, so the hard sleep had been great. I got out of bed and took a piss I slipped into my running shorts and shoes, grabbed my cell phone and Bluetooth earbuds and went out to run. I planned on taking a different path today, just in case there were any more random couples fucking on the picnic table.

This path took me more through camp and was hillier than the one I'd taken the day before. People often think running up hills is harder than running down them, but I disagree. Sure, you may exert more physical energy running up a hill, but you weren't likely to lose control. Someone could easily move too fast running downhill, which could cause them to trip and fall. I took my time running down hills, watching to make sure each hit of the pavement was safe for me. I waved at a couple of guys who were out walking or jogging. One guy, who was sitting on his porch drinking coffee, yelled something at me and shot me a rude and highly suggestive gesture. I didn't need to hear him to know that he'd just offered to do any number of things to my body. I kept running.

I got to this one part with a steep hill on the other side of camp. About halfway up the hill, I noticed Isaac wheeling himself. As I neared, I looked down and practically gawked at the size of the guy's triceps. I hadn't really seen him shirtless yesterday during our massages. After catching an eyeful of his monstrous cock, I had closed my eyes like a little kid. But now, I looked at him in his tank top with his shoulder and arm muscles trying to push himself up the hill. I was impressed and slightly turned on.

I was maybe twenty-five yards from him when he lost his grip on the wheel. He started rolling backward. I watched as he grabbed the wheel brake, but he fishtailed. His wheelchair tipped sideways, and he tumbled to the ground. He was still strapped into the thing. I made it to him in seconds.

"Are you okay?" I asked, running up to him and bending down. "Can I help? Are you hurt?" I hadn't meant to rapid-fire the questions at the poor guy, but I wanted to make sure he was responsive.

"I'm fine...just stupid," Isaac said as he turned his head to look up at me. "I knew the second I overcorrected I'd fucked up. Can you help me get upright?"

"Sure." I leaned down, and he threw his arm around my shoulder as I pulled him and his chair into a vertical position. I looked him over and didn't see any blood. There was a slight scratch on his arm where he'd hit the path, but nothing that wouldn't fade in a day.

"I hate asking, but what were you doing trying to go up this hill?"

"You mean because I'm in a wheelchair?"

"I didn't say that." I looked down at Isaac. He stared up at me defiantly. "Okay, maybe I implied that. But really, this hill is hard for anyone to even walk up. I can't imagine how hard it is to push yourself up that hill. And why were you doing it alone?"

"To see if I could."

I shook my head. I didn't think that was a great answer, but something in his countenance told me it was the truth. "Are you all right? Is the chair usable?"

"This bad boy is indestructible," Isaac said, patting the side with one of his gloved hands. He wore leather gloves with no fingers. He jutted his hand in my direction. "I don't think we've been properly introduced yet. I'm Isaac. You're friends with that Darrin guy. The one I rolled over on the first night we were here." I grabbed his hand and shook it. "Is your friend actually all right? He said he was yesterday, but you know how men can be."

"He's fine. He saved someone on a hike yesterday and helped carry the guy out of the mountains."

"I heard about that. I didn't know Darrin was involved in the rescue attempt. I heard it was that guy Chad and his twink friend."

I rolled my eyes. "Avery."

"Huh?"

"The twink. His name is Avery. And yes, Chad helped Darrin and Mano. Avery basically carried a backpack."

"And where were you during all this?"

"I ran back to camp to call EMS and get the ambulance here."

"That makes sense. You clearly have a runner's body," Isaac said, appraising me. Wearing only my short running shorts, I was practically naked standing in front of him.

"Where are you heading?" I asked.

"Back to my cabin."

"Where are you?"

"I'm in the blue cabins."

"That's right down from the green cabins. That's where I am. Mind if I walk with you?"

"Suit yourself." We went down the hill and picked a different path that would be a bit more gradual back to the center of camp.

We walked and chit-chatted for a few minutes before I got up the courage to fan boy on him. "I have to admit something to you."

Isaac kept rolling, but he turned his head and looked at me. I stared down and watched as his trapezius muscle in his shoulder moved under his skin. I had to admit, his arms were fucking amazing.

"What?" he asked.

"I knew who you were before we met this weekend. Hell, I had a poster of you in my bedroom growing up."

A smile ruffled Isaac's lips. "Oh, really? Was I your teenage fantasy? Did you jerk off staring into my picture?"

I looked at him and found myself speechless for a second. "I don't know how to respond to that. I was a teenager. I probably got off looking at any hot guy I came across. And since you hung on my wall..." I let the words hang between us.

He burst out laughing. "I'm just busting your balls." We started moving again before he said, "So you were a fan?"

"I was."

"Thanks. Most of the guys around here do not know who I am... Well, was. I kind of appreciate the anonymity."

"I grew up in Poughkeepsie and was a huge fan of football. The second I saw you, I recognized you. I followed your career from when you played in high school through everything else."

The 'everything else' was the part of the story Isaac didn't want to go into. He'd gone from Poughkeepsie to a full ride at Notre Dame and was then drafted into the NFL, playing for the Patriots. He had a decent first year in the league, but it all ended on the first day of training camp the following year. They had been practicing, and he'd gone in for a tackle, but the quarterback had moved backward at the last second and another player smacked his shoulder into the middle of Isaac's back, crushing his seventh and eighth thoracic vertebra. It had been a complete freak accident. The Patriots had gone on to win the Super Bowl that year.

"What was it like after it happened?"

"After the accident?" He left out a quick breath and wheeled along. "Life sucked. I played the 'woe is me' game for months while in rehab. I'd been so scared because my career was over. Everything I'd worked for was gone in an instant." He snapped his fingers for emphasis. "I didn't want to see anyone. And before long I'd totally isolated myself. I found myself in a hospital bed with no friends. Well, no real friends. I had a lot of *friends* in the league, but they stopped dropping by as soon as the season started. I became old news very fast."

"That had to have sucked."

"You have no idea. I contemplated suicide a few times. My family helped me get through it. Finally, my older sister was with me one day, and she looked at me and said, '*You have to find the joy in your life again.*' She then told me she'd known I was gay since I was a kid. She had a friend who worked for one of the trade magazines, and they wrote a delightful story about my injury and my coming out. I was contacted by *Outsports* almost immediately and became one of their celebrity spokespersons. It took a long time for me to find my joy, but I did."

"That's pretty fucking inspiring."

"Thanks. What inspired me was porn."

"Huh?"

"More specifically, I watched Kenneth Connin, a paraplegic guy, live his full porn fantasy for a popular website. Besides making me fucking hot, I was like, if he can be a porn star, I can be whatever I want."

"Oh, so you want to be a porn star?" I said, joking with him.

"Nah. Don't get me wrong. I love sex as much as the next guy, but I don't feel the need to do it for a studio."

"So, do you mind if I ask?" I let the word hang in the air.

"About sex? Yes, I can have sex. And as you learned yesterday, I can get a hard-on," he smiled as he said this, and the heat raced into my cheeks as I blushed. "Just messing with you. As for erections, I have a psychogenic but not a reflexogenic erection. Basically, you can blow me all day long and not get a rise out of me. I don't have the nerve endings down there that work right. But mental images and being with a hot guy makes me rock hard, but I need a cock ring to help maintain it. I also don't experience orgasms the same way."

"Do you miss them?" I said absently but then corrected myself. "I'm so sorry, that came out wrong."

"I miss them. I won't pretend that I don't miss my life before all this," he said, motioning to his chair. "But I'm glad to be alive, and so many parts of my life are better now than before the accident. I don't even know if I would have found my sexuality without the accident. I would still be playing and still be in the closet."

We walked in silence for about a minute before he looked over at me and said, "Want a ride?"

I bent my head to the right and shot him a questioning look. "On your chair?"

"Yep. Come sit in my lap and I'll wheel you back to your cabin. Fulfill your childhood fantasy of sitting in my lap."

I let out a slight groan. "Wow, that was cheesy."

He smiled nonchalantly. "I know. But really, hop on. I've had bigger men in my lap. I can whisk you home."

I felt a little stupid, but thought, *why the hell not*. So, I sat in his lap and let him wheel me around. Even though Isaac wasn't erect, I could still feel the monster lying beneath his shorts pressing into my backside. He had me to the base of the hill leading up to the green cabins in no time.

"Let me off. I'll hike up the last part."

"I can take you all the way."

"I'm sure you could…in more than one way. But the path going up there is not wheelchair friendly."

"Yeah, I haven't even tried going up that hill. The loose rock worries me."

He stopped and I got off his lap. I may have shown him a bit more of my ass than was strictly necessary.

"Thanks," I said. "I can honestly say meeting my number one masturbation fantasy growing up was better than I could have ever hoped."

I bent down to kiss him on the top of the head, but Isaac turned his head, and we locked lips instead. I didn't mind the kiss, but it wasn't his lips I wanted on mine. I put my hand on his chest and gently pushed away. "You cheeky little bastard. That's how you get all the guys…with chair rides and sneaking kisses?"

"You've gotta work with what you have," he said. For the first time, he looked unsure of himself. I could tell that a lot of his bravado was still an act. But hey, fake it till you make it.

"Trust me. You're still one of the hottest guys. And if I wasn't already falling all over myself for someone who isn't available, I'd be all over you. Again, you're my wet dream made flesh. And I would love nothing more than to let you wrap those arms around me, but…"

"I get it. My loss. I wish we had met before you'd found Mr. Right."

"Well, I don't know if he's that. Hell, I don't even know if he's into me."

Isaac raked over my body with his emerald eyes and said, "If you tire of pining for your mystery man, come find me. Remember...I can stay hard for hours with a Viagra and a cock ring. And you don't have to worry about premature ejaculation with me at all."

"You're assuming I'm a bottom," I replied.

"Well, when most guys see my cock, it's amazing how quickly they want to hop on for a ride."

I remembered his cock pointing at me yesterday, and I just had to know, "How big is it?"

"Ten inches, cut and thick."

"Impressive. I'll keep that in mind. I'll see you around," I said before starting the climb to my cabin."

"I love watching you walk away from me. Those shorts would look great on my bedroom floor."

I laughed and turned around. "Not going to happen. But thanks for the offer."

"I'll wheel back to my cabin and take matters into my own hands, thinking about the little lap dance you gave me on the way up here."

"Bye, Isaac. I'll see you later." I reached to the waistband of my shorts, lowered them quickly and shot him a glance of my ass as I walked up the hill.

"Oh, come on! That's so not fair," he yelled after me. "Don't forget. You have an open invitation to my lap any time."

I had a wide smirk on my face, but I didn't turn around and gloat. I just continued to hike. I heard Isaac wheeling away. I was ready for a much-needed shower.

Chapter Thirteen

As the water in the shower ran over my body, I reeled because I'd just met my high-school crush, taken a ride in his lap and been offered a different type of ride. And in a different world, I would have hopped on him and ravaged him from head to toe. It's not every day one passes up their biggest wet dream from their teen years. And while Isaac was still fucking gorgeous, I couldn't get Darrin out of my mind.

Ahh, Darrin... Remembering his tan ass from yesterday caused my cock to grow. I stroked it as the water flowed over me. I imagined Darrin's ass in front of me as I plunged into him over and over again. But in my fantasy, suddenly, I had Isaac taking me from behind. His giant cock invaded me while I was in Darrin. I imagined myself in the middle of one fucking hot, awesome man sandwich. I hadn't fully appreciated the size of Isaac's cock yesterday, but I had felt the slumbering beast beneath my shorts when I sat in his lap. And if his flaccid dick was any indication of how big he could grow, damn, it would be like having a bowling pin shoved up my ass. I don't even know if I could take a regular eight-inch cock, let alone the massive thing like Isaac had between his legs. But fantasies are just that...fantasies. I forced myself back to my mental threesome and found myself coming all over the shower.

"Needed that," I said to no one. I washed and got out of the shower then I looked over at my watch, which sat on the table charging. I threw on a pair of shorts and T-shirt and a pair of sandals. My long feet looked nice in them. And some guys enjoyed seeing feet. *I wonder if Darrin likes feet?*

I left the cabin to head to the dining hall. I turned and locked the door. Avery and Chad were standing nude on Avery's porch.

"Geez! Can you at least put on some clothes when you're outside?" I asked, scrambling down my steps as if running could somehow wash that image out of my head.

"Stop being such a prude," Avery said to my back. "We're in nature, so we're being natural."

"You're being a slut," I said under my breath, but I didn't turn around. *Don't engage. You're not going to change him. It's not worth your time.*

The more I thought about it, I realized that Avery and Chad made the perfect couple. I don't think either of them could get enough sex. They clearly liked sex with each other, and they had no qualms about adding other people to the mix. *Guess it takes all kinds.*

I got down to the dining hall and walked in. I looked around to see if Darrin and his friends had made it there yet, but I didn't see them. I grabbed my tray and made my way over to the breakfast bar. There were eggs, hash browns and buckwheat pancakes.

A guy noticed me eyeing the label. "Don't. I grew up in West Virginia. Buckwheat is nasty. There's not enough maple syrup in New England to make those things edible."

"Thanks for the warning," I said. "Toast it is."

With food on my tray, I looked for a place to sit. I looked around and found Isaac sitting at a table with some other guys. I caught his eye, and he waved me over.

"Please, take a seat," Isaac said. "And this time, it doesn't have to be in my lap."

"Please don't tell me you fell for the *'sit and my lap and I'll take you for a spin'* come on?" one of his friends said.

"Don't listen to him, Jordan. Ignore Carl. He's just jealous he's never gone down on my pole before."

"Well, that makes two of us," I said.

"Jordan was a fan of mine when he was growing up. He told me all about how he used to jack off to me as a teen."

"That's so hot," Carl said. "Did he live up to all your expectations?"

"And exceeded them," I said, tossing some scrambled egg into my mouth.

"That's okay," another one of Isaac's friends said. "I jerk off thinking about how this man wrecked my ass all the time. Did you see the size of it?"

"I may have accidentally gotten an eyeful yesterday during couple's massage."

"You did?" Carl asked.

"That's right," Isaac responded. "I totally forgot you were on the mat next to Owen and me. I may have snuck a peek or two at you yesterday."

"What?"

"Hey, it was hard not to look at all the nude guys. I think I even got an eyeful when you turned over," Isaac said with a wink.

"Well then," I said, chewing on some hash browns.

"I could have reached across and grabbed that pole of yours when it was sticking up. It looked like it needed a hand," Isaac said.

There were two Isaacs—the pretty cool and chill Isaac I had talked to earlier, and there was the sex-crazed and overly flirty Isaac. And under different circumstances, I would gladly take this Isaac back to my cabin for the rest of the weekend.

I looked across the dining hall and made eye contact with Darrin, who had gotten his breakfast while I had been distracted by table talk. Darrin had diverted his eyes from me. *What was that about? He's acting like I caught him doing something wrong. Is he jealous? Was it because I wasn't sitting with Darrin and his friends for breakfast? Maybe he doesn't like someone at this table?* I'd have to ask him later.

Darrin

After seeing Isaac and Jordan, I took a longer route to the Mug Slug Café for my morning coffee. I hadn't bothered to go back to my cabin and grab my watch and cell phone. I figured I'd get them after breakfast. By the time I made it down to the center of camp, it was already time for breakfast, so I headed over to the dining hall and found Bryce and Richard standing in line. I'd ultimately made a peanut butter and honey sandwich for breakfast. I needed to eat something, but I wasn't in the mood. Inside I saw Jordan sitting with his *new* friends, and a pang of jealousy swept over me.

What right do I have to be jealous? He isn't my boyfriend. We're friendly acquaintances. Of course, I was lying to myself. Something in me was deeply drawn to Jordan, and it was clear now that I'd lost my chance.

"What bee got in your bonnet this morning?" Bryce asked between his bites of oatmeal.

"Nothing. Just didn't sleep very well last night."

"Why don't I believe you," Bryce said. He'd phrased it as a question, but it wasn't.

My sandwich was half-eaten. "I think I'm done." I pushed my chair back from the table.

"Perfect timing," Bryce said. "I'm done, too. Why don't we go for a walk?"

"I'll be done in a minute. I could join you two?" Richard offered.

"Take your time, honey. This will give Bryce and me a chance to catch up." With that, Bryce stood then kissed Richard on the top of his head before following me to the kitchen area to deposit our trays.

We took the side exit and headed out into camp. There were still a few stragglers making their way to breakfast. Mostly, the grounds were empty except for a gardener we passed who was pruning trees in the early morning air.

"Out with it," Bryce said after we'd been walking for a few minutes.

I took a loud breath in through my nose and let it out with an audible sigh. "I have a crush, and I think I totally blew it by not doing anything about it sooner."

"The local kid?" Bryce asked.

"Jordan," I corrected. "His name is Jordan. And yes, it's him."

"Good for you."

"Huh?"

"I'm glad you're feeling something for another man again. I know life hasn't been easy for you after Chance."

"What would you know about that?" I questioned a little more sharply than I had intended.

"A lot more than you think I do." Bryce stopped and turned to meet my eyes. His gaze looked like a parent about to scold a petulant child. I winced. "You don't know that Richard wasn't my first love."

"Really?" I asked. I had kind of assumed Bryce and Richard had always been together.

"Really," he responded. "Let's take a seat."

He motioned to a stone bench in an alcove created by a large arched wooden arbor. It was covered in green vines with white flowers, providing a quiet place to sit in the shade out of the sun, not that we needed it in the morning light. I sat down on the bench, and Bryce sat next to me. He crossed his legs. His foot moved slightly back and forth, the only hint of his nerves.

"When I was in my early twenties, I was in love with a Puerto Rican guy named Alejandro. After dating for a month, we had moved in together. We were discussing marriage before we hit the one-year anniversary. Now, mind you, I was doing all this while in medical school. Despite my crazy hours and life, Alejandro was there. Hell, he was my rock during the first two years of medical school."

There was a lull in the story, so I urged him to continue with a simple gesture of my hand.

"I had just started rotations and my attending was a bit of a jackass, so I got home late. I walked in the door and found Alejandro on the floor, seizing."

"Holy shit."

"I stabilized him and called nine-one-one."

"What was it?"

"A grade four glioblastoma multiforme."

"Ahh, Bryce." As soon as he said the word, I knew where the story would end — a highly aggressive brain tumor with less than a five-percent survival rate at five years. Seventy-five percent of patients with a diagnosis passed within one year. "I'm so sorry."

"Thankfully — if you can call having a tumor thankful — he didn't last long."

"Oh my God. I'm *so* sorry."

"I argued for a very aggressive treatment. I wanted Alejandro to fight it with every tool modern medicine had. I wanted him to undergo surgery and chemotherapy. I knew that this would increase his lifespan to fifteen or sixteen months, but I wanted those months."

"What happened?"

"He let me dictate his treatment plan with his oncologists. I almost think the oncologists were a little too giddy that I wanted them to push the limits with Alejandro. If there was something new, I wanted them to try it. Finally, after seven months of undergoing all kinds of indignities, Alejandro looked at me and said, '*I can't take it anymore. Please, let me die.*'" I stared into Bryce's face as tears welled in his eyes. He reached up and wiped them away before continuing. "I remember sitting on our bed together, stunned. I wanted to argue with him. I wanted to force him to keep fighting. But when I looked into his pleading eyes, there was no fight left in him. All I could do was let him die in as much comfort and dignity as possible. The next morning, I called hospice, and we stopped treatments. He was gone within a month."

Tears welled up, and I let them fall. I reached out, embraced my friend and we held each other, knowing we both still grieved the loss of our first loves. After a minute, Bryce let go and pushed himself back. He pulled out a hanky from his pocket and wiped at his tears. I wasn't sure which I was surprised by more, Bryce's emotional catharsis or the fact that he had a hanky in his pocket.

"So, there you have it," Bryce said. "I know more about what you're going through than you ever knew. About a year later, I met Richard. Trust me. I did everything in my power to not love Richard. I didn't think I deserved love after I let Alejandro die. That's how I saw it. I blamed myself for not having enough strength for both of us. I know that's stupid now, but when you're in the throes of grief, logical thinking isn't exactly there."

"Tell me about it."

"That's my story," Bryce said. "You're still writing yours. And from how it sounds, this Jordan guy is part of it."

"Maybe. Who knows? I don't."

"You don't have to. Go with the flow. See where life and love take you. If Jordan isn't the next great love of your life, he's at least opened you up to the possibility. And I think that's a gigantic leap in the right direction."

"I feel like I'm betraying Chance's memory," I blurted.

"Whoa," Bryce said. "I knew Chance longer than you did. I know for a fact he wouldn't have wanted you to mope around pining for him for the rest of your life. You know that, too."

"Cognitively, I know it. But I—"

"But nothing," Bryce responded. "So, why do you think you've lost your chance with Jordan?"

I told Bryce what I'd witnessed that morning.

"The old 'let me take you for a ride on my wheelchair' trick. Isaac's been using that one for years. He's a huge flirt, but for the most part, he's harmless. Besides, I think Owen has been occupying Isaac's free time—if you know what I mean."

I chuckled. I'd seen how touchy-feely they were during couple's massage.

"Well, I need to go get ready for rock climbing," Bryce said. "What's on your agenda today?"

"Remote viewing."

Bryce barked out a laugh. "Have fun with that. If you see any of my relatives in Croatia, tell them I said hello."

I stood up and offered my hand to help Bryce off the bench, which he accepted. We then hugged and went our separate ways.

I pulled out my handy-dandy schedule. My remote viewing workshop was in the Central Sanctuary, so I headed off in that direction. When I walked in, I found Jordan sitting with Isaac and Finlay. I walked over and took a seat on the other side of Finlay.

"Good morning, gentlemen," I said in the most cheerful voice I could muster.

"Good morning," Finlay said.

"Morning," Jordan added, but he didn't look at me.

"Good morning," Isaac said. "How's the foot? Again, I'm sorry about that the other night. I'm usually very conscious of other people around—"

"It's fine," I said. "There's been zero pain since Thursday night. No harm, no foul."

"So, anyone know what this is about?" Jordan asked. "I've never heard of remote viewing."

"Oh, honey," Finlay said, "you're in for a treat."

Gong! The sound of Roodra's entrance into the building was signaled. Like yesterday, he strolled down the aisle with his posse in tow. When he got to the front, he leaned on a stool that had been already placed there.

"Good morning, my children," Roodra said with a ridiculously enormous smile.

"Good fucking grief," Finlay muttered.

"Today, we are going to explore the world of remote viewing. For those of you new to the world of psychic phenomena, remote viewing was originally coined by physicists Russell Targ and Harold Puthoff at the Stanford Research Institute in the early nineteen-seventies. Of course, psychic phenomena have always existed in our world. They've even been studied by the US military's Stargate Project, which ran from nineteen-seventy-five to nineteen-ninety-five. Remote viewing uses the mind to sense people and places that are otherwise inaccessible by sensory means. For example, let's say I want to check in on my brother in Oregon. I can use remote viewing to sense him and see how he's doing."

"What the fuck?" Jordan said under his breath.

"My thoughts exactly," Isaac agreed.

"Today we will learn the same techniques the Central Intelligence Agency has used to train its remote viewing operatives. I cannot confirm or deny whether I have trained with the CIA to learn these techniques. Let's just say Langley, Virginia, is gorgeous during cherry blossom season." There was a polite chuckle from Roodra's acolytes, but the rest of the room remained silent.

"I cannot confirm or deny that Roodra is RuPaul in disguise," Finlay whispered. I bit the inside of my cheek to stop from laughing out loud. Isaac busted out laughing, which drew condemning looks from Roodra's acolytes.

Roodra continued, "I will hand everyone a pad and pencil. I have a friend named Stephanie, and she's currently in the city looking at something specific. I want you all to attend to her. Find her in your minds and draw what she's looking at."

A guy in the front row raised his hand. Roodra gestured to the young man. "How can we attend to her if we don't know her?"

"Great question. She will be sending you purposeful thoughts. You should be able to find her wavelength by focusing on her name and her intentions."

The young man nodded his head, but I could tell that nothing of what Roodra had said made any sense. Roodra then provided some explanations for how the exercise would go.

"Let's do this," Roodra said excitedly. His acolytes stood and started handing out pads of paper and pencils. I thanked the man who handed me my pad and pencil. Roodra looked at his watch. "Stephanie should start transmitting in five, four, three, two, draw."

I closed my eyes as instructed and let my pencil move over the page in front of me. I sensed jack shit. I moved my pencil and spent the time thinking about Jordan. As soon as this was over, I needed to pull Jordan aside and talk with him.

After what seemed like an eternity, Roodra clapped his hands. "Let's see how you did." Roodra walked around the room, commenting on the drawings. He looked down and said, "Well done." I had drawn what looked like a stick. "You are remarkably close. You must have some clairvoyance to have such an accurate depiction."

When Roodra moved on, Jordan asked, "What did you draw?"

I showed him my drawing.

"It looks like a dick," Isaac said.

"You must have been remote viewing into Chad and Avery's cabin by accident," Jordan joked. He looked at me, and a grin sprang across his face. My heart flipped.

"Or maybe he's just remote viewing that monster in your pants, Isaac," Finlay added.

"Well," Isaac said, looking at me, "you can remote view inside my pants any day."

"Silence!" followed by a loud clapping at the front of the room, brought our attention back to Roodra. "Overall, many of you clearly have natural psychic abilities. You should learn to foster these."

"So, what were we supposed to see?" the same young guy who'd spoken early asked.

"Stephanie was in Central Park staring at Cleopatra's Needle."

"What's that?" Jordan asked.

"An Egyptian obelisk," Finlay said. "I used to sit on a park bench near there and eat lunch when I worked at a temp job when I first moved to New York."

"Focus," Roodra's booming voice said over the chatter in the room. "For our second remote viewing opportunity, I will have you focus on my friend Diana, who is currently in San Francisco."

Jordan

We had a double dose of Roodra. After remote viewing, I wasn't sure what to expect from the next session. I stared at my schedule and asked, "What the fuck is Angelic Alchemy? I mean, I know what both words mean, but not together."

"Yeah," Finlay said, coming up behind me. "Why don't you and Darrin join Isaac and me for yoga?"

"And deviate from our schedules?" Darrin joked.

Finlay started walking to the yoga pavilion, and we followed him. "So, have either of you done yoga before?" Finlay asked.

"Nope. Well, not really. I think we may have tried yoga in physical education during middle school," I admitted.

"Yeah, I've usually just hit the gym. So, I've mostly lifted things or used a treadmill," Darrin said.

"Well, I think this will be good for you both."

We walked into the yoga studio, and Finlay had us each grab a rubber mat from a stack and lay them on the ground. I grabbed one for Isaac and rolled it out for him.

"Now, Isaac has been coming to my studio in the city for a while, so don't be surprised when he does a few more advanced moves. Let's start."

He made us take off our shoes and socks. He also said that we should tuck in our shirts or take them off completely to avoid them flapping around our heads when we were in some positions. I wasn't even sure what a 'position' was.

"We're going to start with a simple sun salutation." Finlay swept his arms over his head, bent at the waist and lowered his hands to the ground. I cocked my head to the side as he bent himself in half.

"Yeah, I don't bend like that," I said.

"Just go as far down as you can with straight legs. If you must bend your legs a little, that's fine, but you should feel the stretch in your hamstrings."

I swept my hands over my head, bent at the waist and made it like three-fourths of the way to the ground before my hamstrings laughed at me. I glanced to my right and Darrin wasn't doing much better than me at bending in half.

We ran through that simple stretch and bent in half a couple more times before he then said kick back into a low runner's lunge. That was a position I understood. So, I pushed my left foot back and kept my right knee at a ninety-degree angle. That part was simple. Then he said to raise both hands over our heads straight up past our ears to the sky. I started wobbling worse than when I stood on a balance board.

"We call this position 'warrior one'. Let's switch into a 'warrior two' pose." Finlay showed the next position, which didn't involve as much balance as the last one. I glanced over and watched Finlay working with Isaac through different poses.

Before I knew it, Darrin and I were adding the first three poses together, then Finlay asked us to push back into a downward-facing dog.

"You're making that one up," I said, looking at him from my still-wobbly warrior one position.

"It's an actual position. Place your hands down on the mat and lower yourself into a plank." I watched as he smoothly transitioned to the plank. "Then curl your toes under and push back through your arms. You want to make your back flat while lowering your heels to the ground."

Finlay made it look effortless. Getting to the plank was easy, so was curling my toes under. My hamstrings and calves did not think yoga was a great idea when I pushed back. I think I was doing more of a flying monkey pose than a downward-facing dog.

Finlay came behind me, grabbed me by my hips and pulled them back. "You look more like a crab. You need to push your ass away from your hands with a flat back. You don't want to make a triangle with your ass up in the air," he informed me. My hamstrings burned.

"Darrin, work your heels into the ground. If you can't get both on the ground, work them down one at a time."

I looked over from my ass-up position and stared at Darrin's legs. His legs were lightly hairy, and his muscles moved as he worked his well-defined calves into the mat. I wished I had positioned my mat behind his. I could have had a complete eye view of his ass up in the air.

"Wow, both of you have really tight legs," Finlay said. "I guess neither of you is putting your ankles behind your head anytime soon. No missionary for you."

I was glad I was looking at the ground. I was sure I'd turned beet red. I immediately had images of me grabbing Darrin by his ankles with his quads pushed against his chest as I lowered myself into him. I wouldn't mind helping Darrin stretch out his legs in that manner. Maybe he'd rest his knees around my shoulders as I fucked him repeatedly. Then he'd turn the tables, and I'd get the stretch of my life.

"I know a muscle I'd like to stretch," I muttered.

"What was that?" Darrin said from next to me.

"Sorry... Talking to myself."

I wasn't sure if my face was red because I was blushing or because all the blood was racing to my head in the downward dog position.

"Now, I want you to sweep your left leg into the air as high as possible."

I looked ahead and my jaw dropped as Finlay's leg pointed at the sky. I barely got my leg past my hip before I finally teetered over. "Fuck!" I crashed to the right, sending my sprawling body smashing into Darrin, who wasn't having much more luck balancing himself than I was, and we both tumbled to the ground. I untangled myself from Darrin. "Sorry about that."

"I thought I would fall in your direction a couple of times."

"What am I going to do with you two?" Finlay sighed as he shook his head.

He worked with us for the next thirty minutes before allowing us to get on the floor and informed us it was time for some partner work. I was a hot, sweaty mess. My shirt was sticking to my body. Darrin had taken off his shirt at some point, as had Finlay.

"I thought yoga was supposed to be relaxing," I said as he had us sit on our mats with our legs pointing in a wide V on the ground.

"I'm totally relaxed," Isaac said. "And I've been enjoying the show."

"Isaac," Finlay scolded. A look crossed between him and Isaac that I couldn't quite decipher. "Darrin, why don't you get behind Jordan and add your weight to his back to help him stretch deeper. Just be slow and safe. The goal is to stretch, not hurt."

"Okay," Darrin said. He got off his mat and stood behind me.

"Now, put your chest to his back and lean your body into Jordan." The heat of Darrin's bare chest immediately combined with my back, and I slowly stretched closer to the ground.

"Let me know if I'm hurting you," Darrin said. His breath fluttering over my ear made my whole body get tingly.

"I'm fine," I said. My voice was almost breathless. "I can take more of your weight." I wasn't sure if I could, but I wanted to feel him against my back. I had an erection already growing and it made bending a little more complicated, but I didn't care. Then something else was poked into my back. *Holy shit, he's as hard as I am.* Suddenly, Darrin shifted his weight, adjusting himself so his cock wasn't grinding into me anymore. I wanted to tell him it was okay, but I did my best to pretend I hadn't noticed.

"Am I late for hot nude yoga?" a chipper Scottish voice said, walking into the yoga studio. I glanced up to see Darrin's friend Owen walking into the studio. "Nope, too many clothes are still on. But damn, Darrin. If you don't put that thing away, you're going to poke that poor kid's eye out—unless you're hoping to poke him somewhere else with it."

Immediately, the pressure on my back released as Darrin stood quickly.

"I didn't mean to… It was an accident. I…"

I glanced up to see Darrin looking at me. I got an eyeful of his covered cock at eye level, barely contained by his shorts. He didn't say a word. He grabbed his shirt and shoes and was out of the room before I could catch my breath.

"Owen! Why did you have to go there?" Finlay said. "Those two were connecting just fine before you got here."

"What?" I gasped. "Wait a second… Did you two cook this up?" I asked, looking between Finlay and Isaac.

Isaac shrugged and Finlay smiled before explaining, "We didn't think you two would ever make a move on your own. You were naked yesterday and obviously wanted to jump each other's bones, but you were both so — so I don't even know what to call it."

"Clueless?" Isaac offered.

"Not clueless," Finlay corrected. "But it didn't look like either of you would make the first move. So, Isaac and I concocted this while you were remote viewing."

"We were like school kids passing notes back and forth when Roodra or his lackeys weren't looking."

I didn't know what to say. I needed to find Darrin. After grabbing my shoes, I got out of there.

Chapter Fourteen

Darrin

As soon as I was away from the yoga studio, I sat down on the path and put on my shoes. I got up and started running. I didn't know where I was heading. I wanted to run. I passed Kieran and some guy holding hands coming in my direction, so I ducked down a different path and kept moving. Up ahead, Bryce and Richard talked with another couple. Bryce's arm was thrown over Richard's shoulders as Richard's head rested on Bryce's. I turned a different direction and found Mano and Jaxson making out in a flowery alcove. Everywhere I turned, guys were holding hands or sucking face. I saw Roodra and his two acolytes making out on a blanket. *Guess your session ended early – or this is part Angelic Alchemy.*

I turned and headed down a path I thought led up to the green cabins. A few minutes later, I could see the green cabins. Chad was fucking Avery on his porch. Avery leaned over the wooden porch rail as Chad nailed him from behind. *What the fuck is wrong with these people?* The two men saw me crest the hill. Avery waved. Chad leaned over and whispered something into Avery's ear before they retreated inside.

Instead of heading to my room, I followed a hiking path to my right. The trail headed off into the forest, so I took the turn and kept moving. It felt good to feel my feet pounding the dirt trail beneath them as I fell into a steady rhythm. I needed to let off some steam. *What am I running from?* Was I embarrassed that I'd gotten an erection? *No. Erections happen.* I was a little embarrassed Jordan had witnessed my erection, but I think I could have lived with that. I kept running. Was I worried I was disrespecting my memory of Chance? No. What Bryce had said earlier was right. I ran for a long time. A river of sweat ran down my back.

I stepped in a pile of shit. "Fuck!" I yelled at the top of my lungs. A flock of birds rose from the trees nearby because of my sudden outburst.

I looked around my feet and found a fallen branch. I picked it up and did my best to clean the crap off my shoe. *What the hell made that?* I looked closer. It was filled with berries. *Fuck!* It was bear scat.

Only then did I realize that I didn't know where I was. I figured where there was bear scat, there were bears nearby somewhere. I needed to be careful. Running aimlessly through the forest was probably not the brightest idea I'd ever had.

I looked around me in a wide arc. I couldn't see the trail I'd been running on anywhere. All around me was overgrown brush blooming in the spring sun. I tried to remember which direction I'd come from before I'd almost stepped in the scat, but I wasn't one-hundred percent sure. I looked around and tried to find my tracks. I look down at the ground, looking for a tennis shoe indent. I found bear tracks leading off in one direction, so I decided the wisest decision was to head in the opposite one.

Jordan

As Darrin ran through the camp, I tried to follow him. I wasn't sure if he was running away from me, but he kept turning and going in different directions. I lost him twice, then saw him running on a path that led up to our cabins.

"Hey, Jordan," a voice called. I looked around, and Cody Benton was headed in my direction.

"Hey, Cody. Any word about Phil?" I asked.

"You know I can't talk to you about a patient," Cody said as he gave me a quick hug. "Thankfully, he's not one of my patients. Phil was released from the hospital this morning after two rounds of antivenom treatment yesterday. The docs in Kingston were very glad your friend Darrin stabilized Phil before he was carted down the mountain to the ER."

"I'm glad to hear that Phil is on the mend." I looked past Cody to see if I could still see Darrin, but I didn't see him anymore. *Must have gotten to his cabin.*

"Speaking of Darrin," Cody said, forcing me to look him in the eyes. "How is his foot really doing? Physicians are notorious for being horrible patients. I want to make sure he's not further injuring himself to prove he's a big man."

"I don't think he would do that," I said with some hesitation. "I mean, don't get me wrong. He was a bit of a jerk at Urgent Care, but he really has seemed fine.

He's walked…and run all over the place without a limp."

"I guess that's a good sign."

"Well, I need to catch up with Darrin. I'll talk with you later," I said as I sidestepped whatever Cody's next question would be. I ran up to Darrin's cabin. The dynamic duo next door sounded like rabbits again. "Shut the fuck up already!" I yelled at them before knocking on Darrin's door. There wasn't a response. *If he's in the shower, he probably wouldn't hear me.* I looked down at the sweaty shirt that clung to my body. I needed a shower myself.

I started walking down the stairs when the door to Chad's cabin flung open.

"What the fuck is your problem?" Avery yelled at me.

He was sweaty and still hard.

"What's my problem? You're the ones who fuck constantly and so loudly that people in the next county can probably hear you."

"Let 'em! If you weren't such a prude—"

"I'm not a prude. I believe someone's private life should stay private."

"Whatever. It's not my fault you're not getting laid. But with that attitude of yours, I'm not surprised."

I took two steps forward toward him on Darrin's porch. "What the fuck did you just say?"

"Oh, now you're going to be all tough and macho again and attack me?"

"Avery," Chad said, coming out of the cabin. He at least had taken the second to grab a pillow, which he now held in front of him. "Come back inside."

"No, this asshole," Avery said, gesturing in my direction, "is threatening me with violence—like I knew he would."

"*He's just a scorpion.*" Darrin's voice sounded in the back of my head.

"You're not worth it," I said. I turned and looked at Chad. "If you're happy with him, I'm happy for you. But please, for the love of God, tamp it down a bit. You have neighbors."

I didn't wait for a response. I turned around and took three steps off Darrin's porch, walked over to my cabin and headed inside. As soon as the door was shut behind me, I turned, pressed my back against the wall and let out a breath I didn't even realize I'd been holding. I took the high road.

I slipped out of my shirt, shorts, underwear and shoes and socks before heading into the shower to take a shower...a freezing one.

* * * *

After my shower, I put on my next outfit. At the rate I was going, I would have to run home and do laundry before the end of the weekend. I was used to taking multiple showers a day, but not on my fucking vacations.

Once I was put back together. I exited my cabin and walked over to Darrin's and knocked. Nothing. I knocked again.

"He hasn't been here, as far as I know," Chad said, exiting his cabin.

"Sorry about earlier. Avery has a way of pushing my buttons."

"I can see how. But he's a nice guy. He comes off as all privileged and spoiled, but that's an act. If you get to know him, he's just a guy scared of his own shadow. He had a father who roughed him up when he found out he was gay. I think your more confrontational nature reminds him of his father."

"That still never gave him the right to grope me."

"You're right. He shouldn't have done that. There's no excuse for how he acted the night you met him. I won't apologize for him, but just know he's more than that."

"I'll take your word for it, but I still don't want to be around him."

"I can understand that." Chad looked at me and nodded before turning around and going back inside.

A loud gong caught my attention. *Lunch time.* I decided that the dining hall was probably the best place to find Darrin, so I headed down the stairs and away from the cabins toward the dining hall. I quickly fell in with the men of all ages, shapes and sizes who were ready to eat.

When I got into the dining hall, I bypassed the line. I started looking around to see if I could find Darrin.

"Hey, Jordan. You, okay?" I turned my head and saw Finlay heading in my direction, with Isaac rolling behind him.

"I'm fine. I was trying to find Darrin."

"You haven't found him yet?" Isaac asked.

"Not after that little debacle in the yoga room," I said, staring between both men.

"Sorry about that," Isaac said. "We shouldn't have hatched that plan. We didn't want to see either of you pass up the opportunity without at least giving it a try first."

"And while I can appreciate what you did, I'm not sure Darrin does."

"What's his deal, anyway?" Isaac questioned.

"You didn't tell him?" I asked, looking at Finlay.

"I don't know myself. I know he's here with a married couple, and he knows Owen, but that's the extent of what I know about Darrin. We've talked a few times but never got into a serious conversation," Finlay informed me.

"It's not my story to tell," I said. "I don't want to violate Darrin's confidence, but he's dealing with some stuff."

Finlay looked like he wanted to ask a question, but he stopped himself. Instead, he said, "Why don't you join us for lunch? Just us three."

I looked around and didn't see Darrin anywhere, so I said, "Sure. Why not?"

We headed to the line and piled on vegetarian stir-fry over rice. I scooped up a large helping before following Finlay and Isaac to a table in the room's corner. We sat down and didn't say anything at first.

"So, what do you like about Darrin?" Isaac asked. "I mean, we can tell that you two are clearly infatuated with each other. I'm trying to figure it out."

"I'll be the first to admit that we're very different people. We're just like Aesop's Fable of the town mouse and the country mouse, but I was drawn to him from the minute I got to see past his infuriating exterior." I told them about our trip into urgent care and how I'd wanted to kick him out of my truck at first but then I realized that was his way of controlling his situation.

"Do you think he may not be ready for a relationship?" Finlay asked.

"Well, that came out of nowhere," I responded.

"Really? You're surprised by that question?" Isaac said, a dubious look crossed his face.

I let out a huff before saying, "No, but I'm afraid it's true. What if he's not ready to be in a relationship? After what he's gone through, I don't know if he'll ever be ready for one again."

"And what has he been through?" Isaac asked.

"Good try," I said. "You already know I'm not going to tell you that. Like I said, it's not my story to tell."

"It was worth a shot," Isaac said as he gave me a one-sided smile and shrugged.

We spent the rest of lunch talking about boyfriends and love. We also spoke about Finlay and his passion for yoga.

"I was on a college volleyball team, and I injured myself. Part of my physical therapy was yoga. Before I knew it, I was doing yoga full time, quit the volleyball team and dropped out of college altogether, much to my parent's dismay."

"Well, you definitely seem to be adept at downward-facing doggy style," I joked.

"Sadly, no downward-facing doggy for me," Isaac said, and a hint of mischief gleamed in his eyes. "But I can do a mean cobra if you want to mount me from behind," he hissed at me before sticking his tongue out in rapid succession.

"Still not interested," I said, but I had to smile at him. "I promise I'll let you know if that changes, my friend."

"Jordan." I looked up as Bryce headed toward the table. "Have you seen Darrin?"

"Not since this morning. He ran off. I haven't seen him since before lunch. I had hoped he was with you."

"Hmm... Did something come up?" Bryce asked.

"You could say that," Isaac joked.

I shot Isaac a 'shut it' look before turning back to Bryce. I told him the bare bones of the story and how Darrin had run off.

"I'm sure he's fine," Bryce said. "Probably just needed some time to cool off and put his thoughts together. He gets like that some days. Maybe he's up in his cabin?"

"I was there before I came down to lunch. Honestly, I'd hoped I would find him here hanging out with you."

"Hmm... I'm sure he'll turn up."

"I hope so. If you see him, tell him I'm looking for him," I said.

"I will. And if you see him, please tell him to find either Richard or me."

"I will as well."

By the time lunch ended, I still hadn't found Darrin, and no one I asked had seen him, either.

Chapter Fifteen

Darrin

The midday sun was bearing down. The tree cover provided me with a lot of shade. Of course, the problem with all the trees was I couldn't see anything but a shit ton of them. Maybe it was the Texas boy in me, but I'm used to seeing a skyline in every direction. We have trees in Texas. There are Ashe juniper, bald cypress, chinquapin oak, Shumard oak, southern magnolia and pecan trees, but they don't grow right on top of each other. There are just trees, trees and nothing but trees up here in the Catskills. In every direction I looked there was a sea of fucking bark and green.

I looked down at my wrist for like the twentieth time to see what time it was, only to remember I had left my watch and my cell phone in my cabin. I was desperately lost. I tried to remember my Boy Scout training. Most of my outings had been in the rolling grasslands of the Blackland Prairie region or the weird mix of prairie, savanna and woodland ecosystems that make up the

Cross Timbers region. Even the more forested areas of the Cross Timbers region differed quite a lot from the Catskills.

"Okay, Darrin. Keep it together. When you get lost in the woods, you're supposed to STOP—stay put, think, observe and plan." I hoped saying the acronym out loud would help me keep myself focused. Step one, I needed to find a place to hunker down. If someone was going to find me, my stumbling around in the woods would not make it easy. After walking for a few minutes, I found a clearing. I needed to have enough room to see what was in my immediate surroundings. There was all kinds of wildlife out there. I wanted to make sure they could see me, and I could see them. The last thing I wanted was to stumble into a black bear and her cub.

Step two, I needed to think. *What resources do I have? Not many.* I had my wallet, but there wasn't anything in there that would be of any practical use. I don't think I could defend myself against a bear attack with a credit card.

Which led me to step three. I needed to do a better job of observing my area. I took a good twenty paces in any direction from the tree I planned on hunkering down nearby. I wanted to make sure there wasn't anything dangerous in the immediate area. I didn't find any scat, which was a good sign.

The last step was to plan. By this point, I assumed it was midday to early evening. I still had plenty of time to get my act together and prepare for nightfall. I started by locating some larger rocks that I could use to make a small fire ring near the tree's base. The fire would help rescuers spot me in the dark—if it came to that. The fire would also stave off the cold. With my small ring built, I started locating twigs and branches. Unfortunately, many of the twigs and branches I found weren't overly dry, so getting them to burn was going to be a pain in the butt. I also knew, from experience, that creating a fire by rubbing sticks together would not be easy. They always make it look easy in movies. Even though it was still daylight, I decided I might as well get the fire going.

I put my kindling into the little circle then I found a couple of sticks. I removed the shoelace from one of my shoes to create a bow. I twirled my bow around a stick that I could use as a drill to help build friction against a larger block of wood that I kept steady with my left hand while I started pumping the bow back and forth with my right hand in a sawing motion. After what seemed like forever, I started seeing a little bit of smoke. I eventually had a small glowing coal and immediately transferred it into the tinder bundle I had sitting in the fire ring. Once that caught fire, I added my twigs and eventually the larger pieces of wood.

"Yes! I have fire," I yelled into the wilderness. I looked at the pile of logs I'd created to keep my fire burning and decided I should probably get a few more before the evening hit. I searched forty paces in any direction, looking for more logs. After Phil's run-in with the rattler the other day, I didn't take any chances. I found a long wizard-staff-like piece of wood and used it to poke at any logs I found. I yipped once when I rolled a log and a snake slithered away into the forest. Once my heartbeat calmed down, I realized it was a simple garter snake.

When I rolled another log, I found a bunch of earthworms underneath. I glanced down at the worms.

That's protein. And immediately added, *I'm not that hungry or desperate yet.*

Before long, I had a stack of wood that should keep me through the night. Now that I had a fire, my biggest concern became dehydration. I hadn't passed a river, stream or pond while wandering through the woods. Because of the surrounding mountains, I could be near a pond and have no idea. All I could do was hope that I would be rescued long before dehydration set in. As a rule, I could survive for at least a couple of days without water. Still, my crazy running around and exercise to get the fire going could make my dehydration symptoms come much faster. I was already thirsty, which wasn't a great sign.

With nothing else to do but wait, I leaned my back against a large, solid tree. Exhaustion set in. *How could I be this stupid?* I pulled my knees up to my chest and leaned my head between them. Part of me wanted to cry, but I forced back the tears, because the last thing I needed to do was lose even more water.

Jordan

When the gong for dinner rang, I practically raced down to the dining hall. I still hadn't seen any signs of Darrin, and I was getting worried. I was also a little pissed off that no one else was taking Darrin's disappearance as seriously as I was.

As soon as I entered the dining hall, I made a beeline for Bryce and Richard's table. "Have you seen Darrin yet?" I asked, not bothering with a polite greeting.

"No," Bryce said, looking up from a tofu meatloaf. "He hasn't returned to his cabin?"

"No, he hasn't. I've been sitting on my porch waiting for him to get back."

"He was a Boy Scout. I'm sure he's fine."

"He was a Scout in Texas," Richard said, "where it's flat."

"Don't encourage the boy," Bryce said. "I'm sure Darrin is fine. If he needed help, he could use his cell phone to call for help."

"You're presuming he can get a signal," I said. "You're also assuming he even has his cell on him."

"Good point," Richard said. "Maybe you should let Jaxson and Mano know, just in case."

Bryce rolled his eyes, but he didn't contradict his husband. I nodded and turned to find the other couple in the sea of faces.

I spotted Jaxson and Mano sitting at a table with a group of men I didn't recognize. Jaxson looked up as I approached the table and asked, "What's wrong?"

"It's Darrin Betancourt. He's missing."

"What do you mean by missing?" Mano asked.

"No one has seen him since about mid-morning."

"Is he in his cabin?" Jaxson questioned.

"No. I've been there all afternoon, waiting for him to return."

"And you've talked with his friends?" Mano said after finishing a bite of his meatless meatloaf.

"I talked to them," I said with more exasperation than I intended. "After mid-morning yoga with Finlay, he disappeared." Mano's eyebrows raised at that tidbit of information, but he didn't say anything.

"You're really worried," Jaxson said.

"Of course, I'm worried. He could be lying in a ditch somewhere with a broken leg. He could have been mauled by a bear or bobcat."

"Okay," Mano said in a voice that was trying to be soothing but irked me instead, "let's not get ahead of ourselves. You're from up here. You know animal attacks are very rare."

"True. But if he was injured, he could look like easy prey," I added.

Mano looked at me for a second. I recognized the moment he figured out I wouldn't let this go. He sighed. "Let's talk to the camp manager." He then looked down at Jaxson. "I'll be right back."

Mano pushed his chair back and stood. I followed him through the dining hall then a side door leading to the kitchen. At the far end of the kitchen was an office. Mano knocked on the doorframe before poking his head in. "Hey Hal, do you have a minute?"

An older-looking man looked up from a stack of papers on his desk. "Mano, how can I help you?"

Mano and I stepped into the office. "We may have a missing camper situation." Mano ran through what we knew about Darrin.

"Any chance he left?" Hal asked.

"No," I replied. "He's here with friends. He doesn't have a vehicle of his own, so he really doesn't have a way to leave."

"Okay," Hal said as he steepled his hands under his chin. "Let's go check out his cabin. If his stuff is still there, that should let us know something."

Hal stood and led us out a backdoor from the kitchen. We followed him all the way to the green cabins with no conversation. Thankfully, no sex sounds were coming from the last two cabins when we got there.

"Which one is he in?" Hal asked.

"The second one," I said. "I'm in the first."

Hall climbed the stairs and pulled out a large keyring, searched through the keys and slipped one he picked into the lock.

"Mr. Betancourt?" Hal said into the opened doorway. Once he was satisfied that Darrin wasn't there, he turned to Mano and me and said, "For privacy purposes, I will ask both of you to remain out here." Mano and I stood in the doorway as Hal walked into the room. Hal checked the bathroom. "He's not in here, but his stuff is still here. His watch and cell phone are sitting on the nightstand."

"Well, fuck," I mumbled.

Hal pulled out his cell phone. After a few seconds, he said, "Hey, Jenny, we may have a missing camper. Can you make an announcement for Mr. Darrin Betancourt to report to the administration building?" Hal turned to us and said, "Hopefully, he'll hear the announcement and come to the main office. Let's head down in that direction."

Hal locked up Darrin's cabin, and we headed back down into the heart of the camp to the main offices. While we were walking, a female's voice was heard across the camp, asking for Darrin to come to the administration building. *God, I hope he's there.*

Unfortunately, there was no sign of Darrin when we got to the admin building. A young blonde woman was standing on the front porch of the building, waiting for us. "Hey, boss," the woman said to Hal. "No one's showed up yet."

"We'll give it a few more minutes." Hal gestured to a set of wooden chairs.

"Can I get you anything?" Jenny asked.

"I'm fine," I said. "Thanks."

"I'm going to go update Jaxson," Mano said. "I'll be back in a few minutes."

The sun was setting, and it was going to be dark soon. Most people don't get how dark a forest can be at night with only stars and the moon providing light. I grew more worried that Darrin was lost in the woods with each passing minute.

"Don't worry, hon," Jenny said, looking at me. "We haven't lost a camper yet. And we won't lose your friend."

Twenty minutes later and there was still no sign of Darrin. By this point, a small group had congregated at the administrative building. Jaxson and Mano were there talking in hushed tones with Hal. Bryce and Richard had shown up and were sitting next to me. They sat together on one of the wooden chairs. The chair wasn't meant to be a two-seater, but Bryce and Richard had squeezed onto it together and made it work.

"I'm not sure if going out in the dark is a smart move," Jaxson said. "What if we lose even more people?"

"Honey, we have a missing camper. We can't wait until daybreak to look for him. If something happened…" Mano's voice trailed off as he shot me a look.

"I'm not a huge fan of mounting a night search party," Hal said. "But I'm going to agree with Mano on this one. I don't think we have any great options presently, but we should try."

Having heard enough, I finally said, "I'm going to go looking for him. The longer we sit here debating what to do, the worse his situation could be." I started to rise but a hand grabbed my forearm. I looked over to see Bryce looking at me.

"We're with Jordan," Bryce said. "If something has happened to Darrin, every second we sit debating what to do could put his life in further jeopardy."

The group debated the pros and cons of mounting a night search party, but eventually, those who favored going out into the dark won out.

Within twenty minutes, we started forming groups. More campers appeared from the woodworks. Kieran showed up with Owen. Even Avery and Chad showed up to help with the search, which blew my mind.

Six teams of two were organized. I paired off with Kieran. Each group was provided with a walkie-talkie and a satellite GPS device, so we'd know where we were located and could tell basecamp exactly where we were when we checked in.

"I expect each group to report in every twenty minutes," Hal said. "We want this search to be swift and organized. I do not want anyone else to go missing. Remember… You are entering the forest and there are a variety of animals out there. Most are perfectly harmless, but some are not."

Jenny provided each search team with flashlights, bear spray, bottled water and a backpack containing a small first-aid kit. Once each group was outfitted and ready to go, we headed off into the night.

Chapter Sixteen

Kieran took charge of the handheld GPS device. Honestly, I'd never used one before. I knew my boss, Dale, had one of those contraptions. He'd used it to walk to work one day. Let's just say that hadn't gone according to plan.

I've been around the Catskill forests my entire life, but I don't go hiking in them when it's dark. The high-beam flashlights that the camp had given us to help us trek through the woods provided a ton of light.

"Do you have much experience in search and rescue, mate?" Kieran asked.

"Not really. I once worked with a community group when a child got lost in the forest. We found her in under two hours and before it had gotten dark. You?"

"I have a little experience. Before moving to the US and after I'd left the New Zealand military, I worked for the NZ Emergency Management Assistance Team. Basically, anytime there was a major disaster, we got called in to help support the local community — kind of like the US' Federal Emergency Management Agency."

"FEMA's been up in this area a few times when there's been blizzards, floods or hurricanes. A few years back, we had this ice storm that hit most of the western part of the county. We had almost three-fourths of an inch of ice covering everything. I'd never seen so many downed trees and power lines in my entire life. Nothing says home sweet home when your refrigerator is warmer than your house."

Kieran laughed, and I heard a bird fly away in the night. "Primary thing is to keep your eyes on the ground, looking for tracks. Since we're sticking to paths, that may be difficult because there are so many tracks. Look at the path's edges to see if you see footprints leaving the path. That could be a good sign that Darrin took off into the forest."

"Sounds like a plan. I'll look on the left side, and you look on the right."

We walked like that in silence for the next ten minutes. There was a burst of static at my hip, which caused me to let out a squeal.

"Basecamp. Time for a check-in," the walkie-talkie said. I recognized Jenny's voice.

I pulled the device from its clip and said, "Kieran and Jordan, checking in. Nothing so far."

"Thanks, Team One." Jenny had assigned each of us a team number. I didn't think it was necessary since there were only six pairs of guys out wandering the night looking for Darrin. I listened as the other five groups checked in and said the same thing. No signs of Darrin. We kept walking.

"Why did you move to the US?" I asked.

"New Zealand is amazing and progressive, but that doesn't mean there aren't a few backwoods types. When I transitioned, I had your usual hatemongers telling me I was going to hell and whatnot. Part of my family disowned me, and I needed a new start. Besides, after riding out the pandemic for a year on lockdown, I wanted to be somewhere else."

"What was the pandemic like for you guys on the other side of the world?"

"We shut down. Any hint that the virus had gotten to New Zealand and we clamped down harder than a twink taking his first cock up his ass."

"Thanks for the added mental picture."

"You're welcome. It was interesting because I was so used to being out and about in nature. A buddy and me, also a transman, had been hiking the Routeburn Track on the South Island. We did not know anything was going on. After a week of roughing it in the bush, we made our way back to the Routeburn Shelter and found the place deserted. I swear. It reminded me of one of those old western movies, and I half expected dust and a tumbleweed to float by, even though we don't have tumbleweeds—or one of those Christian movies where suddenly someone finds out the rapture has happened and they're the last person left on the planet. There wasn't a person in sight and not a vehicle in the carpark."

"What did you do?"

"We stayed put for about a day. We figured someone would eventually come by. Our rations were running low, so we were going to hike out the next day when a minivan pulled up. And when people got out all in gloves and masks, I was truly like *'what the fuck?'*" Kieran stopped for a second to examine something on the ground.

"What'd you see?" Kieran shined his light into a pile of scat right off the path. "Bear scat from the looks of it.

See those red berries? The bears love those suckers. They also love blueberries, raspberries, strawberries, blackberries and acorns. They're omnivores, so they'll eat almost anything they can scavenge."

"More things we never had to contend with in New Zealand. There are no bears, snakes or wolves there. We have some shit spiders that will try to kill you and some aquatic life, but not like Australia or even here in the States."

We started walking again. "You didn't finish your story," I said.

"Oh yeah, where was I?"

"A van had pulled up, and a hazmat team basically walked out."

"Well, I wouldn't go that far, but they were fully masked, wearing gloves and face shields. They shouldn't have been out and about because they'd violated the country-wide lockdown, but they figured the fresh air for their school-aged kids was more important. At first, we were like, '*hey!*' And they looked at us like we were patients zero in a horror flick. The mother had yelled, '*stay away from us.*' We held up our hands and tried to look as unassuming as possible. The father was a bit more reasonable. He told us what was going on and promised to call NZ EMAT as soon as they got back to their house. They'd taken off shortly after that.

Honestly, I gave our chances of them sending help a fifty-fifty chance. We were about to hike out when an NZ EMAT truck pulled up. Unfortunately, I knew the people in the truck, but they didn't recognize me post-transition, which I guess was divine intervention because I bet they would have just left us there. Anyway, it was drizzling, but EMAT guys wouldn't let us in the cab in case we were infected. They drove us to Christchurch and threw us on a plane back to Auckland. The entire plane had maybe ten people on it, and we were asked to keep our distance from each other. Of course, by this time, we had at least been allowed to shower and get into new clothes. We'd also been provided PPE, so..."

"Yeah, it was scary living up here when the city had the first major outbreak. It reminded me of that movie *Contagion*. Thankfully, the people didn't start rioting and looting. We didn't have martial law imposed by the President, but it was scary. My whole family was glued to the television every day. We watched the infection rates skyrocket, and the hospitals became overwhelmed. I thought we were at the end of the world when they created a hospital tent city in Central Park then converted the Javits Center to ICU beds."

"Scary times for everyone. Now look at us. We're vaccinated, boosted and hiking around in the dark."

We continued in silence for a few minutes until I noticed something off the path to the left. "Stop," I said. I inched closer to the edge of the path and recognized a shoe print in a pile of bear scat. Nearby there was a tree branch thrown to the ground. It looked like there was scat on the end of the branch.

"What are you thinking?" Kieran asked.

"Looks like someone hit that patch of scat and tried to clean their shoe with that stick." We backtracked a little, trying to see the direction the shoe had gone. Whoever scraped the scat with a stick hadn't done a bang-up job because there were smushed berry tracks leading in the opposite direction...off the path. I pulled my walkie-talkie off my belt and phoned it in.

"Are you sure it was a human shoe?" Jenny asked after I called basecamp.

"Yeah, we could see the tread marks in the scat."

"What are your GPS coordinates?"

I handed the walkie-talkie to Kieran, who read her the coordinates from the device.

"Hal says it looks like you're in one of the old streambeds. They can easily be mistaken as paths if you're not paying attention. Since you're leaving the main path, check in every ten minutes. We'll redirect a team from the south to your general location."

"Thanks," Kieran said before handing the walkie-talkie back. "At least we have a direction to head in now."

We followed the old streambed, and Kieran started noticing more signs that someone had ventured from the path and run in this direction. "Whoever we're following, they weren't going slow. You can see by the stride that they were either ridiculously tall or running."

We walked in that direction for ten minutes and called it in. The stream went around a bend. A hoot overhead caused me to career into Kieran as I jumped. Kieran took it in stride, laughing. "Don't let a little owl scare you."

I didn't respond. I was more embarrassed than anything. I felt myself getting a little twitchy. I know black bears aren't inherently aggressive toward hikers, but that's not to say they wouldn't protect their cubs if we somehow found ourselves between a mama and her babies.

"What's that?" I asked. Up ahead, there was what looked like a glimmer of light. I couldn't be sure if I was imagining something or not.

"Not sure. Probably nothing. Phone it in, just in case."

"Basecamp, this is Team One. Over?"

"Team One, this is basecamp. Status?"

"Are there any humans out here besides us? We think there may be a light in the distance, but we're not sure." She asked for our GPS location, and Kieran read it off.

"Hal says where you are should be uninhabited. Approach with caution."

"Will do," I said before clipping the device back to my waistband.

Darrin

My fire wasn't what I'd call large, but it was enough to provide light and keep me warm against the cooler night temperature in the mountains. I wasn't likely to die from exposure to the elements this time of the year, but that didn't mean I wanted to let my body temperature drop too low during the night.

Unfortunately, the fire only provided maybe ten to fifteen feet of light. I was glad my back was against a tree but was also freaked out something would stalk me from behind or jump down on me from above. My mind was playing tricks on me. More than once, I swore I heard an animal walking back in the dark. I'm sure it was nothing, but my mind was racing with every way I could die before someone found me out here. That was assuming anyone had even noticed I was missing. I can't believe I ran off because someone laughed at my boner. *"How did he die? Eaten by a bear after someone pointed at his dick and laughed. I'm such a fucking moron."*

I sat there for what seemed like hours with my knees huddled to my chest. Finally, I needed to pee. I went right to the edge of my fire circle, not wanting to go any farther than that. I pissed out into the black. My eyes hadn't adjusted to pitch-black night. I flicked the last couple of drops to the ground when a pair of glowing eyes were about ten feet ahead of me. I stumbled backward and crab-walked back to the fire. As I stared out into the black night, those same eyes blinked on and off, on and off. *Fireflies.* I looked down at my unzipped pants and chided myself for letting my mind get the better of me. I stood and zipped up before sitting back down at my position beneath the tree.

I stared into the fire for what seemed like eons. Periodically, I'd drop another log on the fire to keep it stoked.

In the distance, I heard a rustling sound. *Your mind's playing tricks on you again. Keep your shit together.* I doubted anything would come charging out of the night to attack me, but I didn't like the feeling of being so exposed sitting out in the elements like this. More than once, I swore I would never venture into nature again if I survived this. I also promised I'd take a nature survival course and turn myself into the next Bear Grylls if I got out alive.

"Darrin?" My head spun in the voice's direction. Seconds later, Jordan came running into the campfire light. I barely stood before he'd thrown himself around me. He clenched to me like I was a life preserver, and I was the only thing preventing him from drowning. I reached up and grabbed the back of his head and held it against me.

"I'm fine," I said.

He let go of me, then looked up into my face and smacked me upside the side of my head. "Ow! What was that for? I'm the victim here."

"No, you're the idiot who went running around in a forest with no one knowing where you were going and no provisions."

"Hey, Darrin," Kieran said from his position on the other side of the fire. I could see his curved lips with just a hint of teeth. "Need some water, mate?"

"Yes," I said immediately. "I haven't had anything to eat or drink since breakfast."

Kieran pulled off a backpack, unzipped it and handed me a water bottle. "Any injuries?" he asked.

"Just to my pride."

"You fucking scared a lot of people," Jordan said. I looked at him. Something about how the fire twinkled in his eyes made me reach out with both hands, grab his face and plant a long, passionate kiss. Kieran turned his head to avoid watching us as Jordan threw his arms around my neck and held me.

"Team One. Report. You missed your check-in," a woman's voice broke through the silence.

Jordan reached down and pulled a walkie-talkie from his hip. "This is Team One. We have him. He's safe. There were no apparent injuries besides where I lopped him upside his damn head for scaring us."

"Hal is moving in on your location. Stay there. He'll guide you out the fastest way possible," the voice said.

"Who's Hal?" I asked.

"Hal is the camp manager," Kieran said. "I have a protein bar if you're hungry." I accepted the protein bar with my free hand. My other hand was intertwined with Jordan's.

Chapter Seventeen

Jordan

I stood in the clearing holding on to Darrin while we waited for Hal to show up. I had a million and one questions I wanted to ask Darrin, but I didn't think grilling him in front of Kieran was the most brilliant move I could make at the moment. Instead, I stood there and tried to be as jovial as possible. Once Darrin had downed the protein bar and the water, I felt better. He was far from dehydration or starvation, but watching his basic needs get met made me more comfortable.

After what seemed like forever, Hal showed up with Cody in tow. "So, you're the one who caused all the trouble this evening?" Hal asked, looking Darrin up and down.

"Sorry about all this," Darrin said sheepishly. "I went running and got myself lost."

"Be glad your friend here," Hal said, gesturing to me, "was so insistent. Let's get you all back to camp."

Hal handed Darrin a flashlight before he started putting out the campfire. "Not a poor job you did there. I would have cleared the brush farther from the fire pit to prevent stray sparks from catching anything on fire, but it's workable."

Once the fire was doused to Hal's liking, the group trudged after him. Darrin and I continued to hold hands.

"Darrin," Cody said, coming up beside us, "are you good? Anything I should worry about?"

"Nah," Darrin said. "The only thing damaged in all this was my pride."

"Did you drink or eat anything out here?"

"I hadn't broken down and gone native—if that's what you're asking. The first time I had anything to drink or eat was when Jordan and Kieran rescued me."

"That's good. Unless you're familiar with the plant life here, I wouldn't recommend eating anything straight from the vine. Some of the plants around here are more likely to make you sick than alleviate your hunger," Cody admitted. "Well, I'm just glad you're all right. Gave us all a bit of a scare."

"I promise you, I'm fine. I feel like half my weekend has been telling you I'm fine." Darrin sighed. "Trust me. This is not how I envisioned my camp experience."

"Stop all that yammering back there," Hal said from in front of us. "I want to be home before eleven."

We quickened our pace and caught up with Hal and Kieran. We made our way through the wooded night. A couple of times, Hal stopped and pointed something out that we would have missed without his expert guidance. I quickly learned that Hal knew more about the plants and fauna of the Catskills than anyone I'd met, which said a lot.

Before long, we could see the camp's lights. "Before we do anything," Darrin said as we walked, "I want a shower, a change of clothes and to throw these tennis shoes in the garbage."

"Just to let you know, your shoes led us straight to you. If you hadn't stepped in the bear scat, Kieran wouldn't have figured out which direction you'd headed," I let him know. I shivered slightly. The cool mountain air was getting to me. The whole time we searched for Darrin, I hadn't noticed the temperature drop. But now that I had him, I was feeling many different things.

"Well, score one for bear scat," Darrin joked. "These tennis shoes are going right in the garbage. Even if I got them cleaned, I don't think I could ever wear them again without smelling that horrid smell."

When we hit the first of the camp paths. I thanked Hal and Cody for guiding us. I shook both men's hands, and Darrin did the same.

"Shit, I don't even have my keys. I forgot about that," Darrin said.

"Here, take this key," Hal said, turning to Darrin. "Bring it back once you've let yourself in." With that, Hal and Cody turned and started walking away.

I turned to Kieran, "Thanks for everything tonight." I let go of Darrin's hand so I could wrap my arms around Kieran in a bear hug.

"You got a real keeper here, mate," Kieran said when we let go. "He cares a lot about you." Kieran turned to me and said, "And you, don't let him sulk in his cabin all night. Get him down to the party, will ya?"

I looked at Darrin and said, "I promise we'll get him there. Tell everyone to give us like thirty minutes." Kieran nodded his head once. Kieran shook Darrin's hand, then headed off after Hal and Cody, who had already started making their way toward the administration building.

A static sound at my hip caused me to jump. "Oh shit," I said. "Kieran," I yelled and started running after him. "I still have the walkie-talkie." I got to him and handed him the device before turning around and walking back toward Darrin. When I got there, I threw my arm around his waist, he threw his arm around my shoulders and we walked up to the green cabins.

"Take it. Take it. Take it. Take it," Chad stammered in rapid-fire as we rounded the bend toward the cabins. Avery was bent over the railing on his porch, getting nailed by Chad from behind.

I rolled my eyes, glad no one could see the look on my face. I was sure it was a cross between disgust and a complete lack of surprise.

Avery looked over at us when we walked up to Chad's porch. "I see you found him. We got back about ten minutes ago. Once we got the 'all clear', we headed back." He said this in between breaths as Chad pounded him.

I couldn't help but stare for a second. Avery's cock swung in the air with each of Chad's thrusts.

"Thanks for your help," I said.

"Sorry to worry everyone," Darrin added.

"It's cool," Chad said as if he was sitting in his grandmother's parlor drinking some lemonade on a summer eve. "Fuck, I'm gonna come. Uhh...fuck... fuck... Fuck!"

I could have gone my entire life without seeing Chad's "O-face."

"My turn," Avery said. "But let's take it inside."

Avery grabbed Chad by the little Chad and dragged him into the cabin. Darrin was still fiddling with the key in the dark, but I heard the tell-tell sign of the door opening, then Darrin flipped on the switch.

"Why don't you come in," Darrin said as he kicked off his shoes on the porch. "I'm going to run through the shower."

"That's cool," I said. I sat down in one of the stuffed chairs near the window. Darrin grabbed a duffel bag and rummaged through it for a second before pulling out a pair of Under Armour boxer briefs. *Guess that answers that question.*

"I won't take long."

I pulled out my phone and checked my messages. Not too much was going on. Had a text from Talgat asking me how the weekend was going. I shot him back a quick response.

Busy weekend. It's been an adventure. I'll tell you all about it on Monday. Having a great time. Maybe met someone.

I half expected an immediate response from either Dale or Talgat, but my phone sat quiet, which was fine by me. I leaned my head back on the chair and let my eyes close.

* * * *

There was a field. In the distance, I could see Darrin yelling for me. But I couldn't hear what he was hollering. He pointed to the left. Avery was fucking Chad in the meadow. I looked to the right and Dale and Talgat applauded the show. Then the earth shook. Is this an earthquake?

There was pressure on my left arm as I snapped my eyes open and stared into the most gorgeous pair of brown eyes I'd ever seen. "Sorry. That took longer than expected," Darrin said. "Seems like you put the time to good use. I almost didn't want to wake you."

I looked up to find Darrin fully clothed and standing over me. "Hey," I said, trying to keep the sleep out of my tone of voice. I lifted my hands and rubbed at my eyes, trying to get them to open as I let out a deep yawn.

"You must have fallen asleep because of adrenaline fatigue."

"Huh?"

Darrin offered me a hand and I grabbed it. He leaned back and helped me out of the chair as he kept talking. "You were probably stressed out trying to find me, which made your adrenals overtaxed by excess cortisol. Once you got back to no longer being stressed, your cortisol levels dipped, causing you to become tired. People who live in a state of stress often see this yo-yoing effect, which can screw with their sleep and circadian rhythms."

I looked at Darrin and said the only thing that came to mind, "Nerd."

He grinned goofily. "And proud of it. Let's get out of here."

He grabbed his key, cell phone and wallet before we left his cabin. Since the night air had cooled off, I ran back to my cabin to grab a sweatshirt while Darrin locked up.

Darrin waited for me at the foot of the stairs. I walked down and grabbed his hand and pulled him in for a quick kiss. The fresh minty taste of toothpaste on Darrin's lips was a welcome surprise. *I should have used some mouthwash.* Oh well, too late for that now.

We walked down to the heart of the camp. There were many people out and about walking around. There were guys walking hand in hand, arm in arm or around each other's waists. Everyone we passed and said hello to was physically connected to someone else.

In the central part of the camp, there was a giant field. In the middle, a bonfire blazed.

Darrin let out a low whistle. "Puts my flimsy little fire to shame."

"Yeah, but you did that by hand. I'm sure they had gas and matches."

"True. I can honestly say, I never thought I'd need to know how to build a fire by hand before. Score one for being a Boy Scout!"

A golf cart pulled up next to us. "You're looking back to normal already," a voice said. We turned and Hal and Jenny were sitting in the small vehicle.

"I thought you were going to get out of here," I said, looking at Hal.

"I'm trying to."

"Hey," Darrin said, reaching into his pocket. He pulled out the single key Hal had given him earlier. "Thanks for letting me borrow this." Darrin handed the key over.

"You're welcome. I'm glad we found you quickly. Well, you two, have a good night." Hal didn't wait for a response. He sped away. Jenny waved politely.

"He's definitely old school," I said. "I grew up with a lot of guys like that. My grandfather had a group of friends who remind me so much of him."

"Shall we?" Darrin motioned toward the bonfire.

We were immediately surrounded by people checking in to make sure Darrin was all right.

"I'm fine. I'm fine. Just a little ego bruising is all," Darrin admitted when Bryce and Richard finally got to him. "Nothing some wine won't fix."

Darrin had let go of my hand when the other two men had hugged him, but then he immediately pulled me back into his side when they were done. He was taller than me, so I let him snake his arm around me and rested my head against his shoulder. Part of me was still trying to wake up from the catnap I'd taken.

"Well, why don't you two join us?" Bryce said. "Richard brought down a second blanket. He was going to curl up in it if he got cold."

"Yeah, we were so close to the fire at first," Richard added. "I thought my skin was going to melt."

"Hey, you two," another voice cut in. I turned around to see Jaxson and Mano making their way over. "I see you got him back in one piece," Mano said.

"Yep, my hero," Darrin replied, giving me a squeeze.

"Did you need something to eat?" Mano asked. "I'm sure there's food around here somewhere."

"No need," Darrin said. "I had a protein bar earlier, so I'm good till morning."

Jaxson looked at Darrin and asked, "Is that going to provide you with enough energy for later?" He then diverted his eyes to me. It took me a second to realize what he was insinuating.

Darrin laughed. "Trust me. I've had plenty of stamina on far less food. I'll be fine." He then raised his eyebrows for a second before shooting me a mischievous smile that made me tingle.

We walked over to the ground, where Richard set out a blanket for us. Darrin propped himself up and pulled me down between his legs with my back leaning against his chest. He wrapped his arms around me.

"Well, you two are looking chummy?" Richard asked. "It's about fucking time. We wondered how long it would take for you to stop playing googly eyes with each other."

"What can I get for you?" Bryce asked. "We have a cabernet sauvignon or a moscato."

"Cabernet for me," Darrin replied. "And for you?" he said, turning to me.

"I'll have the moscato."

"Dry and sweet, like you," Darrin replied.

"If you keep up that kind of talk, I'll make you sit on the other side of the fire," Bryce groused.

"Party pooper," Richard said, chastising his husband. "He's never been a big fan of sweet talk or public displays of affection."

We sat. We talked. We laughed. And through it all, we kept on drinking. Once we had our wine in hand, I took a sip and let the fruity flavors swirl around in my mouth.

Darrin

I probably should have eaten something a bit more substantial. The wine entered my bloodstream and went straight to my head since there wasn't any food really in me. My face tingled with the pleasant feeling of a light buzz. I was relaxed and happy for the first time in months. Jordan fit between my legs so comfortably. It was like we'd been in that position for decades. He leaned his head back and gazed up at the stars, and I leaned down and planted a kiss on his forehead.

I wanted to rip his clothes off and have my way with him on the blanket, but I wasn't so completely gone that I'd lost all sense of decorum. But as the night went on, we became a little friskier. It started with him scooching himself back even closer to me. His back was pressed directly against my torso, which immediately made me go hard.

He'd turned his head and curved his lips upward. He hadn't said anything, but I could tell he knew from the way he moved his ass more firmly against me. Of course, I had my arms around him as his cock jabbed into my forearm. I wanted to get up and run back to the cabin, but I also didn't want to embarrass either of us with giant walking hard-ons as we walked away. There would be no hiding our arousal, even in the firelight.

We talked and drank some more. Eventually, another blanket was thrown down next to us. Finlay, Kieran, Owen and Isaac sat and started drinking with us. It didn't take us long to realize that Finlay and Kieran had a thing for each other while Owen and Isaac were also getting chummy. I thought back to earlier that morning when my jealousy had gotten the better of me.

"So, I gotta ask. Why were you riding around on Isaac's wheelchair earlier?"

"Oh, that," Jordan said. "Did that make you jealous?" he said sarcastically as his eyebrows made this incredibly adorable wiggling motion.

"Of course not," I lied. "Just curious."

"Well, if you must know," Jordan said. While he was talking, I leaned my face against his. I could feel his jaw move next to mine as he spoke. "I had a minor crush on Isaac growing up."

"You did? How did you know him? Was he in a boy band or something?"

"You don't know who Isaac Robinson is?"

"Not a fucking clue," I admitted.

Jordan gave me a complete bio of Isaac, which included all his stats from both college and the NFL. I nodded my head.

"You have no idea what I'm talking about," Jordan said.

"Nope. Football was never my thing."

"How can you have grown up in Texas, the home of *Friday Night Lights*, and not be a football fan?"

"Very easy. As you delicately put it, I was a nerd. I was captain of the mathlete team. I didn't exercise till I was in college. I was always a string-bean guy. I got tired of being the skinny kid in college, so I took a weightlifting class as an undergraduate and started bulking up. This body is meant for pleasure, not playing sports."

"Oh, really?" Jordan said, turning his head slightly to look into my eyes. He reached his hand around, placed it on the other side of my face and drew me in for a kiss. "I like the sound of pleasure."

"I feel like I'm supposed to make a tight end or wide receiver joke now," I joked when we pulled away. Jordan stuck his tongue at me jokingly. "Is that an invitation or a promise?" I asked.

"Take me back to the cabin and find out," he whispered into my ear before letting his tongue trace around the outside. The look in Jordan's eyes was earnest. Something had switched on inside him, and it made me want to throw him over my shoulder and fireman carry him while I ran up to the cabin.

"Bryce, Richard, I think we will call it a night," I snapped.

"Don't worry about folding your blanket. I'll grab it before we go," Richard said.

"Thanks. And again, sorry about running off like that."

"Water under the bridge," Bryce said. "You two have fun. Don't do anything Richard and I wouldn't do." Richard hit his husband on the arm lightly. "What? I didn't say anything bad."

"Leave 'em alone," Richard said. "Let the young kids have their fun without our commentary." Richard leaned over and kissed Bryce. When he pulled away, he looked at Jordan and me before saying, "Quick. Run while he's still speechless." Richard turned back to Bryce and kissed him some more.

I didn't have to be told twice. I jumped up and practically lifted Jordan off the ground and started pulling him away as I jogged through the field to the main path. Jordan and I exited the area laughing at our harrowing escape.

We started our hike up. We got to the light pole in front of the Central Sanctuary, and I nuzzled Jordan's back against the light pole before pressing my body into his to kiss him. I gripped his face as I traced the outline of his lips with my tongue. Jordan's head bent backward slightly, exposing his Adam's apple, so I took it as an invitation to lick around that area.

I took a sharp intake of breath when Jordan slipped his hand under my shirt and pressed against the small of my back, drawing me closer to him.

"Sorry," he said. "Cold hand?"

"Just a little," I said before nibbling on his ear. I started grinding my erect cock into his stomach. I wanted the clothes to disappear. "We need to run, or I'm going to rip your clothes off and have you on that porch," gesturing with my head to the front of the sanctuary.

"As much fun as that sounds, I want you to myself and not on full display for just any passerby to watch."

He pushed me away. "Last one to the cabin gets fucked!" And darted up the hill.

I didn't need to be told twice. I ran after him. I, however, am not a trained long-distance runner, so our little race was rigged. When I got back to the cabins, Jordan was sitting on his porch, his legs spread wide. "I can't wait to fuck that hot ass of yours."

"Only if I get to return the favor."

He stood up, bounded up the stairs and opened the door with me right on his heels. We didn't even bother with the light. I bumped the door behind us closed with my hip, then kicked off my shoes before launching myself on top of Jordan, who had already made it to the bed. I rested my weight on my forearms with him below me so I could kiss him repeatedly. Before long, I pulled his sweatshirt and T-shirt off and started licking every inch of his torso. I began by licking his clavicle and spent a good five minutes teasing his nipples with my fingers, tongue and teeth. He squirmed beneath me. And his cock responded by getting harder. I licked down his abs, lapping over each of his abdominal muscles.

I lowered myself off the side of the bed and pulled Jordan forward. He sat up. His feet were on the ground, with me kneeling between his legs. He knew what came next. I knew what came next. I gazed up at him and he lowered himself to kiss me before he laid back and rested his head on his arms so he could watch.

Before I popped the button on his shorts, I kissed every inch of his waist. I reached up, grabbed the zipper then pulled it down slowly before gently pushing his pants down around his ankles. Jordan's cock popped straight up out of his boxers without his clothes holding him back.

"Someone's happy to see me." I rested one hand on Jordan's abs while grabbing his balls with my other hand. I teased his cockhead, making sure I licked every part of it. I drew my tongue down the underside of his cock from the frenulum down to his balls. Jordan's breath caught when I flicked my tongue back up in one quick motion before engulfing his entire cock with my mouth. I sucked him down about halfway before I gagged a bit.

Jordan reached up, grabbed the back of my head and shoved his cock down my throat farther and started face-fucking me. The gagging went away as I got into the rhythm. He shoved it down my throat even farther, and I gagged and coughed as he pulled out. My spit dripped off the end.

"One of us has way too much clothing on," Jordan said. He reached down and lifted me until I stood in front of him, then pulled my shirt up and over my head. A second later, a soft thump of fabric hit the floor as my shorts fell.

"We can probably lose these, too," I said, pulling down my boxer briefs, fully freeing my dick. My fat, nine-inch uncut cock looked quite large compared to Jordan's thinner, seven-inch cut one. I knew seven inches going inside my ass would sting like a motherfucker.

"Get on the bed on all fours," Jordan said.

I didn't hesitate, even though I am very much not a bottom. Something about his take-charge attitude made me want him inside me. I wiggled my ass slightly at the edge of the bed. The head of his cock rubbed back and forth over my crack, then poked tentatively at my hole.

"Got lube?" I asked.

"Of course." I heard Jordan walk into the bathroom then return a moment later. I heard the squirting sound of lube before I felt him rubbing cool material against my hole. I took a sharp breath in as a single figure inched into me. I let out a breath and gave into the sensation. Before long, I could sense a second finger joining the first and working in and out of me.

After what seemed like forever, Jordan withdrew his fingers and poked his cock against me. He slowly started to push in.

I thought I was being impaled by a telephone pole. "Holy shit!"

"Just breathe," Jordan encouraged. "Don't fight it. I'm going to leave my cock here for a minute to let you adjust."

He gently ran his hand down my back a few times before he grabbed my hips and shoved every inch of himself inside me. I was rock hard. I could have jerked off with him just resting his cock inside my ass and been perfectly happy. But Jordan dragged out his cock. He almost had all of it out before he shoved forward again. The light slapping sound of his balls connecting with my ass was the only sound besides our breathing.

Before long, Jordan built up steam and was fucking me like a piston on an old railroad. My ass was on fire. "Where do you want me to come?" he asked.

"Wherever—"

I didn't get to finish my sentence before the first wave of Jordan's cum flowed inside me, followed by the second, third, fourth… I lost count of how many thrusts he made with cum flowing into me. When he was done, he pulled out slowly. When the head of his cock exited, I felt empty, like something that belonged inside me had been removed. He flopped down on the bed beside me.

"Don't get any ideas of sleep," I said as I kissed him. "It's my turn. As they say, it's better to give than to receive. And I'm ready to give you everything I've got."

I reached down and, with one fluid motion, flipped Jordan onto his stomach. I scooched him farther up the bed to lie down between his legs. I nudged his legs into a wide V before spreading his ass cheeks with my hands then lowered my tongue into his ass. I darted my tongue in and out of his hole, trying to drive it deeper into him with each thrust. I knew from experience that it took a bit of opening up an ass before a guy could handle both the length and girth of my cock, so I licked one of my fingers before placing it at Jordan's hole. I slowly pushed it in — one knuckle, then two. I let my finger fuck him while I licked his taint. I soon replaced one finger with two, then three.

"Fuck me already!" Jordan practically screamed.

"With pleasure."

I found the bottle of lube on the bed, so I lathered it on myself then coated Jordan's hole before taking a few more minutes to finger him. Once I felt he was loosened enough to take me, I hovered my cock over his hole before slowly letting him feel the head of my cock inside him.

"Holy fuck!" Jordan said. He bucked his hips under me slightly, but I held him in place.

"As you said, breathe. When you're ready, push back. I won't thrust into you until you're ready."

True to my word, I let him adjust for a second before he took me fully into him. We started and stopped a couple of more times until I had my entire cock buried inside him.

"That's it," I said. With my cock in, I pulled him up and spun him around. I wanted to sit with him on my cock to watch him. But first, I wanted to kiss him. I love making out with a guy with my cock sitting up inside them. It has always turned me on—not fucking them, just letting my thick, hard cock sit nestled inside a guy's tight hole as he got used to me being there.

I wrapped my arms around him so he couldn't escape or buck. I wanted to control this fucking. He threw his arms around my neck and kissed me. In that position, I moved my hips slowly into the bed before pulling them back, slowly sliding my cock in and out of him—not the entire way, but just enough to get his ass used to my cock moving back and forth inside.

He looked at me and pushed my torso back before getting onto his feet. He grabbed my hands for leverage as he started riding my cock. His leg muscles lifted him up and down repeatedly. When I came, we both grunted with exhilaration. I shot my first load, and Jordan shot his second.

Now that we were both spent, we curled on the bed, the sheets scattered around us and our sweaty bodies intertwined. For the first time in forever, I had no desire to take a shower or change the sheets. We lay there in our sweaty mess until sleep took us both.

Chapter Eighteen

I lay in bed, not wanting to open my eyes, but my bladder told me it needed me to move soon. I rolled to my back and looked up at the ceiling before glancing around the room. *Where am I?* More awake, I sat up and took in my surroundings. Only then did I realize I was also butt-ass naked. Images of the previous evening started slowly piecing themselves together — getting rescued, hanging by the bonfire and having sex with Jordan.

The flushing sound from the bathroom drew my head in that direction. I reached for the sheets on the bed and raised them to cover my lower half as Jordan sauntered into the room, still naked.

"Hey, good morning, sunshine," Jordan said with a sly smile. "Hope I didn't wake you."

I shook my head, trying not to let my eyes linger too long on the lower half of his body. Seeing his cock dangling there in front of me reminded me of… *That's why my ass hurts.* It was like my body was trying to catch up with everything. The more I considered it, the more the stinging sensation in my ass reminded me of how he'd fucked me from behind.

"It looks like someone's having a good morning," Jordan said, glancing at the tent that had sprung under the sheet.

"Sorry…just remembering last night."

"Well, would love to have round two when you're ready. For now, I'm going to go for my morning run. Want to join me?"

"No thanks. I probably need to get back to my cabin and clean up."

"Suit yourself." Jordan reached into his bag, pulled out a pair of running shorts, bent over and slipped them on. The sight of his ass reminded me of other things we'd done last night, which caused my cock to grow even more. Jordan then sat on the edge of the bed and put on his tennis shoes. Before he left, he crawled over to me and kissed me. He grabbed my dick under the sheet and said, "I can't wait to feel you inside me again." He then patted my stomach, sighed and got off the bed. He was out of the door.

I sat there for a moment. The room reeked of sex. I'm sure I smelled like a brothel myself. I walked into the bathroom and forced myself to take a leak, which was always difficult when trying to do it through a hard-on. Once my bladder was relieved, I came back into the bedroom and searched for my clothes. Most of them were scattered in a tight circle around the bed. I got dressed and slipped out of the cabin.

"Walk of shame, eh?" Chad's voice called from his porch. "It's about fucking time you two hooked up. Avery and I had a bet going on whether you'd do it before the end of the weekend."

I looked at Chad and tried to tamp down my face-splitting grin. With a little shrug, I walked over to my cabin. I took a quick shower, where I jerked off to the memories of last night. Once I was put together, I headed down to the café, not waiting for Jordan to return. I needed some time to process what had happened, and I needed a large cup of coffee to do it. Once I had my coffee, I made my way to the Central Sanctuary. I needed someplace to think.

I walked in and was glad the area was empty. There was still the faint whiff of incense in the air. For the first time, I took in the room's beauty. The domed window ceiling let the morning light flood the place. Along the walls were a range of spiritual sayings from various people who had taught in that room. I didn't recognize any of them, but the pictures and biographies next to the expressions let me know these were probably some of the best minds in the New Age world.

"Good morning," a voice came from behind me.

I spun to see Roodra Rahim standing in the entrance. "Sorry… I was looking for a place to think."

"No need to apologize. That's exactly what I'm doing here. Usually, this place is a ghost town first thing in the morning."

"I'll… I'll leave —"

"This room is large enough for two people to sit in quiet contemplation."

I looked at Roodra, who was wearing shorts, tennis shoes and a polo. If I hadn't seen him before, I'd have assumed he was another camper hanging out for the weekend. Without thinking, I blurted, "What's the deal with the guru-shtick?"

"What do you mean?" Roodra said, acting like he didn't know what I was talking about.

"You know what I mean. I grew up in the South. I've seen a lot of religious leaders. You're like one part televangelist and one part Buddhist mystic."

"Why are you hiding from the world in here?" Roodra countered.

"I'll tell you mine if you tell me yours," I clapped back.

Roodra eyed me for a moment and pointed to a couple of chairs. "Might as well get comfy."

We took our seats and stared at each other for a moment. It was like we were waiting to see who would blink first. Finally, Roodra said, "As you already know, my birth name is Jeremy Smith. And yes, Fin and I dated." I gestured for him to continue. "When I was in my early twenties, I wasn't sure what I was doing with my life. I had just finished law school and was going to set out to work for one of the big firms in the city. After working sixty-to-eighty-hour work weeks, I was burning out quickly. A friend convinced me to take some vacation time, and we went to Burning Man. While I was there, I dropped some shrooms and had a spiritual trip. When I came down, I knew my goal in life had to be to help people not end up like me."

"But why the guru schtick?"

"The 'guru schtick', as you call it, is part reality and part theater. Do I believe what I teach? Yes. But if I came in here dressed like this, people wouldn't take me seriously."

"Really? You think the white toga made people take you seriously?"

"Okay, that may have been over the top, I'll give you that, but it made an impression. People will talk about that little demonstration for years. And maybe, just maybe, a few of them will more deeply explore their own sexuality. If they do, then I was successful."

"What about remote viewing? Come on... Do you believe in that?"

Roodra wrinkled his forehead. I could tell he was trying to plan his answer. "Do I believe there are phenomena that exist in this world that are unexplainable? Most definitely." I was about to say something, but he cut me off and kept going. "Some things that were at once mystical later have scientific justifications. Other things, we still have no good explanations for them. Have I ever accomplished remote viewing? No. Have I witnessed people who have a talent that I can't explain? Yes."

"How can you teach something like that if you can't do it yourself? Why not be honest about that?"

"I know the mechanisms for how it's supposed to work. You probably know how an airplane flies. That doesn't mean you know how to pilot one? And who knows? Someone in that room the other day may have awakened a latent talent they never knew they had."

"But why the assuredness when you're not completely sure yourself?"

"This coming from a surgeon? How often have you acted confident in front of a patient, even though you didn't know what to do?"

"That's different—"

"Really? People want their gurus, whether spiritual or medicinal, to be competent. They want to know that we have their best interests at heart and that we're trustworthy. We both put on shows for the benefit of the people watching."

I wasn't entirely sure I believed his answer. Personally, it sounded like a copout, but I didn't want to contradict the man.

"So, Darrin, what's your story? Why are you hiding in here this morning?"

"I'm not hiding." Roodra inclined his head to the left, narrowed his eyes and gave me a 'who are you kidding' look. "Maybe I am hiding. Long story short. I had sex with a guy last night."

"Who didn't?"

"But I think I may have actual feelings for this guy. I lost my husband last September, and this is the first time I've felt something."

"Ahh...feeling a little widower guilt?"

"If you mean do I feel like I'm stepping on the memory of Chance? Then, yes. I know Chance would want me to keep going and make the best life for myself possible, but it's hard to do when I miss him every day."

"Back up. I'm missing pieces of the story. Do you mind telling me?"

I took a deep breath and told Roodra everything. Honestly, he was a fantastic listener. When I finished telling him, I realized Roodra would have made an excellent therapist.

"My advice..." Roodra started. He formulated what he wanted to say next. "Think of your budding relationship with Jordan as honoring Chance's memory by learning to love again. What better legacy can any of us hope for than spreading love? We live in a fucking scary world. And if any of us can find respite in the chaos of life in the arms of another man, we must embrace those opportunities. I'm not talking about casual sex, though. Sex is simple. Intimacy is hard. What you had last night wasn't just about sex, was it?"

"No. Sure, it was passionate and crazy, but it was like I couldn't bear to wait for Jordan's touch. I had to get to know him…all of him. But—"

"No buts. There will always be buts. And as a top, I should know. There are thousands of 'butts' out there, no pun intended. If you get the chance to love—even if it's just a passing chance—never pass it by. Our lives are too short to pass on love."

We sat in silence for a few minutes. Despite my misgivings about Roodra, he had a lot of insights into the human psyche, which I guess made his line of work a little easier. Roodra glanced down at his watch.

"Are you going ziplining? We're supposed to be at the vans like ten minutes ago."

"Oh yeah, I totally forgot about that."

"Well then, we best get our butts out there and hope the last van hasn't left yet."

We walked over to the parking lot. Both of us were comfortable in the silence. A van passed by on the road before we crossed into the parking lot.

I recognized most of the guys in the group boarding the last van.

"Guess we're just in time," I said to Roodra. "Thanks for the conversation."

"Any time." Roodra walked over to his two acolytes, who were dressed for the excursion.

Avery and Chad stood off to the side. I think it was the first time I had seen both dressed since we'd gotten there. I walked over and said, "Good morning." Avery smiled at me knowingly. "Yes, I got laid last night."

"I know. Honestly, I think the whole camp knows," Avery said. "It's about fucking time, too."

I rolled my eyes but couldn't help myself from smiling. Only then did I realize Avery and Chad were holding hands. *Interesting.*

"Have either of you seen Jordan?"

"He was on the van that just left. He was looking for you, too, but wasn't sure if you were going ziplining. He said you hadn't shown up for breakfast."

Jordan

I got down to the dining hall in time to scarf down some food before I needed to get to the van for the ziplining excursion. I kept hoping I'd see Darrin but figured I'd missed him. Part of me had hoped he'd still be naked in bed waiting for me when I got back from my morning run, but I couldn't say I was too surprised when I returned to an empty cabin.

I made my way to the parking lot and found a bunch of guys already milling around. I poked my way through the crowd until I got to Bryce and Richard.

"Good morning," Bryce said as I approached. "Did you wear Darrin out last night?"

"Bryce!" Richard chastised.

The joy inside me probably beamed outward through my smile. I didn't care who knew that Darrin and I had absolutely mind-blowing sex last night.

"I haven't seen him since I left the cabin this morning."

"I'm betting Darrin needed some alone time," Richard said. "Darrin may be processing. He tends to need solitude occasionally. Having sex with someone he has feelings for isn't something he's done in a while."

I nodded my head in understanding. Before long, we boarded the van. Most of the guys in ours were people

I recognized. Finlay was there and so were Owen and Isaac. I wasn't sure how that would work, but apparently, the Catskills Zip Tours were accessible.

"We should be at Overlook Mountain in about fifteen minutes," the van driver said.

I looked out of the window as we pulled away from the parking lot. Across the street, Roodra and Darrin stood there looking pretty chummy.

"Looks like Roodra got his hooks into another minion," Finlay said behind me.

I crossed my arms and tried to get images of Roodra, his minions and Darrin having an orgy out of my head.

"I'm sure there's a logical explanation," Richard said, leaning toward me. "Don't let Finlay's past with Roodra color your judgment of Darrin."

"Thanks," I said. Richard was probably right, but a pang of jealousy still struck me.

I leaned back and closed my eyes. The guys around me got more excited at the prospect of ziplining, but I sat there in a bit of a pouty funk.

The van pulled up at Catskills Zip Tours and we all piled out.

"Good morning, Namast-Gay," the tour guide said as we huddled around him. "We're excited to have you here this morning. My name is Chip, and I'll be your tour guide. I see that we have one tourist who needs a little help on the trail," acknowledging Isaac. "Don't worry. We are one-hundred percent accessible. We're ready to accommodate a broad range of needs here."

Chip then ran through a series of safety protocols. Then he showed how the zipline harnesses worked. I had to admit that Chip was fucking gorgeous. He had a down-to-earthy, woodsy feel. The stubble around his face made my dick twitch. Before long, the group was outfitted with harnesses, helmets and GoPro cameras to capture our adventures.

An ATV showed up to haul Isaac up the mountain. The rest of us hiked up a nature trail to the first zip.

"How long have you worked here?" I asked Chip as I matched his stride.

"This will be my third summer up here. I'm a student over at Bard."

"Where are you from originally?" I asked.

"Poughkeepsie, so I didn't get very far."

"I know that feeling. I grew up in Woodstock."

"Ahh, so you're not one of the citidiots," Chip said.

"Nope. Total local."

"How'd you end up with this lot?"

"I'd heard about Namast-Gay, and it sounded like fun."

"Who knows, maybe I'll join you guys next year. It looks like an entertaining bunch."

Thank God, my gaydar isn't broken. I smiled at Chip. Chip was the perfect guy — gorgeous, outdoorsy and from the area. He was the antithesis of Darrin.

"Where do you live now?" I asked casually.

"I'm over in Palevile. Maybe we should hang out sometime since we're both local."

"Could be fun. We could go hiking or climb the Gunks."

"Definitely," Chip said, drawing out the word. "Do you climb often?"

"Not really. I've been a couple of times with friends, but I'm not much of a rock climber."

"Well, if I'm not up here working, I'm usually over at the Gunks, so I could definitely show you around the cliffside."

Up ahead, I saw the first staging platform. Isaac and Owen were already there waiting for us.

When Chip and I climbed up to the platform, Isaac said, "Took you long enough," with a big grin. "I was wondering if you got lost in the woods like Darrin. Too soon?"

I didn't have a witty comeback, so I stuck my tongue out at him. *Real mature.* The rest of our group made it there, too.

Chip huddled the group and said, "That was the end of our hiking for the day. Everything else is downhill from here." He broke out into the safety protocols again. "Remember... If you get stuck on a line, don't freak out. I'll climb out and drag you in. It happens from time to time. There's nothing to worry about."

We then lined up. The guide who had brought Isaac and Owen to the top zipped across first to help everyone on the next platform. First up was Isaac, who screamed the word 'fuck' as he flew through the air, which caused the entire group to bust out laughing.

I hung back and was the last one to go. Chip checked my gear, strapped me to the zipline and said, "You're good." I took the leap of faith and stepped out into the open air as I suddenly was flying. The wind rushed around my face, and I burst into a giggle fit. The sensation of soaring over the trees made me feel like Superman. The end of the zipline approached and I pulled on the break as we'd been instructed. I slowed smoothly and stood on the wooden planks with no problems. The guide unhooked me and pointed to the other side of the platform, where the next zipline waited for us. I heard Chip land behind me. The next time, Chip went first, so I volunteered to go after Isaac and Owen. The tour contained seven ziplines, so we were off and running.

Chip went first again on the sixth platform, and I followed Isaac and Owen. I was getting to the end of the run, and I slowed down. About twenty yards from the platform, I came to a complete stop.

"Just give me a second," Chip yelled.

"I'm not going anywhere," I yelled back, hanging in midair.

Chip hooked his harness to the zipline, then pulled himself up onto the steel cord. He wrapped his ankles around the line and pulled himself out to my location. When he got to me, he hooked a D-ring to my harness and dragged my ass back to the platform. I had to admit, the view of Chip's ass and his muscled arms pulling me to the platform was as lovely as the mountain scenery around me.

"What happened?" I asked when we got to the platform.

"Gravity, probably.

It happens. Or you just wanted me to save you." Chip winked at me before turning to help the rest of our group land safely.

"If I had known I'd get a show like the one you just got, I would have pulled the break early on every line," Isaac said. "I'm kind of jealous."

"What did he say caused it?" Owen asked.

"Gravity."

"Must be that runner's body of yours. You need a little more meat on your bones," Isaac said as he flexed his biceps.

The rest of the group got to the platform, and we took off for our last trek down the zipline.

Chip once again was going to be the last man down, so I waited. We casually talked while he waited for each camper to make it to the other end. When I was the last one there, he said, "Ready to go?"

"Of course."

"When we get to the bottom, we should totally exchange information."

"I would like that."

Chip double-checked my harness, and I took my leap of faith. I enjoyed the last seconds of mountain scenery and the amazing sensation of flying through the sky.

I neared the other platform and pulled on the brake. Nothing happened. I pulled on it harder. The other guide yelled at me to slow down.

I screamed.

Chapter Nineteen

Darrin

We boarded the van a few minutes after Roodra and I got there. I was introduced to his two minions, err...boyfriends? Honestly, I wasn't entirely sure what they were. Standing around waiting to board, I had found out they were a throuple, and their names were Asher and Baron. Just listening to Asher and Baron for a couple of minutes, I could tell they were trust fund babies.

I sat in a row with Avery and Chad, of all people. The happy throuple were all cozy on the bench behind us. I stared out of the window as we pulled out of the parking lot. Jaxson sat in the passenger seat and Mano sat in the row behind him with a couple of older guys I'd never seen before. A group of four skinny twinks I hadn't met were crammed into the back row together. We had the fifteen-passenger van at its limit.

I looked back to ask Roodra a question and found Avery and Chad making out on the seat beside me.

Avery's eyes were open and met mine. He pulled away abruptly from Chad.

"What's wrong?" Chad asked.

"We have an audience," Avery said.

Chad turned to look at me. I just smiled.

"Oh, yeah. Sorry about that. Forgot you were there." I tilted my head. "When I'm with Avery, I seem to forget about everything else around me. I'm glad we met."

"Me, too," Avery said. "He's a keeper." Avery threw his arm around Chad and drew him in.

"We totally have the same outlook on life," Chad said.

What? Fuck half the population before you die? I kept the snarky comment to myself. "I'm glad you two found each other. I hope you're happy."

"Don't worry, Darrin. I can still come by for our little get-togethers when you're on Grindr."

"Thanks. But if things work out with Jordan, I hope to not need your help anymore."

"You never know," Roodra said, leaning between Chad and me. "You might find that you like having a second boyfriend. They have their benefits."

"I think I'm a one guy kind of man. Trust me... I could barely keep up with my husband, and I can already tell Jordan's going to give me a run for my money."

"Don't knock it till you've tried it," one of Roodra's boyfriends said. I couldn't remember if it was Asher or Baron who was speaking. They both kind of looked alike to me. "I would never have guessed I would end up in a three-way relationship with men. Until I met Roodra, I was a straight stockbroker working on Wall Street. I got fired during one of the massive bank layoffs. I was going throw myself off the pier into the Hudson River down at Battery Park." *I wonder if he realizes people can survive a jump from a pier?* I smiled and nodded my head. "Roodra spotted me and started talking to me. The next thing I knew, I had broken down into tears and Roodra was taking me back to his place to meet his boyfriend. I had nowhere else to go, so Roodra took me in. Here I am two years later. I have a new family and a better job than before."

"And it's more than just sex," Roodra's minion number two said. *I should pay attention to names more.* "I know some people think we're a sex cult with Roodra as our leader. It's not. Roodra helped both of us realize that we have more to offer the world than sex. I was a sex addict party boy when Roodra met me." From what I'd seen and heard this weekend, the man was probably still a sex addict, but I kept my mouth shut. My mother would be so proud of my newly learned ability not to say whatever the fuck I'm thinking. "We think all three of our souls have had relationships in past lives. It wasn't until Roodra found us that our souls finally became complete again."

I didn't have to respond to that one because the van slowed as it took a turnoff. I read the painted sign 'Catskills Zip Tours' as we pulled into the parking lot. When the van stopped, Jaxson hopped out of the passenger seat and opened the door for those of us sitting in the back. We didn't waste any time piling out.

"Hello, everyone, and welcome to Catskills Zip Tours," a woman with short-cropped black hair said. "We're happy to have our last group of Namast-Gay campers join us today. My name is Trish, and Brian and I will be your guides. Brian will meet us up at the top. Let's get started by discussing a few safety issues."

"Hey, look! It's Isaac!" either Asher or Baron said.

We watched as Isaac screamed his little head off, flying down the hill before landing smoothly. A good-looking guy helped him down and sat him on a bench on the platform.

"Sorry about that," Mano said to Trish. "That's some of our group."

"No problem. We can watch the group zip down before I continue. It happens all the time with larger groups that are broken up."

We watched as the rest of the group zipped and zipped. Owen, Bryce and Richard landed successfully on the platform. And there he was, flying over the world, looking like he was having the time of his life. I wished I could see Jordan's hair blowing in the breeze, but his bright orange helmet stopped that from happening.

Jordan screamed before I had a chance to realize something was wrong. *He's not slowing down!* I watched in horror as the guide on the platform dove out of Jordan's way before Jordan smashed into the tree supporting the platform. I didn't think. I just ran.

I took off toward the tree, hoping to find the stairs up to the platform. A group of people pooled at the bottom outside the fenced-off area. I pushed my way through them and jumped the turnstile.

"You can't go up there," someone else yelled after me.

Thankfully, someone from the camp said, "He's a doctor, and I think that's his boyfriend."

I made it to the platform. Another Zip guy tried to get in my way, but Bryce barked, "Let him through. I need him."

"I'm going to take off his helmet," some Zip guy said, kneeling near Jordan.

"Don't you fucking dare," Bryce said.

"What do we have?" I said, taking a deep calming breath and putting on my game face.

"Stabilize his neck. He has multiple leg fractures."

I looked down Jordan's body. A bone protruded from the skin on Jordan's left leg. I froze. I couldn't look away from Jordan's blood on Bryce's hands. *Get it the fuck together! He's not Chance. You're a trauma surgeon, for crying out loud. Do your fucking job.* I looked away from Jordan's leg and focused on stabilizing his neck.

"Let them do what they do best," Richard said, pulling the Zip guy up. I looked over and read his name tag, '*Chip.*'

"Thanks, Chip. I work with Bryce. We have the scene until the EMTs get here."

"It's all my fault. If I hadn't been flirting with him, I should have known something was wrong when he got stuck the first time."

"Get him out of here," I said calmly to Richard.

He nodded and got Chip off the platform before he did anything else to Jordan by accident. I looked down at my patient and immediately ran through the stabilization protocol. I conducted an initial analysis of Jordan's throat. There was no discoloration or open wounds.

"Gloves?" I asked. A guy with the Zip people handed me a box of latex gloves. I expertly donned them before checking Jordan's neck. His trachea was fine, which was a good sign as far as I could tell. I lowered his jaw and ran my finger around the inside of his gum to make sure there was no bleeding or loose teeth. "We need rolled-up towels," I said.

I heard someone bark an order.

I focused on Jordan's breathing. His breaths were shallow, but it didn't look like there was an obstruction. I palpated Jordan's neck, evaluating him for a possible hematoma, a pulsatile mass or subcutaneous emphysema.

"I think we're good on my end," I told Bryce.

"How are things down there?"

"I'm applying pressure. He's lost a lot of blood. Not sure if you saw the break."

"I did."

"Then you know it's bad."

A zipline worker arrived with more bandages, towels and ice packs. Bryce took the bandages and icepacks, and I took the towels, rolled them up and placed them on either side of Jordan's neck to prevent it from moving. The last thing we wanted was more trauma, because we didn't have a scan.

In the distance, I heard the siren.

"Do we need to switch?" I asked Bryce.

"I'm fine. Go get the EMTs."

I ran down the stairs and jumped over the turnstile again.

Roodra stood in the crowd and asked, "How bad is it?"

"Bad," was all I said as I ran up to the ambulance as it pulled in. The EMT was barely out of the passenger seat when I started barking orders. "We have a high-velocity trauma to the left side of the victim's body. Possible spinal injury. The victim has a comminuted open fracture on the left side." The EMTs grabbed the stretcher and started wheeling it toward the entrance. "Follow me," I snapped and the EMTs fell into step behind me. "Clear a path," I yelled as we neared the group of onlookers.

We got the EMTs up the stairs quickly. Bryce and I helped transfer Jordan to the stretcher, then helped the EMTs lower Jordan's body. I kept looking down at Jordan's unresponsive form. I wanted to scream. *Keep your head in the game. I can freak out later.*

Once we transferred the backboard to the stretcher, we exited via an open gate. To the left of the turnstile, Bryce talked to one of the EMTs about Jordan's leg, and I told the other about Jordan's possible neck and back trauma.

Finally, the EMT I talked to asked, "Who are you guys?"

"Yeah, sorry about that. He's the chief of emergency medicine at an ED in the city, and I'm one of his trauma surgeons."

"This guy must be special to have two ED docs on hand."

"He is," I said.

We helped the EMTs lift Jordan into the ambulance and let the EMTs strap in the stretcher before I climbed in after him.

"I'm going with them," I told Bryce.

"We'll find out where you're going and meet you there," Bryce told me as the back ambulance doors shut.

The EMT hooked Jordan up to a set of monitors. I watched Jordan's EKG and oxygen levels and was glad to see they both looked normal.

"How can I help?" I asked the EMT.

"Just stay out of my way. I got it from here, doc."

I reached down and grabbed Jordan's right hand and watched as the EMT inspected our triage.

I let myself cry.

Jordan

Every inch of my body hurt. Even though I wanted to open my eyes, they were weighed down in pain. I convinced them to open halfway. My left leg hung from a suspension in a cast. *That can't be good.*

I tried to talk, but my mouth was dry, so only a strange sound came out.

"Drink," someone said, "slowly."

A white straw was pressed between my lips, and I sucked in some water.

"Where am I?" I asked, pushing the straw out of my mouth.

A light flashed into my eyes. "Follow my finger," the voice said. I did as he'd commanded.

"You're in Kingston. You had an accident."

My eyes focused and I recognized Cody Benton staring down at me.

"Hey, Cody," I scratched out.

"Let me get your doctor."

A couple of minutes later, Darrin walked into the room. He was wearing a pair of blue scrubs. "Who let you in here?" I joked.

"I got emergency privileges when I came in with you. I wasn't about to turn over your care to anyone else."

"What happened? I don't know."

He walked around to the right side of my bed and grabbed my hand. "What was the last thing you remember?"

His touch. I remember how he touched me. "Last night," I said with a wolfish grin. "I remember us…together."

"Don't freak out, but that was two days ago."

"What?" I barely got the word out as a sharp pain from my leg shot through my entire body.

Darrin pressed a button into my hand. "When you feel pain, push this button. Don't overdo it, but don't hesitate if you feel pain. Got it?"

"Yeah."

"You had a compound fracture. The orthopedic surgeons here are damn impressive. You were ziplining and something happened to your harness. You slammed into a tree. You were probably going somewhere between thirty to forty miles-per-hour on impact. From what Bryce told me, you kicked out with your left leg to brace yourself, which is why your bone shattered in multiple places."

"That explains that," I said, gesturing to my foot raised in the air. "It's bad, isn't it?"

"It will take some time and physical therapy to get you back to normal." Darrin then uttered a series of medical words that I don't remember hearing in my biology one-hundred class in college.

"Just kiss me," I said.

Darrin smiled, bent over and pressed his smooth lips against mine. He was hesitant at first. I pulled away and said, "I'm not that fragile." I reached up and pulled his head into mine. *How wretched must my breath be?* But despite the horribleness of my mouth, Darrin didn't pull away.

"Knock, knock," Talgat sang as he knocked on the hospital room's door frame.

"Come in," I said as Dale pulled back the curtain.

"You're supposed to wait a second before letting them know we're here, or the ruse doesn't work," Talgat said. He looked down at me and asked, "How's the patient?"

"Yeah, we totally caught you two making out, but Talgat didn't want to interrupt, so he thought his knocking ruse would help," Dale said. "I'm glad you're awake. Took you long enough."

"Darrin, meet my bosses—"

"We've met," Darrin said. "I've actually spent the night at their place."

"You did?" Jordan asked.

"Bryce, Richard and Owen had to get back to work. I'm still technically on vacation, so I stuck around. Dale and Talgat were kind enough to loan me their guest room."

"Please," Dale said. "Don't let him fool you. I think he's been there twice to shower and take a catnap before hopping back into his car and driving like *Speed Racer* to get back down here. We've practically had to pry him away from your bedside."

"I'm going to go check on getting you something to eat," Darrin said. "I'll be right back."

Darrin nodded his head at Dale and Talgat as he exited the room.

"Look at you," Dale said, coming over to lay a hand on my shoulder. "Found yourself a doctor, and you only had to break a leg to do it. I practically had to get mauled by a bear to find my farmer." He flashed his eyebrows as he smirked down at me.

"Don't listen to him. Sometimes, I wish the bear would have gotten to you first," Talgat joked. He turned and looked at me and added, "Just know, Darrin seems like a keeper."

"I think so, too," I admitted.

"Hurry and get better," Dale said. "I don't know how we'll manage the farm all summer without you."

"Sorry about that."

"Ignore him," Talgat said. "We want you to be healthy."

"And don't worry, your insurance is pretty fucking great," Dale said. "I'm glad I took out those policies on all my workers. Your expenses and rehab are totally covered. And you can either do your rehab up here or in the city. Let's say…your doctor friend has talked about getting you into someplace near him in the city — if that's something you'd want."

Sounded like fun, but I didn't know what I wanted right then. I would be in the hospital for a little longer before I needed to decide that.

Before long, Darrin came back into the room with what I guess was dinner. We sat around while I ate. Mostly, I felt okay. I hit my pain button twice, but it didn't make me feel like I was drugged.

"Non-hospital people, my patient needs his rest, which means all of you need to get out. That includes you, Darrin," Cody said, breezing into the room. Darrin started to protest. "He's awake. He needs sleep. *You* need sleep. You need to go back to Dale and Talgat's and get rest. I don't want to see you in here for at least eight hours. Is that understood, mister?"

"Wow, I never knew Cody was such a pushy bottom," Dale joked.

From the glint in Cody's eyes, I could tell that he had a comeback on the tip of his tongue, but he didn't say anything. He looked at Dale and said, "Out."

Once Dale, Darrin and Talgat had left, Cody checked back in on me.

"Okay, you," he started, "we're adding a mild sedative to help you sleep through the night. Currently, your body is healing. You need your rest. If you need anything, you push that buzzer."

"What if I need to pee?"

"I guess you didn't notice the catheter yet," Cody said. He lifted a bag of yellow fluid up to show me before replacing it with an empty one. "Now, please heal quickly. I don't think I can put up with Darrin in my hospital much longer."

"Yeah, he's definitely an alpha male when he wants to be."

"I'm sure your ass likes it like that," Cody joked.

"Oh, don't you know? Alphas are the first to bend over in the bedroom."

Cody laughed all the way out of the room. He turned off the lights, and there was a soft click of the door shutting behind him.

I breathed in and out. In minutes, I was in blissful sleep.

Chapter Twenty

Darrin

I looked up ahead, took the turnoff of Interstate 87 toward Kingston and continued the roundabout until my new Nissan Rogue was pointed toward Woodstock. My iPhone was playing whatever playlist Jordan had curated for us. I was pretty good with anything he wanted to play, as long as it didn't have country music or death metal.

"It feels weird being back up here," Jordan said as he gazed out of the window.

"Well, it's been a few months of rest, relaxation and physical therapy down in the city."

"Again, I can't thank you enough for getting me into rehab with Daria. I googled her. Did you know she has a waiting list of clients a mile long trying to get in with her?"

I ignored the question. "I saved her sister's life, and we became friends. She jumped at the opportunity to pay me back, even a little bit." I reached over and grabbed Jordan's hand.

The past three months had been crazy. Once Jordan had been well enough to transport, I had him moved to my place in the city. At first, Daria had come over every day to work with him. Eventually, she had only needed to come over three times a week. Once we had gotten him mobile, he went to her office to continue rebuilding flexibility, mobility and strength in his leg. Jordan had bounced back much faster than expected, and he was ready to show off his new bionic leg—as we called it—at Dale and Talgat's wedding.

I pulled into the small bed and breakfast we'd found online, The Serenity Inn. The old Victorian looked like it had in their 3D walkthrough of the place. It was run by an older gay couple who had worn matching knitted sweaters on their website. I wondered if they'd be wearing matching outfits today. *Fingers crossed!*

I grabbed our luggage from the trunk. "You don't need to carry mine," Jordan said.

"Daria said you're still not to bear any extra weight. That includes luggage."

"It's maybe ten pounds."

"No extra weight means no extra weight. Now, up those stairs." I gestured toward the stairs, and Jordan rolled his entire head, not just his eyes, to show me he thought I was being a bit too insane about his rehab.

"Welcome!" one of the proprietors of the B&B said as he opened the door for us. "I'm Tom. Charlie is around here somewhere. You must be Darrin and Jordan."

"That we are. How'd you guess?"

"You're our only guests this weekend. We do more business in the fall during leaf season and the winter when people want a cozy getaway. Early August isn't our busiest time."

"Well, we're glad to be here," Jordan said.

We checked in, and Charlie showed up at some point. I almost squealed when he was wearing the same polo shirt as Tom, just in a different color. I found the idea of matching outfits both disgusting and cute. Talk about weird relationship goals.

We were staying in the master suite on the second floor, so I schlepped the luggage upstairs and Jordan followed me, complaining the whole time that he could carry something. Once we were in the room, it was time for quick showers and a change of clothes before we needed to head off to the wedding.

Jordan ran through the shower first because it would take him a bit more time to get ready. His leg was doing better, but it was still finicky, depending on the day and the hour. With Jordan showered, I ran through the hot water as rapidly as possible. The shower was much larger than I had imagined. There was a bench that sat on one side of the wall. A giant waterfall shower head in the middle with three different spray jets coming at you from various angles. You could control everything from a built-in touchscreen monitor. Tom and Charlie had clearly spared no expense when they'd remodeled this place.

Once I was squeaky clean, I headed into the bedroom with a towel wrapped snuggly around my waist. Jordan stared at himself in the mirror, trying to figure out how to tie his bowtie. He'd downloaded an app that was supposed to walk you through the process step-by-step, but the tie was clearly not wanting to cooperate.

"Let me," I said.

I walked up behind him and did my best not to let my still-glistening torso touch the back of his starched white tuxedo-shirt. I made quick work of the bowtie. I'd had to go to enough black- and white-tie events that I'd gotten pretty good at bow ties over the years. I amazed myself at how easy it was to get Jordan's bowtie fixed.

"I got you a little something," I said. Walking over to my bag, I pulled out a light blue box. There was a sudden look of shock on Jordan's face. "Don't worry. It's not a ring. I don't think we're there yet. But I wanted to mark this occasion—"

"You didn't—"

"I know. But I wanted to." I handed him the box and he opened it to find a pair of gold cufflinks I'd had engraved with his initials.

"Wow. These are gorgeous."

"I wanted the most gorgeous man in the world to have something special. Let me put them on you." I showed Jordan how cufflinks work since this was his first experience in a tux outside of prom.

Once he was ready, I threw on my tux. Where Jordan's was more traditional, I had a tuxedo suit. It was a steel-blue suit with black satin trim. I made quick work of my necktie. "Can you help me with my cufflinks?"

"Sure." Jordan walked over and helped me secure my double cuff. "When did you get these?"

"They were a present from my parents when I graduated from medical school. I only pull them out on special occasions." I did one more look in the mirror. We made a fucking gorgeous couple. I reached over and grabbed his face with both my hands and kissed Jordan's tender lips.

"What was that for?" he asked when we separated.

"Just because I can." I could tell that I was grinning like a kid who had been told he could buy anything he wanted in the candy shop.

"If I had my way, I'd be ripping that tux off you in nothing flat," Jordan said. The glint of sexual arousal beaming off his face.

"Likewise. But we must get moving. Grab your coat." I'd already told Jordan not to put on his coat until we got to the Devereux Farm. There was no need to wrinkle the coat while we're in the car.

We left our room and headed out of the B&B. A loud whistle caused me to spin my head in its direction. Tom and Charlie were on the front porch with a pitcher of lemonade sitting between them. "You two make one mighty handsome pair," Tom said. "Now get going. Have fun at that wedding of yours."

"We will," I said. "Trust me. We will."

I pulled out the keys and opened the car. I hung my coat on the hook behind the driver's side and Jordan did the same with his on the passenger side. I got into the driver's seat, started the vehicle and blasted the air conditioning. I put the car in reverse and pointed us in the farm's direction.

Jordan navigated, and we found ourselves at the Devereux Farm in minutes. The farm looked amazing. A giant white tent had been erected right in front of the barn. We drove a little past it to a massive parking lot. I found a space, parked and we got out. I reached into the back, grabbed my coat and slipped it on. I glanced over and found Jordan doing the same.

"Ready?" I asked.

"Let's do this. I hope we don't outshine the grooms."

We walked to the front and were immediately accosted by a young woman. "It's about time you got here," she glanced at her watch. "You're supposed to be here in ten minutes."

I cocked my head in confusion, but Jordan chuckled. "Ayala, this Darrin. Darrin, this is Ayala. She's turned into the mistress of ceremonies. And according to my watch, we're early."

"One person's early is another person's late," Ayla countered.

"What does that even mean?" Jordan asked. "Take a breath. It's all going to go fine today. You've got this under control, I'm sure."

"Well, I'm freaking out a little," she admitted. "Since you couldn't make it last night to the rehearsal, I've been a little stressed."

"Sorry about that," I said. "That was totally my fault. I had a charity dinner—"

"No offense, boyfriend. I don't care. I'm glad you're here. You," she said, looking at Jordan, "go to the administration building." She then turned to me. "As for you, you can go into the tent, and someone will seat you."

I kissed Jordan goodbye and did as I'd been told. Something told me that today was not the day to cross Ayala Kudaibergen.

I walked beneath the white canopy and was greeted by an usher who asked me if I was on "Team Dale or Team Talgat."

"I'm on Team Jordan," I said.

"Team Talgat it is," the usher said, leading me to a row and sitting me next to a couple of twinks before handing me a folded sheet of paper with a picture of Dale and Talgat on the cover.

The young guys nodded politely as I sat. I opened the program and started to read the order of the afternoon's service.

"How do you know Talgat?" one twink asked me.

"I don't," I admitted. "I'm dating one of his groomsmen."

"Well, we know it's not Rasul, so you must be Jordan's new boyfriend."

"Well...yeah... I guess that's me," I stammered. I turned my head and looked at the couple for the first time.

The other twink said, "It's a small town. Everyone knows everyone's business around here." He extended his hand saying, "Dylan Holland. And this is my friend Wes Phelps. He's dating one of the groomsmen on Dale's side."

I shook both of their hands, saying, "Darrin Betancourt. It's nice to meet you both."

"We met once back in May, I think," Wes said as we shook hands. "Jordan and you came into the coffee shop I work in for dinner."

"Oh, that's right. Wow, that's been a while."

"So, I hear you saved Jordan's life," Wes said. "That's one way to land a boyfriend."

"Hey, you're the last one to talk about how they landed their boyfriend," Dylan joked back. I didn't ask, but I could tell there was a story behind that statement, because Wes blushed.

"I also heard that you saved Phil Tucker's life," Wes said, clearly trying to steer the attention away from him and his dating life.

"Phil?"

"The pharmacist?" Wes asked.

"Oh, yeah. Wow, I forgot about that."

"You save so many lives that you forget about them?" Dylan asked.

"I work in an emergency department down in the city. Saving lives kind of comes with the territory."

"Interesting," Dylan responded. "But I bet you don't take most of the guys you save home with you."

"Wow, word gets around in this town."

"It's small," Wes said. "And the gays love to gossip."

The string quartet started, and the groomsmen walked down the aisle to Etta James's *At Last*. Jordan beamed at me as he walked by.

Once the four groomsmen were in place. Wes leaned over and said, "The older guy? That's my boyfriend, Roger. The one next to him is Greyson something or other, Dale's best friend."

"That would make the other guy standing with Jordan, Rasul?" I questioned.

"Yep. That's him."

The string quartet switched to an interesting arrangement of Lady Gaga's *Bad Romance*.

"That was Dale's idea," Wes told me. "After Talgat and him binged *Bridgerton*, he had to have that to walk down the aisle."

Jordan

My leg was getting tired, but I stood there like a good little soldier. I sort of half-listened to the minister and half-watched Darrin in the back. He was sitting with Wes and Dylan, who I'm sure were keeping him entertained.

"By the power vested in me by the State of New York and the Universal Life Church, I now pronounce you husbands in the eyes of God and man. Please share with us your first kiss as a married couple."

Dale grabbed Talgat's head and laid one of the sloppiest, most over-the-top kisses on his new husband I think I'd ever seen. I could tell that Dale had been planning that one. When he pulled away, the smirk on his face told me he knew there would be hell to pay later for it.

After the hooting, hollering and laughter died down, the minister said, "The couple would now ask you to move into the barn for the reception."

After the ceremony, the wedding party hung around for a few more minutes taking pictures. Darrin stayed in his seat and waited for me. There were pictures of the grooms together, photos of Dale with Greyson and Roger, then pictures with Talgat, Rasul and me. I wondered if the photographer would ever run out of memory on his camera. He'd taken what seemed like thousands of pictures.

"Listen up," Ayala said, cutting through the chitchat going on in the tent. "We're now going to make our way over to the reception. You are all sitting at the front table. The groomsmen and their dates will walk in first. They will be followed by Dale and Talgat. Don't sit until everyone is in there. Any questions?" Hearing none, she said, "Let's do this."

I grabbed Darrin and stood behind Rasul and some girl I hadn't met yet. We then were led like an army going off to war by Ayala. People applauded as we walked into the barn. We did exactly as we had been instructed. When Dale and Talgat entered, everyone stood and clapped even louder as they walked to the front table.

Once they were there, Dale immediately grabbed Talgat's hand, and the married couple sat down. Those at the front table then sat, and soon everyone else in the room was sitting. As if on cue, the wedding caterers started delivering our meals.

Dinner was a lot of fun. Once things started to wrap up, it was time for the speeches. Rasul toasted his brother, and Greyson toasted Dale. The rest of the evening was a haze of partying and dancing.

I had a bit too much to drink, but Darrin was right at my side the entire night.

"How's your leg? Are you okay? Are you doing too much?"

"I'm okay at the moment. I may regret it in the morning, though."

"We'll ice your leg when we get back to the B&B."

"Yes, Doctor," I said with a sly smile. I gave Darrin a hard time about his doctoring, but I secretly loved how he took care of me. Darrin was about to say something else, but I grabbed him by the neck and drew him in for a kiss.

We danced, drank and ate until the wee morning hours. By the time Darrin rolled me back into our room at the B&B, I was exhausted and ready for a good night's sleep. I wanted to remove Darrin's tux slowly and have my way with him, but I was just too exhausted. From the looks of things, Darrin was on the same page.

"You know, we should totally take a shower together in the morning. That thing has plenty of room for both of us," Darrin said as he slipped out of his pants.

"You, me and a small football team." I undid my bowtie and did my best to hang my new tux on its hangers neatly as I stripped. Before long, I was in my boxers, and Darrin was in his boxer briefs. We both ran through the bathroom then collapsed on the bed. I took the little spoon position and wrapped Darrin's arm around my stomach while holding his hand.

"Do you miss it up here?" Darrin asked as he kissed the back of my neck.

"I miss the people, but I also enjoy what we're building in the city. And besides, it's not like Woodstock is in another country."

"True."

"And I'm going to be at NYU for the next two years, so we'll see where life takes us. Dale has already told me I can get a job in the corporate office in Manhattan at any time. I promised to come up on the weekends in the fall to help with the masses of apple pickers. I can catch the bus Dale will charter in the morning and take the last one back, so I won't even need to rent a car or have you drive me up here."

"You know, I'd drive you up here anytime," Darrin countered.

"I know you would." I squeezed his hand. "I don't want to be a burden on you. That's not who I am."

"You're not a burden. You'll *never* be a burden." Darrin kissed the back of my neck again. And if I wasn't exhausted, I would have flipped around and started making out with him. "You know, I could see myself working in a small town like this one day. I never planned on dying in New York City."

"Really?"

"There's something nice and peaceful about life up here. I could always keep the house in the city and get an apartment or another house up here. Many people I know do that."

"Ah, yes, the weekenders," I said. "Sorry. It's weird to think I may become a weekender one day."

"I don't think you could ever be—what do you call them—a citidiot."

"God, I hope not," I said with a chuckle. "If that happens, take me to the farm…stat!"

With that, I snuggled a little closer to Darrin. I knew the moment he'd fallen asleep because his breathing changed. I lay there for a few more minutes, realizing how ridiculously happy I was in that moment. I didn't know what the future held. But for that moment, life couldn't have been more perfect.

Want to see more from this author?
Here's a taster for you to enjoy!

Up on the Farm:
Catching the Composer
Jason Wrench

Coming May 2023

Excerpt

I looked around my studio apartment again to ensure I wasn't missing anything. *Cell phone charger? Check. Laptop? Check. Clothes? Check. Toiletry bag? Check.* I couldn't think of anything else I'd need for a weekend in the country. My wrist buzzed. Glancing down at my smart watch, I saw it was my business partner calling, so I grabbed my cell out of my pocket. I call her a business partner, but she's my librettist slash lyricist. I'm a musical theater composer.

"Good morning, Janice," I said into the phone. "Only have a minute. I'm finishing up packing for my weekend getaway."

"Morning, Stephen. I totally forgot this was your weekend up in Woodstock with Kenya. Going to get all hippy on me?"

"Don't worry. I don't plan on coming back Monday singing the lyrics from *Hair*. So, what's up?"

"I wanted to find out when I should expect new pages from you." She said it like a statement, but I could tell there was a different question behind it. *"Have you actually written anything yet?"*

"I promise to have new music for you by the end of next week… I *promise*."

"I'm holding you to that. Anyway, have fun in hippy land."

"I'll try." I hit the call button. *Well, fuck!* I hadn't even started writing.

God, I needed this vacation from my life. When my best friend, Kenya Abrams, invited me to spend a couple of nights in upstate New York, I thought it sounded like a lot of fun. And I definitely needed to get away from the city. Don't get me wrong, I loved NYC. It's everything I imagined it would be and more. I grew up in San Jose, California. After getting my bachelor's degree in musical composition from San Jose State University, I moved to NYC to pursue my MFA from the Graduate Musical Theatre Writing Program at New York University.

I had been in high school when I'd watched my first Broadway musical. I had been flipping channels and landed on PBS, of all things, just at the beginning of a *Live from Lincoln Center* episode. A woman had been conducting an orchestra, so I had stopped to see what was happening. Then the words "Florence, Italy. 1953" had crossed the screen. Immediately, the aria sung by Katie Rose Clarke, who had played Clara in the PBS version, had filled my ears and applause erupted in the auditorium as Victoria Clark walked on stage. I hadn't known what I was watching, but I was transfixed. I'd been in a couple of school plays, so the stage at the Vivian Beaumont Theater at Lincoln Center intrigued me. I'd never seen a thrust stage before. The music had swelled, and Craig Lucas and Adam Guettel's masterpiece *The Light in the Piazza* played out before my eyes. By the time the absolutely gorgeous Aaron Lazar—who was played Fabrizio Naccarelli—had caught Clara's hat as it floated on the wind, the world around me had faded away, and I was transported to Florence, Italy...nineteen-fifty-three. That day... That show... My life had been changed forever.

A vibration in my pocket caught my attention. I reached in and grabbed my cell.

About a block away. Get your butt downstairs.

Aye, aye, captain, I texted back.

Hefting my duffle bag on my shoulder, I conducted one more mental checklist before I left my apartment. I lived on the fifth floor of a twenty-two-story building, so it was easier to take the stairs most days. I exited my building in time to see the 'purple people eater' turning the corner, which was what I called Kenya's bright purple SUV. It pulled up to the curb, and I threw open the door behind the driver's seat to toss in my bag before heading to the passenger side.

You've gotta be fucking kidding me! In what was supposed to be my seat sat a man I had not expected— Noah Miko.

"You should probably sit behind me," Kenya said. "There's more legroom."

I climbed in behind her and did my best not to look disgusted.

Kenya pulled into traffic before I buckled up.

"Well, this is *unexpected,*" I said, drawing out the word.

Kenya looked at me through the rearview mirror and shot me a warning look.

"Hey, Steve. Good to see you again," Noah said as he turned and gave me one of his brilliant smiles I'd seen on the pages of several magazines. Noah was a model and wannabe actor. I'd seen him last year in an Off-Off-Off-Broadway show, and he wasn't good. He might have been pretty, but he couldn't act his way out of a bag.

"It's Stephen," I said. "No one calls me Steve."

"That's right," Noah said. "Sorry about that."

He wasn't sorry. We'd had this very conversation at least a half-dozen times since Kenya brought him into the friendship circle about two years ago. In retrospect, I think Kenya only befriended Noah because she wanted his sperm. Kenya had decided she wanted to get pregnant almost a year before. As a junior partner in a law firm, she'd tried going out with various guys, but she didn't exactly have too much time for a very successful romantic life. She even dated other lawyers, but quickly realized lawyers were boring conversationalists over dinner.

So, about ten months ago, Kenya informed me that come hell or highwater, she wanted to be a mother.

"I'm going to have a baby," Kenya had told me when she'd first raised the idea.

"You're not pregnant?"

"Oh, God, no," Kenya had said. "But I am getting in vitro fertilization."

"Oh, are you using one of those services to find the perfect baby-daddy?" I had joked.

"No. I've already picked out my donor."

"Oh, really?" At first, I had grown anxious because I feared she was about to ask me for my little swimmers.

"Noah Miko."

"Oh, come on," I had responded. "He may be pretty, but what else does he have going for him?"

"He has good genes. I figure between the two of us, my child will get my brains and his good looks. Kind of the best combination possible."

I had wanted to say, *"What if he gets your looks and his brains?"* Thankfully, I'd stopped before I put my foot in my mouth.

A couple of months later, Kenya was pregnant. The Woodstock trip was to be our last big hurrah before the baby came. She didn't look like she was quite ready to pop, but she was getting there. I had assumed it was going to be Kenya and me, so finding the sperm donor in the SUV was a shock.

"What a *pleasant* surprise," I said, putting as much venom behind my words as I could muster.

"Well, it's good to see you, Steve," Noah responded. He was wearing sunglasses, so I couldn't see his eyes, but I did see his smug look reflected in the front window.

"Play nice, boys." Kenya once again looked at me through the rearview mirror. "This weekend is for me, so cut the gay drama shit."

She glanced over at Noah, who nodded. I started to roll my eyes.

"Don't even think about rolling your eyes at me, Stephen," Kenya warned.

"There's no way you could see that," I said as a form of protest.

"I know you and those classic eyerolls too well. I don't need to see them to know that's your go-to whenever you don't get your way."

"Fine. I promise to play nice with the muscle queen. Just don't expect me to like it."

"Oh, you were checking out my muscles?" Noah asked. He didn't look at me from his seat, but he twisted his head enough so I could see the smirk on his face.

"It's hard not to notice your nude portrait in Times Square." Noah was the fresh face for Alessandro Cattaneo's latest menswear line, but the billboard had made me wonder what clothes the Italian designer was advertising. It was basically a nude of Noah standing in a pair of Cattaneo's briefs with the designer's name at the bottom of the billboard. The underwear was pulled so low on Noah's hips that it left little to the imagination.

"Yeah, that was an interesting photo shoot. The photographer kept having me pull the briefs lower and lower. I wondered if I would have to tuck myself like a drag queen to get them low enough. Thankfully, the guy's a genius, and the pics turned out amazing. The billboards in London, Rome and Tokyo will go up later this month, so my pretty face will be worldwide. My agent expects that I will have a lot of job offers coming through."

"Yip dee doo," I said under my breath. "Does this mean you'll have to miss the birth? I mean, if you're going to have jobs all over the world..."

"Nope. I already told everyone I had to be in New York for the birth."

"You remember you're not the father?" Kenya asked.

"That's right." I shot Noah a smile. "You're just the baby-daddy. Maybe a spuncle, at best. You have no legal entanglements with Kenya or the baby." Kenya had written an ironclad contract when she'd sought Noah's sperm services.

"I remember. I'm not there to be a father. God knows, no one needs me as a daddy figure. I need to be there for Kenya. You know...to show her support."

"As long as you remember I'm the one who gets to be with her in the delivery room."

"Don't worry, my man. I don't want to step in on your parade. I know you've been attending all those Lamaze classes with our Kenya."

"So, who wants to listen to some music?" Kenya asked before I could say anything else. She plugged in her phone, and immediately the latest anthem from some pop diva that I'd never heard of blared through the car.

Great! Pop music...my favorite. If it wasn't recorded on a cast album, I probably hadn't heard it, nor did I desire to. People have a range of eclectic musical tastes. I liked people who knew how to sing without damaging their vocal cords. Even better, I preferred singers who could enunciate, so you knew what the hell they were singing.

I tried to listen to the pop diva screeching out her tune. Both Kenya and Noah were singing and car dancing right along with the pop anthem. I pulled out my AirPods, threw on the latest score from the newest Jason Robert Brown show and lost myself listening to a woman who could hit a sustained F6 while belting about divorce. Mixing her chest voice and head voice leading to the F6 was seamless. How she pulled that note off eight shows a week was beyond me.

I opened my eyes. Kenya and Noah were still enjoying their front-seat concert. Kenya could sing, but I had no idea about Noah, so I pulled out one of my earbuds to see if Noah came close to hitting the right notes. I might not have known the song, but I could tell he was in tune. I listened to him belt for a second. *Dammit. He can sing, too.*

My real problem with Noah Miko was that he was perfect — gorgeous beyond belief. I mean...he was a fucking underwear model. But beyond being flawless, he knew he was the gay physical ideal. And he never seemed to miss an opportunity to let everyone know. Before Kenya dragged Noah into my life, I had run into him on Scruff, one of my favorite dating apps. I had a headless pic of my big, burly self. I clicked the 'woof' button because…why the hell not? He had messaged me almost immediately. *"Why do you think I would even bother with someone who looks like you? Look at your pic, then look at my pic. Get real. Oh, and stop shoving food in your face, you fat fuck."* Then he'd blocked me before I could reply.

So, when Kenya brought him into our friendship circle a couple of months later, my hatred toward the asshole had only grown. Some would say I should have given him a chance, but why bother? He lived up to the ever egotistical, braindead stereotype I had dreamed up for him before I'd met him. Somehow, he'd gotten his claws in Kenya. God only knew how that had happened. I was drawn to Kenya in the first place because she wasn't like that. She was a biracial woman from Louisiana who'd earned her undergraduate at Tulane before getting her JD from Columbia. She was sexy. She was smart. She was cultured. And, most importantly, she loved musical theater as much as I did.

That's how we met. I had been working as a pianist in a Broadway-themed piano bar. Kenya would come in and belt out *Seasons of Love* like nobody's business, and we slowly became friends. She had been in law school, and I was finishing up my post-MFA stint at the BMI Lehman Engel Musical Theatre Workshop. We had quickly started doing things outside the piano bar. Before I knew it, she had become my best friend.

My first commercial production was *The Lair of the White Worm*, a musicalized version of Bram Stoker's nineteen-eleven novel. A producer had seen one of our workshops of the show at BMI and signed us up for an Off-Off-Broadway run in a tiny theater in the West Village. It was a sixty-seat black box in a church basement, but it was my New York debut. When the show opened, Kenya was the only one in the world I wanted as my plus one. The critics loved the show. My next show, *Manhattan Transfer*, based on the nineteen-twenty-five novel by John Dos Passos, was produced Off-Broadway by The Public. Currently, I was stuck in the middle of a score for a revision of Currer Bell's—Charlotte Brontë's penname—eighteen-forty-nine novel *Shirley*. The Public had already inquired about the piece, but I also had a few commercial producers who were interested. There had already been talks about taking it out of town and maybe opening on Broadway. But I couldn't find the heart in the show.

Shirley may have been written in the eighteen-forties, but the book's themes were highly relevant today. Instead of the musical taking place in the Yorkshire textile industry, we'd refocused it to an automotive plant in Detroit. In the novel, the villain—who is a textile plant owner—is bringing in new machinery that will enable him to eliminate jobs. Sound familiar? For our version, we updated it to people losing jobs to robots. The story is sadly timeless and prescient. There are two central romantic affairs, Caroline and Robert and Shirley and Luis. And for the life of me, I couldn't get the love affairs right. No matter how hard I tried, nothing seemed to mesh. The music didn't sound right. The love seemed fake. But then, it's hard to write a romance when you've never had one.

About the Author

Jason Wrench is a professor in the Department of Communication at SUNY New Paltz and has authored/edited 15+ books and over 35 academic research articles. He is also an avid reader and regularly reviews books for publishers in a wide number of genres. This book marks his first full-length work of fiction.

Jason loves to hear from readers. You can find his contact information, website details and author profile page at https://www.pride-publishing.com

PUBLISHING

Sign up for our newsletter and find out about all our romance book releases, eBook sales and promotions, sneak peeks and FREE romance books!